T0144716

The Sky Man

The Sky Man

Henry Kitchell Webster

MINT EDITIONS

The Sky Man was first published in 1910.

This edition published by Mint Editions 2021.

ISBN 9781513283531 | E-ISBN 9781513288550

Published by Mint Editions®

MINT
EDITIONS

minteditionbooks.com

Publishing Director: Jennifer Newens
Design & Production: Rachel Lopez Metzger
Project Manager: Micaela Clark
Typesetting: Westchester Publishing Services

Contents

I

The Man with Wings

For many hours—Cayley was too much of a god today to bother with the exact number of them—he had been flying slowly northward down a mild southerly breeze. Hundreds of feet below him was the dazzling, terrible expanse of the polar ice pack which shrouds the northern limits of the Arctic Ocean in its impenetrable veil of mystery.

Cayley was alone, as no man before ever had been alone, for the planet which spun beneath him seemed to him, aloft there in the empyrean, as remote as Mars or as the Pleiades. Its mountains, its crevassed valleys and its seas, the little huddled clumps of houses called towns, the small laborious ships ploughing their futile furrows,—all amused him with a whimsical sense of pity. And most of all, those human dot-like grubs, to whose family he had belonged until he found his wings!

A compass, a sextant, a bottle of milk and a revolver comprised, with the clothes he wore, and with the shimmering silken wings of his aeroplane, his whole equipment. His nearest base of supplies, if you could call it that, was a twenty pound tin of pemmican, hidden under a stone on the northeast extremity of Herald Island, three hundred miles away. The United States Rescue Station at Point Barrow, the extreme northerly point of Alaska, the place which he had called home for the past three months, was, possibly, half as far again away, somewhere off to the southeast.

But to Cayley, in his present mood, these distances were matters of small importance. Never again, perhaps, would the mastery of the air bring him a sense of happiness so godlike in its serenity, so ecstatic in its exhilaration. For the thing was perfect, and yet it was new. Only with his arrival at Point Barrow at the beginning of this summer had his flight been free from the thrill of momentary peril. Some sudden buffet of wind would tax his skill and nerve to the utmost. A flight before the wind, even with a constant, steady breeze, had been a precarious business.

But for these past weeks of unbroken Arctic sunshine, he had fairly lived a-wing. The earth had no obstructions and the air no perils. Today, with his great broad fan-tail drawn up arc-wise beneath him, his planes pitched slightly forward at the precise and perilous angle that only just did not send him plunging, headfirst, down upon the sullen masses of ice below, he lay there, prone, upon the sheep-skin sleeping bag which padded the frame-work supporting his two wings, as secure as the great fulmar petrel which drew curiously near, and then, with a wheel and a plunge, fled away, squawking.

Cayley would not say that he had learned to fly; he would still insist that he was learning. And, in a sense, this was true. Almost everyday eider, gull, cormorant or albatross taught him some new trick of technique in steering, soaring or wheeling, perhaps, in a tricky cross-current of air. Even that fulmar, which had fled in such ungainly haste, had given him a new idea in aerostatics to amuse himself with.

But for all practical purposes Cayley had learned to fly. The great fan-driven air ship, 100 feet from tip to tip, which had long lain idle on his ranch at Sandoval, would probably never leave its house again. It had done yeoman service. Without its powerful propellers, for a last resource, Cayley would never have been able to try the experiments and get the practice which had given him the air for his natural element. He had outgrown it. He had no more need of motors or whirling fans. The force of gravity, the force of the breeze and the perfectly co-ordinated muscles of his own body gave him all the power he needed now.

And what a marvelous power it was! He had never believed before the statement of men of science, that the great gray northern geese can sail the air at eighty miles an hour. He knew it now. He had overtaken them.

Perhaps the succeeding generations of humankind may develop an eye which can see ahead when the body is lying prone, as a bird lies in its flight. Cayley had remedied this deficiency with a little silver mirror, slightly concave, screwed fast to the cross-brace which supported his shoulders. Instead of bending back his head, or trying to see out through his eyebrows, he simply cast a backward glance into this mirror whenever he wanted to look on ahead. It had been a little perplexing at first, but he could see better in it now than with his unaided eyes.

And now, a minute or two, perhaps, after that fulmar had gone squawking away, he glanced down into his mirror, and his olympian calm was shaken with the shock of surprise. For what he saw, clearly reflected in his little reducing glass, was land. There was a mountain, and a long dark line that must be a clifflike coast.

And it was land that never had been marked on any chart. In absolute degrees of latitude he was not, from the Arctic explorer's view, very far north. Over on the other side of the world they run excursion steamers every summer nearer to the Pole than he was at this moment. Spitzbergen, which has had a permanent population of fifteen thousand souls, lies three hundred miles farther north than this uncharted coast which Philip Cayley saw before him.

But the great ice cap which covers the top of the world is irregular in shape, and just here, northward from Alaska, it juts its impenetrable barrier far down into the Arctic Sea. Rogers, Collinson and the ill-fated DeLong,—they all had tried to penetrate this barrier, and had been turned back.

Cayley wheeled sharply up into the wind, and soared aloft to a height of, perhaps, a quarter of a mile. Then, with a long, flashing, shimmering sweep, he descended, in the arc of a great circle, and hung, poised, over the land itself and behind the jutting shoulder of the mountain.

The land was a narrow-necked peninsula. Mountain and cliff prevented him from seeing the immediate coast on the other side of it; but out a little way to sea he was amazed to discover open water, and the smoke-like vapor that he saw rising over the cliffhead made it evident that the opening extended nearly, if not quite, to the very land's edge. It was utterly unexpected, for the side of the peninsula which he had approached was ice-locked for miles.

He would have towered again above the rocky ridge which shut off his view, and gone to investigate this phenomenon at closer range, had he not, just then, got the shock of another surprise, greater than the discovery of land itself.

The little valley which he hung poised above was sheltered by a second ridge of rocky, ice-capped hills to the north, and, except for streaks, denoting crevices, here and there, was quite free from ice and snow. There were bright patches of green upon it, evidently some bit of flowering northern grass, and it was flecked here and there with bright bits of color, yellow poppy, he judged it to be, and saxifrage. Hugging the base of the mountain on the opposite side of the valley, then notching the cliff and grinding down to sea at the other side of it was a great white glacier, all the whiter, and colder, and more dazzling for its contrast with the brown mountain-side and the green-clad valley.

Up above the glacier, on the farther side, were great broad yellow patches, which he would have thought were poppy fields, but for the impossibility of their growing in such a place. No vegetable growth was possible, he would have thought, against that clean-cut, almost vertical, rocky face. And yet, what else could have given it that blazing yellow color? Some day he was to learn the answer to that question.

But the thing that caught his eye now, that made him start and draw in a little involuntary gasp of wonder, was the sight a little clump of black dots moving slowly, almost imperceptibly from this distance, across the face of the glacier. He blinked his eyes, as if he suspected them of playing him false. Unless they had played him false, these tiny dots were men.

Instinctively, he shifted his balance a little to the left, lowering his left wing and elevating his right, and began reaching along, thwartwise to the wind, in their direction.

Presently he checked himself in mid-flight, wheeled and hung, soaring, while he restrained that rebellious instinct of his, an instinct which would have led him to sail down into the midst of them and hold out his hand for a welcome. What were mankind to him? Why should the sight of them make his heart beat a little quicker?

They must be white. He felt sure of that, for this land could hardly have any permanent inhabitants. And, of course, he meant to go for a nearer look. Probably he would descend among them; find out who they were, where their ship was, and if they were in distress, he would then set sail through the air to carry news of their plight to those who might effect a rescue. But not upon that first instinct of his for companionship with his fellow men; not until his heart was beating with its normal rhythm again.

He wheeled once more, and then sailed slowly in their direction. Their laborious progress down the glacier led them away from him, so that he came up from behind, and without attracting their attention. The Arctic sun was too low to cast his shadow across them, and he hung, at last, unremarked, directly over their heads. There was small likelihood that they would look up, until some sound from him should attract their attention, for, among the crevices, the chutes and treacherous ice bridges of the glacier top, they had small leisure to give heed to anything but their footing.

All of the party, but one man, were dressed exactly alike, in hooded bear-skin shirts and breeches, and boots of what he guessed was walrus hide. They moved along with the peculiar wary shuffle of men accustomed, by long habit, to the footing and to the heavy confining garb they wore. So far as he could see they were unarmed.

The other man was strikingly different. He appeared to be clad much as Cayley was himself, in leather, rather than in untanned hide. He seemed slighter, sprightlier, and in every way to convey the impression of having come more recently from the civilized, habitable portion of the world than his companions. He carried a rifle slung by a strap over his shoulder, evidently foreseeing no immediate use for it, and a flask.

Cayley was too far aloft for their conversation to be audible to him, but he could hear that they were talking. The leather-clad man appeared to be doing the most of it, and, from the inflection of his voice, he seemed to be speaking in English.

From moment to moment Cayley kept meaning to hail them, but, from moment to moment, he kept deferring the action. It amused him a little to think how much, in one way or another, that hail might mean to those plodding figures down below. Now, or five minutes from now; it could not matter to them. And meanwhile he could guard that hard-won aloofness from human endeavor, human fears and suffering and limitations, a little longer.

Presently he noticed that the leather-clad man had forged a little ahead of his companions, or, rather—like a flash, this idea occurred to Cayley—that the others were purposely lagging a little behind.

And then, before that sinister idea could formulate itself into a definite suspicion, his eyes widened with amazement, and the cry he would have uttered died in his throat; for this man, who had so innocently allowed the others to fall behind him, suddenly staggered, clutched at something—it looked like a thin ivory dart—that had transfixed his throat, tugged it out in a sudden flood of crimson, reeled a little and then went backwards over the glassy edge of a fissure in the ice, which lay just to the left of the path where he had been walking.

From the instant when Cayley had noticed the others dropping behind, to the last glimpse he had of the body of the murdered man could hardly have been five seconds.

The instant the murdered man disappeared, another, who had not previously been with the party, it seemed, appeared from behind a hummock of ice. There could be no doubt either that he was the assassin, or that he was the commander of the little group of skin-clad figures that remained. The ambush appeared to have been perfectly deliberate. There had been no outcry, not even a gesture of surprise or of remonstrance.

Cayley looked at the assassin curiously. He was dressed exactly like the others, but seemed very much bigger; seemed to walk with less of a slouch, and had, even to Cayley's limited view of him, an air of authority. Cayley was surprised at his not being armed with a bow, for he knew of no other way in which a dart could have been propelled with power enough, even at close range, to have transfixed a man's throat. The assassin's only weapon, except for a quiverful of extra darts, seemed to be a short blunt stick, rudely whittled, perhaps ten inches long.

Obedient, apparently, to the order of the new arrival, the party changed its direction, leaving what was evidently a well-known path to them, for a seemingly more direct but rougher route. And they moved now with an appearance of haste. Presently they scrambled over a precipitous ledge of ice and, in a moment, were lost to Cayley's view.

The world was suddenly empty again, as if no living foot had ever trodden it; and Cayley, hovering there, a little above the level of the ice, rubbed his eyes and wondered whether the singular, silent tragedy he had just witnessed were real, or a trick the mysterious Arctic light had played upon his tired eyes. But there remained upon that vacant scene two material reminders of the tragedy to which it had afforded a setting. One was a smudge of crimson on the snow; the other, a little distance off, just this side the icy ridge over which the last of the party had gone scrambling a moment before, was the strange looking blunt stick which he had seen in the assassin's hand.

Cayley flew a little lower, his wings almost skimming the ice. Finally, reaching the spot where the thing had fallen, he alighted and picked it up. Whether its possessor had valued it, or not, whether or not he might be expected to return for it, Cayley did not know, and did not much care.

He stood for sometime turning the thing over in his hands, puzzling over it, trying to make out how it could have been used as the instrument of propulsion to that deadly ivory dart. There was a groove on one side of it, with a small ivory plug at the end. The other end was curiously shaped, misshapen, rather, for, though it was obviously the end one held, Cayley could not make it fit his hand, whatever position he held it in.

Giving up the problem at last, he tucked the stick into his belt, slipped his arm through the strap in the frame-work of his aeroplane and prepared for flight. He had a little difficulty getting up, owing to the absence of a breeze at this point. Finally he was obliged to climb, with a good deal of labor, the icy ridge up which he had watched the little party of murderers scrambling.

At the crest he cast a glance around, looking for them, but saw no signs of them. Then, getting a favorable slant of the wind, he mounted again into the element he now called his own.

A heavy fog was filling up the cup-shaped valley, like a lake, and when he had towered through it and into the clear, sparkling, unvexed air above it, he found, rolled out beneath him, as far as he could see in every direction, what looked, under the slanting rays of the sun, like a warm, fleecy, rose-colored blanket.

But, somehow, the return to the upper air, even the drawing of that great cloud-curtain across the earth, failed to give back to Cayley that mood of serene happiness which he had enjoyed an hour before. He tried hard to recover it, and his failure to do so irritated him. In vain, he asked himself what those little figures on the ice could mean to him, or he to them. In vain, he told himself that the thing he had seen was nothing but a picture,—a puppet show.

He began wheeling a great spiral in the upper air, higher and higher, until the intensity of the cold and the drumming of the blood in his temples warned him to descend again.

But high or low, some invisible magnet held him over the spot where he had witnessed that unexplained tragedy; an intense curiosity that would not let him go until he had, in some way, accounted for the flying fate that, so silently, had overtaken the leather-clad man down there on the ice.

Five years before Philip Cayley would have passed for a good example of that type of clean-limbed, clean-minded, likable young man which the best of our civilization seems to be flowering into. Physically, it would have been hard to suggest an improvement in him, he approached so near the ideal standards. He was fine grained, supple, slender, small-jointed, thorough-bred from head to heel.

Intellectually, he had been good enough to go through the Academy at West Point with credit, and to graduate high enough in his class to be assigned to service in the cavalry. His standards of conduct, his ideas of honor and morality had been about the same as those of the best third of his classmates. If his fellow officers in the Philippines, during the year or two he had spent in the service, had been asked to pick a flaw in him, which they would have been reluctant to do, they would have said that he seemed to them a bit too thin-skinned and rather fastidious; that was what his chum and only intimate friend, Perry Hunter, said about him at any rate.

But he could afford to be fastidious, for he had about all a man could want, one would think. For three generations they had taken wealth for granted in the Cayley family, and with it had come breeding, security of social position, simplicity and ease in making friends, both among men and women. In short, there could be no doubt at all that up to his twenty-ninth year Fate had been ironically kind to Philip Cayley. She had given him no hint, no preparation for the stunning blow that was to fall upon him, suddenly, out of so clear a sky!

When it did fall, it cut his life clean across; so that when he thought back to that time now, it seemed to him that the Lieutenant Cayley of the United States Army had died over there in the Philippines, and that he, the man who was now soaring in those great circles through the Arctic sky, was a chance inheritor of his name and of his memory.

He had set out one day at the head of a small scouting party, the best-liked man in the regiment, secure in the respect, in the almost fatherly regard, of his colonel, proudly conscious of the almost idolatrous admiration of his men and of the younger officers. He had gone out believing that no one ever had a truer friend than he possessed in Perry Hunter, his classmate at West Point, his fellow-officer in the regiment, the confidant of all his hopes and ideals.

He had come back, after a fortnight's absence, to find his name smeared with disgrace, himself judged and condemned, unheard, in the opinion of the mess. And that was not the worst of it. The same blow which had deprived him of the regard of the only people in the world who mattered to him, destroyed, also, root and branch, his affection for the one man of whom he had made an intimate. The only feeling that it would be possible for him to entertain for Perry Hunter again must be a half-pitying, half-incredulous contempt. And if that was his feeling for the man he had trusted most and loved the most deeply, what must it be for the rest of humankind? What did it matter what they thought of him or what they did to him? All he wanted of human society was to escape from it.

He fell to wondering, as he hung, suspended, over that rosy expanse of fleecy fog, whether, were the thing to do over again, he would act as he had acted five years ago; whether he would content himself with a single disdainful denial of the monstrous thing they charged him with; whether he would resign again, under fire, and go away, leaving his tarnished name for the daws to peck at.

Heretofore he had always answered that question with a fierce affirmative. Today it left him wondering. Had he stayed, had he paid the price that would have been necessary to clear himself, he would never have found his wings, so much was clear. He would never have spent those four years in the wilderness, working, experimenting, taking his life in his hands, day after day, while he mastered the art that no man had ever mastered before.

He had set himself this task because it was the only one he knew that did not involve contact with his fellow-beings. He must have something that he could work at alone. Work and solitude were two things that he had felt an overmastering craving for. And the possibility he had faced with a light heart every morning—the possibility of a sudden and violent death before night, had been no more to him than an agreeable spice to the day's work.

It was not until he had actually learned to fly, had literally shaken the dust of the earth from his feet and taken to the sky as his abode, that his wound had healed. The three months that he had spent in this upper Arctic air, a-wing for sixteen hours out of twenty-four, had calmed him, put his nerves in tune again; given him for men and their affairs a quiet indifference, in place of the smarting contempt he had been hugging to his breast before. Three months ago, at sight of those little human dots crossing the glacier, he would have wheeled aloft and gone sailing away. Even a month ago he would hardly have hung, soaring there, above the fog, waiting for it to lift again the veil of mystery which it had drawn across the tragic scene he had just witnessed.

The month was August, and the long Arctic day had already begun to know its diurnal twilight. A fortnight ago the sun had dipped, for the first time, below the horizon. By now there were four or five hours, out of every twenty-four, that would pass for night.

The sun set while he hung there in the air, and as it did so, with a new slant of the breeze the fog rolled itself up into a great violet-colored cloud, leaving the earth, the ice, the sea unveiled below him. And there, in the open water of the little bay, he saw a ship, and on the shore a cluster of rude huts.

It struck him, even from the height at which he soared, that the ship, tied to an ice-floe in the shelter of the great headland, did not look like a whaler, nor like the sort of craft which an Arctic explorer would have selected for his purposes. It had more the trim smartness of a yacht.

They were probably all asleep down there, he reflected. It was nearly midnight and he saw no signs of life anywhere. He would drop down for a nearer look.

He descended, with a sudden hawk-like pounce, which was one of his more recent achievements in the navigation of the air, checked himself again at about the level of the masthead, with a flashing, forward swoop, like a man diving in shallow water; then, with a sudden effort, brought himself up standing, his planes nearly vertical, and, with a backward spring, alighted, clear of his wings, on the ice-floe just opposite the ship.

As he did so, he heard a little surprised cry, half of fear, half of astonishment. It was a girl's voice.

II

The Girl on the Ice Floe

S he stood there on the floe confronting him, not ten feet away, and at sight of her Philip Cayley's eyes widened. "What in the world!" he gasped. Then stared at her speechless.

She was clad, down to the knees, in sealskin, and below its edge he could see the tops of her small furtrimmed boots. Upon her head she wore a little turban-like cap of seal. The smartly tailored lines of the coat emphasized her young slenderness. Her bootmaker must have had a reputation upon some metropolitan boulevard, and her head-gear came clearly under the category of what is known as modes. Her eyes were very blue and her hair was golden, warmed, he thought, as she stood there in the orange twilight, with a glint of red.

Cayley gasped again, as he took in the details of this vision. Then collected himself. "I beg your pardon," he stammered. "I don't mean to be rudely inquisitive, but what, in the world, is a person like you doing in this part of it,—that is, if you are real at all? This is latitude seventy-sex, and no cartographer who ever lived has put that coast-line yonder into his maps. Yet here, in this nameless bay, I find a yacht, and on this ice floe, in the twilight, you."

She shook her head a little impatiently, and blinked her eyes, as if to clear them of a vision. "Of course," she said, "I know I've fallen asleep and this is a dream of mine, but even for a dream, aren't you a little unreasonable? Yachts are a natural mode of conveyance across the ocean. You find them in many bays,—sometimes in nameless ones—and they always have people on them. But you—you come wheeling down, out of a night sky, like some great nocturnal bird, and alight here on the floe beside me. And then you change yourself into a man and look at me in surprise, and ask me, in English, what in the world I am doing here,—I and the yacht; and ask me if I'm real."

There was a moment of silence after that. Unconsciously they drew a little nearer together. Then Cayley spoke. "I'm real, at any rate," he said; "at least I'm a tax payer, and I weigh one hundred and sixty pounds, and I have a name and address. It's Philip Cayley, if that will make me seem more natural, and my headquarters this summer are over on Point Barrow."

"But that's five hundred miles away," she protested.

"Is it?" he said indifferently. "I've been a-wing all day, and I haven't come down for an observation once. I don't know just where I am. I've been feeling a little unreal for hours, or, rather, the world has. And now, at the end of it, I find a—a person like you here in the twilight—" he finished the broken sentence with a gesture.

"I'm not dreaming, then?" she asked dubiously.

"No," he said; "if either of us is dreaming, it's not you. May I furl up my wings and talk to you for awhile?"

Her eyes were on the broad-spread, shimmering planes which lay on the ice behind him. She seemed hardly to have heard his question, though she answered it with an almost voiceless "yes." Then she approached, half fearfully, the thing he called his "wings."

"It is made of quite commonplace materials," he said with a smile— "split bamboo and carbon wire and catgut and a fabric of bladders, cemented with fish glue. And folding it up is rather an ungainly job. The birds still have the advantage of me there. In a strong wind it's not very easy to do without damaging something. Would you mind slipping that joint for me,—that one right by your hand? It's just like a fishing rod."

She did as he asked, and her smile convinced him that she had at least half-guessed his purpose in asking the service of her. The next moment her words confirmed it.

"You wanted me to make sure, I suppose, that it would not turn into a great roc when I touched it and fly away with me to the Valley of Diamonds." She patted the furled wing, gently, with both hands. "I suppose," she continued, "one could dream as vividly as this, although I never have—unless, of course, this is a dream. But,—" and now she held out her hand to him, "but I hope I am awake. And my name is Jeanne Fielding."

He had the hand in his, and noticed how live and strong and warm it was, before she pronounced her name. At the sound of it, he glanced at her curiously; but all he said just then was, "Thank you," and busied himself immediately with completing the process of furling his wings.

When he had finished, he tossed the sheep-skin down in a little hollow in the floe, and with a gesture invited her to be seated.

"Oh, I've a great pile of bear skins out here," she said, "quite a ridiculous pile of them, considering it is not a cold night; and we can make ourselves comfortable here, or go aboard the yacht, just as you please."

They were seated, side by side, in the little nest she had made for herself, before he reverted to the idea which had sprung up in his mind upon hearing her name. "There was a 'Captain Fielding' once," he said slowly, "who set out from San Francisco half a dozen years ago, in the hope of discovering the Pole, by the way of Behring Strait. His ship was never seen again, nor was any word received from him. Finding you here and hearing your name, I wondered—"

"Yes," she said gravely, "he was my father. We got news of him last winter, if you could call it news, for it was four years old before it reached us. A whaler in the Arctic fleet picked up a floating bottle with a message from him, telling where he was. So we have come here to find him—at least to find where he died, for I suppose there is no hope—never so much as a grain of hope of anything better."

Cayley could not contradict her, and he saw there was little need of trying to do so. She had spoken simply, and very gravely, but it was evident the years had taken the sting out of her grief.

"He told you where he was?" he asked.

"Oh, quite exactly," she told him; "he gave us latitude and longitude, and mapped the coast-line. So you were wrong, you see, in what you said about cartographers. And he gave us the route by which, with reasonable fortune, we might find open water. We had good fortune and we got here safely, but, of course, we were too late. The hut on the shore there is deserted. We have seen no signs of life at all. The men have gone ashore to search, and there is to be a gun-fire if they find anyone alive. But they have been out all day and there has been no sound. You will understand, I think, though, why I did not want to sleep tonight in my cabin in the yacht—why the ice and the dome of stars seemed better."

"Yes," he said, "I understand." Presently, after a moment's musing, he added, "What seems strange to me, incomprehensible altogether, is, that men like your father, and so many others, should risk and lose their lives trying to reach the Pole."

"You can't understand that—" she questioned surprised, "you, a man with wings?"

"I suppose it's because of the wings," he answered her. "I slept there once, early this summer—slept, and rested, and ate a meal."

"*There*—" she echoed incredulously. "Where do you mean?"

"At the Pole, or within a half degree of it,—I won't guarantee my instruments, nor my hit-and-miss observations any more accurately than that—and it seemed a poor place to risk one's life trying to reach.

Just the ice-pack—the eternal ice-pack; nothing but that." Then his eyes lighted a little. "But I should like to go there sometime, in the winter—should like to fly straight ahead, for hours and hours, through the long dark, until I could see the North Star squarely above my head in the zenith, the centre of all the universe. That would be a sight worth having, I should think. Some day, perhaps, I shall try for it. And then one could go straight on across,—a week or ten days would do it all—from Dawson City, say, to St. Petersburg."

"Dawson City to St. Petersburg!" she repeated; "only a creature of wings could put those two cities into the same sentence, even in imagination. And even with you it must be imaginary. You couldn't do it, really—could you?"

"Yes," he said; "I could do it."

"You're tireless then?" she asked. "You could go on flying, flying, without rest, for a week?"

"I don't fly," he told her, "or hardly at all. The birds don't fly, not these great sea birds that live on the wing. They sail; so do I."

"But, then, don't you have to go with the wind?"

"You've sailed a boat, haven't you?" he asked by way of answer. "You put up a sail to catch the breeze, and then you make it force your boat right up into it; make your boat go against the wind, by the force of the wind itself. That was regarded as a miracle once when men first did it."

"Of course," she admitted, "but you do that by tacking."

"That's the way I do it—by tacking, and the force of gravity is my keel."

"And in a calm?" she asked.

"It's never really calm up there; it's always alive, restless, always flowing this way and that, sometimes in great placid, even rivers, with banks as clearly marked, almost, as the banks of a stream of water. And then again, in storms—"

He interrupted himself with a short laugh, and then asked her an absurd question. "Can you imagine a sea of thick molasses? If you can, try to think what it would be like in a storm; and then you will know how water storms seem to me, who live in the air. Those waves in the sky, when they're angry, shoot you aloft for a mile, whirling, and then drop you again, as if off the edge of a precipice, with nothing, nothing at all, but sheer vacancy, beneath your wings. It blows so hard sometimes that even the albatross or frigate-bird can't lie up, hove-to, against it. They have to turn and scud, and give the storm its will with them, just like the lesser fowl. I had to do that once, and it is the only time in my life that I have ever felt an overmastering terror."

She looked at him curiously. "And, yet, you must have faced death a thousand times," she hazarded.

"It wasn't the prospect of death that frightened me," he answered thoughtfully. "It was just plain panic—just the intrinsic terror of the Titan himself, who seemed to be drunk and heaving the world about. That doesn't sound very sensible; perhaps you understand the thing I mean."

She did not answer, but sat for awhile, thoughtfully silent, her chin on her knees, her arms embracing them, and her eyes focused no nearer than on the patch of dusky orange at the horizon.

"How long have you lived like this?" she asked abruptly.

"Really lived? Only three months or so. I spent the better part of five years learning to fly."

"And you have flown all over the world?"

"All over this most deserted patch of it."

There was another silence. Then she said, "And what a contempt you must have for us—for us, poor wingless creatures, who cannot cross a little fissure in a rock or a bit of open water without such toilsome labor. Yes, that must be the feeling—contempt; it could hardly be pity."

"If that's true," he rejoined quickly, "it's only poetic justice. I've only achieved toward the world the feeling which the world held for me."

The words were spoken harshly, abruptly, as if his memory had just tasted something intolerably bitter. The manner of the words, no less than the sense of them startled her, and she checked a movement to turn and look into his face. Instead, she tried to recall it as it had looked when she had first stood confronting him, before the twilight had faded.

It was a strange face, as she remembered it, but this, she reflected, was probably due to the incongruous effect of his deeply tanned skin with his very light, sun-bleached hair. A sensitive face, finely chiseled, almost beautiful,—and young, but with an inexplicable stamp of premature age upon it. It had not struck her at all as a tragic face. And yet the meaning of those last words of his, uttered as they were, had been tragic enough.

"At least you have a magnificent revenge," was all she said. And then there was another silence. She herself was trying to think of something to say, for she realized that his confession had been involuntary, and that the silence must be distressing him.

But it was he himself who broke the silence with a natural, matter-of-fact question. "You say a searching party has set out from the yacht? Have they been long ashore?"

"They set out only a little after sunrise. We came into the bay with the last of yesterday's twilight, and the sight of those huts, at the edge of the shore—" her voice faltered a little, "nearly made us hope that the impossible might prove true. We fired our signal cannon two or three times and then sent up some rockets, without getting any answer. It was too late to go ashore in the dark; so we had to wait a few hours for another sunrise. The few of us who were left on the yacht expected them back today before dark fell. But I suppose there's nothing to worry about in their not coming. They went equipped to pass a night ashore, if necessary. You don't advise me to begin worrying about them, do you?"

He did not answer her question. He was recalling something which his amazing meeting with the girl out here on the ice-floe had, for a little while, put quite out of his mind—the weird, silent tragedy he had seen enacted a few hours before upon the glacier behind the headland. The victim, the man in the leather coat, must have been one of the party from the yacht; but it was impossible that the little band of his murderers could be. No one freshly landed from the yacht would have been dressed as they were, or would have been armed with darts.

With no better look at them than had been possible to him as he hung above their heads, he had been convinced that they were white; certainly, the leather-coated man had been talking to them, freely enough, in English. And yet, if white, they must have been refugees—survivors, if not of Captain Fielding's ill-fated expedition, then of some other, tragic, unreported ship wreck.

But if they were white men—refugees, why had they fled from their hut at sight of the yacht which came bringing a rescue? Why had they driven that one luckless member of the rescuing party who fell in with them, into that carefully prepared ambush, and then murdered him, silently? Even Eskimos would not have done a thing like that.

His long silence had alarmed the girl, and presently, perceiving that this was so, he drew himself up with an affected start. "I beg your pardon. I drifted off, thinking of something else. Living in the sky doesn't seem conducive to good manners. No, I don't believe there is anything to worry about. Any way, as soon as light comes back, which won't be long now, I can set at rest any fears you may have. I'll go and find your party,

HENRY KITCHELL WEBSTER

and I'll search the land, too—for anything else that may be there. And then I'll bring you word."

"You are very good," she said with a little hesitation, "but I can't let you—"

He interrupted her with a laugh. "It's nothing difficult that I am proposing to do for you, you know."

"That's true. I had forgotten your wings. The rocks, the ice, the steep places, that mean so tragically much to them, are nothing at all to you. But what are you doing now? Even you can't find them in the dark."

He had already begun unstrapping the bundle he had made of his wings, and seemed to be preparing for immediate flight. That was what caused her question.

"No," he said; "I shall wait for sunrise."

"But why not here, on the yacht? We can give you a comfortable bed there; better, certainly, than that sleeping bag of yours."

"I am afraid," he said, "that what you call a comfortable bed in a yacht's cabin would be the surest instrument that could be found for keeping me awake all night. No, I shall find a sheltered hollow up at the top of that headland yonder, where I shall sleep deeply enough, you may be sure."

She still interposed a half-hearted objection to his going, and yet she was glad he did not yield to it. The thought of his unfolding his wings and flying away again, just as he had come, seemed fitter, somehow, than the prospect of taking him to the yacht in a dinghy, and bidding him good night, like any other commonplace sort of mortal.

She watched him, silently, while he slipped the steel-jointed rods into place, drew the catgut bow strings taut, until they sang—until the fabric of his planes shimmered in the starlight—quivered, as if they were instinct with a life of their own.

A sense of the unreality of it all came welling up strongly within her, and a touch of an almost forgotten fear of him.

"Good night," she said, holding out her hand— "good bye."

"Till morning," he answered.

A little breeze came blowing across the ice just then. He dropped her hand quickly, slipped his arms into their places in the frame, mounted the ledge of ice, and then, with a short run, sprang forward into the breeze.

She saw his planes bend a little, undulate, rather, with a sort of sculling motion, as he flew forward, not far above the level of her head.

He dipped down again as soon as he had open water beneath him, and almost skimmed the surface of it. Then, gathering speed, he began mounting, on a long slant, in that great starry, domelike sky, until, at last, the darkness swallowed him.

She felt curiously alone now that he was gone; and a little frightened, like a child just waking out of a dream. And she blew a small silver whistle that hung about her neck, for a signal to the men on the yacht to send a boat for her.

Then, while she waited, she dropped down rather limply on her pile of bear-skins. Her hand found something hard that had not been there before, and taking it up she found that it was a curious blunt stick of wood, rudely whittled, and about ten inches long. It must have fallen from his belt while he sat there talking to her. She wondered what he used it for.

III

THE MURDERERS

Two men clad in bear-skins were shuffling rapidly along across the glacier. Dawn was already flooding the Arctic sky with its amazing riot of color,—rose, green-gold, violet, and the ice beneath their feet was rose color with misty blue shadows in it.

The foremost of the two wayfarers was a man of gigantic stature, six and a half feet tall and of enormous girth of chest; yet, somehow, despite his size and the ungainly clothes he wore, he contrived to preserve an air almost of lightness; of lean, compact athleticism, certainly. A stranger, meeting him anywhere and contemplating his formidable proportions, and then looking up past his great, blunt jaw into his cold, light blue, choleric eyes, would be likely to shiver a little and then get out of his way as soon as possible.

He was walking steadily, glancing neither to the right nor the left. Even over the treacherous, summer-glazed surface of the glacier, his great stride carried him along at a pace which his companion found it difficult to keep up with. Besides, this companion made his task the harder by allowing his eyes to wander from the track they were following, and casting little furtive, anxious glances at the man beside him. In any other company he would have been a rather striking figure himself, well above middle height, powerfully made, and with a face that had lines of experience and determination engraved in it. But the comparison dwarfed him.

He seemed to be trying to make up his mind to speak, and still to find this a difficult thing to do. At last, with a deprecatory cough he began:

"What I can't see is, Roscoe, what you did it *for*. It was all right to do it if you were figgering out any gain from it. We'd all agree to that. Anything for our common good, that's our motto. But where's the gain in killing just one poor fellow out of a party of thirty? He seemed a good kind of chap, too, and friendly spoken. We didn't serve you like that, when you come aboard the *Walrus* at Cape Nome."

"It would have cost you four men to do it, Planck, and you were short-handed as it was."

"That wasn't why we didn't do it. You was a stranger and you was in a bad way. There was a mob of men that wanted you mighty bad, and we gave you shelter and carried you off and made you a regular sharin' member of the crew. Of course if we'd had any *reason* to act contrary, we'd have done so. And that's why it seemed to us—to *me* I would say, that you probably had some reason in this case, here. And, well,—we'd like to know what it is."

But the man he had addressed as "Roscoe" strode on with unabated pace, as if he had not heard. For any attention he paid to his questioner, he might have been alone in that expanse of ice and sky.

Planck accepted the silent rebuff as if it had been only what he had expected, but he sighed regretfully. He had once known, and it was only four years ago, that same swaggering trick of contemptuous authority himself. He had been master, the most tyrannical sort of master, some say, to be found anywhere in the world; the captain of an American whaler. And this very man, at whose heels he was scrambling along over the ice, had been one of his crew; had never approached the quarter-deck where he reigned supreme, without an apologetic hand at his forelock, and had always passed to the leeward side of him up on deck.

But the *Walrus* had been destined never to see port again. She lingered too long on the whaling grounds to get back through Behring Strait that fall; and failed in the attempt to make McKenzie Bay, where other whalers in similar plight put in for the winter. Instead of this friendly harbor, she was caught in the pack and carried, relentlessly, north and westward. The milling pressure of great masses of ice crushed in her stout hull, so that the open water they had been hoping for, became, at once, their deadliest peril. The moment the ice broke away, she would go to the bottom like a plummet.

But still, the slow, irresistible drift of the ice-pack carried them north and west into a latitude and longitude which, so far as they knew, no human travellers had ever crossed before. And then in the depth of the Arctic night, bereft of hope, and half mutinous, they found a land that never had been charted, and, most marvellous of all, a human welcome. For here on the shore were Captain Fielding and the two other survivors of his ill-fated expedition.

The fate of the explorer's ship had been, it seemed, precisely that of the *Walrus*. She had been caught in the pack, crushed in it and carried against this coast. Before the coming of spring, and with it the breaking of the ice, Fielding and his men had been able to carry their stores ashore, and of these, the greater part still remained.

Of the *Walrus* people, in all, there were eleven, and these, with the three original castaways, settled down to the prospect of an indefinite number of years upon that nameless coast. "We can live like Christians," Captain Fielding had said, "and we can always hope."

His superior knowledge of Arctic conditions made him, rather than Captain Planck, naturally, commander of the little company. He established the regimen of their life, doled out the stores from day to day, and, as best he could, through that long winter night, provided entertainment for the forlorn little group. He told them of his explorations on the coast, of the lay of the land, of what they might hope to see when the sun should come back to them, marking the beginning of another long Arctic day.

Among other things, quite casually he told them of a ledge in the hills, across the glacier, which contained, he believed, the most extraordinary deposit of gold in the world. So incredibly rich was it, that the rock itself had almost been replaced by solid metal. The Alaska gold, he said, was only the sweepings, in his opinion, of this immense store.

At the sound of the word "gold," the eyes of the man named Roscoe had brightened for the first time since they had taken him, shivering from his long immersion in the cold water, aboard the *Walrus*. He drew into the circle that sat about the reading lamp, and began asking questions. Gold was something he knew about. He had mined it in Australia, in California, and in the Klondike. He questioned Captain Fielding about the exact whereabouts of the ledge, about the sort of ore it occurred in, and about the best means of cutting it out.

To some extent his own excitement infected the others. Even Captain Planck, whose only well-understood form of wealth was whale blubber, began to take an interest in Roscoe's questions and in the explorer's answers to them.

It was a strange and rather pathetic sort of excitement, Captain Fielding thought. To them, in their practically hopeless plight, gold was about the least useful thing they could find; not hard enough to tip lances or arrows with, too heavy and too easily melted for domestic purposes. However, it gave them something to think about, and he, without a suspicion of the sinister direction in which these thoughts might turn, went on and told them all he knew.

When, after a period of tantalizing twilight, the sun again came fairly up over the horizon, they be-sought their commander, with a savage sort of eagerness from which he might have augured ill, that he take them at once to the ledge. They had caught sight of it from a distance, even as Cayley had done, hung in the air above the valley, and had run recklessly on ahead of their leader. When he came up to them, he found them dangerously excited, the man Roscoe fairly dazed and drunken with it.

Finally Fielding had left them to their own devices, and came away with his two companions. And until the light of that short day had begun to fail, they—the *Walrus* people—stayed, gloating over this strangely useless treasure.

For three days after that the man Roscoe never spoke a word. On the fourth day, when the little party assembled for their mid-day meal, the eleven men of the *Walrus* were the only ones to answer the summons. Captain Fielding and his two companions had disappeared.

Captain Planck could not recall that meal now without shuddering, for there at the foot of the table, opposite to him, had sat the man Roscoe, with murder written plain in every line of his face. He had looked a beast, rather than a man, that day. The sated blood lust in his eyes made them positively terrifying, so that the others shrank away from him. He had seemed not to notice it, at least not to take offense at it. He was in hilarious spirits for the first time since they had known him; seemed really to try to be a good companion.

Captain Planck abdicated his leadership that day. He was perfectly conscious of the fact. He had known that to retain the leadership he must take that murderer out and execute him. He knew that if he did not do this, the murderer, not he, would hereafter command the party, and that unless he himself yielded the promptest obedience of any, he would follow the luckless trio whom they were never to see again.

From that day to this there had been no more murders. Roscoe had ruled them with a decision and a truculence which put anything like insubordination out of the question. He had been obeyed better than Captain Planck ever had been. He had worked them fiercely all those four years, cutting, everlastingly, at that wonderful, exhaustless golden ledge, beating the friable ore out of it with heavy mauls, then, laboriously, conveying the great rude slabs of pure metal on rough sledges, over the perpetual ice of the glacier, to a cave near the shore, where they had deposited it. There were literally tons of it hidden there when the smoke from the yacht's funnel was first seen on the horizon.

The moment the news of the approaching steamer was reported to Roscoe, he had entered upon what seemed to his followers a thoroughly

HENRY KITCHELL WEBSTER

irrational and inexplicable line of action. He had ordered them, first, to remove all signs of recent habitation from the hut to the cave where their gold was concealed; then, to cover the cave mouth with a heap of boulders, to secure it against discovery.

Long before the strongest glass on the ship could have made out their moving figures, he took the whole party back to the hills in hiding. He had kept them from answering the hails and the gun-fire from the yacht by the sheer weight of his authority, without vouchsafing a word of explanation.

The next day they had seen the searching party come ashore, and with their knowledge of the lay of the land found it perfectly easy to evade observation, though nothing but the strong habit of obedience kept them from courting it.

Then, along in the afternoon, had happened what seemed to them the strangest thing of all. They had seen a solitary straggler from the searching party coming alone across the ice. He could not see them. It would have been perfectly easy to evade him, but Roscoe now ordered them to go down to him and tell him who they were, and to offer to escort him along the trail down the glacier. And at a certain point they were to lag behind and let him go on alone. That was all any of them knew of their leader's plans, till they saw the flying dart and the smudge of crimson on the snow.

Now, at last, came Planck to the leader, asking the reason why. But his mission, as it appeared, had not prospered.

For a long time Roscoe walked steadily on, until the two had come far up the glacier. Finally, when he did stop, he whirled quite around and stood confronting Planck, squarely in the middle of a narrow path between two deep fissures in the ice. His eyes were glittering malevolently:

"Do you know any reason," he asked in a thick voice, "why I don't pick you up and drop you down one of those cracks there, or why I don't serve you as I served that fellow yesterday?"

Planck thought he meant to do it, but, with the fatalism that marks the men of his profession, he stood fast, and eyed his big opponent.

"You're strong enough to," he said.

"And I'll do it if I want to; you know that," Roscoe supplemented.

"Yes, I know that." The big man nodded curtly.

"Well, I'm not going to now, because I choose not to. Listen. If you had the chance, could you navigate that solid mahogany, hand-painted ship down there?"

Planck cleared his throat, as if something were stifling him. "With a crew, yes," he answered.

"Could Schwartz run those nickel-plated engines he'd find in her, do you think?"

"Yes."

"Well, within two days I'll give you a chance to make good. Now, I'm going to tell you my plan, not because you asked, but because I want you to know. I'd run the whole thing alone if I could, but I want you with me. We're going to take that yacht and we're going off alone in her,—we of the Whaler, alone. Do you understand that?"

"They're better armed than we," said Planck reflectively; "better fed, better everything. And man for man, bar you, they're just as good, and they're three to one of us. It will want some pretty good planning."

"You needn't worry about that," answered Roscoe. "I didn't expect you to make the plans; I knew you couldn't. I've made them myself; they're working right now. Can you keep your tongue in your head and listen?"

Planck nodded.

"That searching party didn't go back to the yacht last night. They're all camped together—about twenty of them—down in Little Bear Valley. There aren't above half a dozen fire-arms in the bunch; none of the sailors from the yacht have any, and they've got about two days' rations. They're all there together, except the one man we accounted for yesterday."

"I see," said Planck; "and you think we can capture the yacht now while they're ashore."

"Don't try to think, I tell you," Roscoe growled. "I'm doing the thinking. There are probably ten able-bodied men left on the yacht. That's not good enough odds, considering the way they're armed. But about an hour ago I sent Miguel down to the shore party to be their guide. He isn't going to say anything much to them, but what he says will be enough, I reckon. He's to pretend he's dotty and can't understand what they say to him."

Planck's eyes widened a little and he did not ask his next question very steadily. "Where is he going to take them?"

"Can't you guess that? He's going to lead them into Fog Lake, of course."

The thought of it made Planck's teeth chatter. Fog Lake was, perhaps, the most curious natural phenomenon upon that strange Arctic land,—a little cup-shaped valley, from which the fog never lifted—had never lifted once in all the four years they had lived there. On days when the rest of the land was clear, the fog hung there, half way up the side of the hills, so that from the ridges surrounding it it really looked like a strange vapory sea. They had explored the edges of it, fearsomely, at times, but had never penetrated far enough to learn the secret of its mystery, if it had one.

"You say Miguel is going to guide them in there?" Planck asked. "How's he going to get out himself?"

Roscoe laughed shortly: "Oh, he's likely to get out. But he's the cheapest man we've got, and that's why I sent him. He's half silly now, and he's likely to go ice-crazy most any time. I've seen it coming on him. Oh, he'll get them in all right. Whether he gets out himself, or not, doesn't matter."

"And then?" Planck asked.

"Why, they'll send out a relief party from the yacht, of course. The yacht's people know what rations the searching party took with them, and when they don't come back in two days, they'll probably set out from the yacht, with every able-bodied man on board, and try to find the first party and bring it in. As soon as they are well out of hearing, we take the yacht. We may not find a living soul aboard her; and we certainly can't leave one there. But we'll steam up and take our gold aboard—all our gold. And then, well—there's where you'll come in."

"But what then, man? My God! what then? Do you suppose we can go steaming into San Francisco, or any other port in the world, with all that gold in our hull and another captain's log and papers? We might just as well hang ourselves from our own crow-jack yard."

"I hope your wits will improve when you get a deck under your feet," Roscoe growled. "On land here you're about as much good as a pelican in a foot race. No, your sailing orders won't be San Francisco, nor any other port that has such a thing as a revenue officer about. But you ought to know the north coast line over there as far east as McKenzie Bay. You must know some harbor there where we can lie up for the winter and not be bothered."

"Yes," said Planck, "I could take the yacht to such a place as that. There's a very good harbor in behind Hirshel Island. But what will we do when we get there?"

"After that, it's my affair," said Roscoe. "We'll winter on the yacht. Then when the weather begins to loosen up a bit, but before the spring thaws, we'll land our gold and our stores; cache all the gold, except what we can carry over the trail, say, about five hundred pounds of it, and we'll leave the yacht's sea-cocks open, so that when the ice goes out, she'll scuttle herself. We shall probably find sledges, and perhaps a pony or two, on the yacht. If we do, it will be easy. It's only a short hike to one of the tributaries of the Porcupine River. Once we reach the Porcupine, it will be easy, for it flows into the Yukon, and that's as good as a railway line. We'll make a raft and float all the way down to Saint Michaels with no trouble at all. The gold we have with us will be enough to take us down to Vancouver, and there we can charter a ship. You take command of her, and we go north through the Straits again that very summer—next summer that will be, of course. We go back to the harbor where we left the yacht. You can figure out the rest for yourself, I guess."

"Yes," said Planck. "It's all very well,—only, won't there be a good many to trust that sort of secret to?"

Roscoe looked at him with a savage sort of grin. "Come, you're improving. But that hike across the mountains to the upper tributaries of the Porcupine is a hard trail. There aren't likely to be many of us left by the time we get started floating down open water. When we get to the Yukon it won't be surprising if there isn't anybody left at all, but you and me."

Planck caught his meaning quickly enough, indeed, a duller man could have read it in Roscoe's savage light blue eyes; and the thought made his teeth chatter. He would have felt a deadlier terror, perhaps, could he have read the thought that lay at the bottom of Roscoe's mind. The gold hunter was not much of a sailor, but he felt confident that on the broad stretches of the Yukon he could navigate a raft alone.

"There's this," said Planck after a moment's silence. "You're planning to maroon that whole party, those that you don't kill, on this forsaken coast. But they came here for a purpose; came to find Captain Fielding, that's clear enough. They won't have come without arranging for a relief ship to follow next summer in case they don't come back. The relief isn't likely to find many of them alive. But it may find a few, and even one survivor would be enough—"

Roscoe interrupted him impatiently. "Why, what could a survivor tell? What could the whole party tell? They don't know there's a living creature on this land besides themselves, except silly old Miguel; and they'll think he belonged to Fielding's party. They'll think the yacht broke adrift all by herself. No, there'll be no possibility of following our trail, unless they set the petrels and loons to watching us."

At that, Roscoe turned and resumed his way along the icy trail, leaving the former captain to fall in behind him. But before he had gone a dozen paces, he whirled around again, suddenly, and shot a blazing, searching look straight into Planck's face. It was as if he had intended to surprise there the inmost thoughts and intentions of his subordinate's mind. He seemed satisfied, however, with the expression he found in the weather-beaten face.

"There's this much more," he said: "you're not to talk to me any more than you can help from now on. You're to take my orders grudgingly. Those other fellows will probably try to start a conspiracy against me. If they do, I want you to be the head of it."

Planck nodded.

IV

The Throwing-Stick

"Oh, I suppose," said Jeanne, "there's no use worrying."

Across the table from where she sat at breakfast in the snug, warm, luxurious little dining-room on the yacht, old Mr. Fanshaw methodically laid his coffee-spoon in the saucer beside his cup, and looked up at her with his slow, deliberate smile.

"My dear," he said, "remember that Tom is in the party. Unless they find everything that, by the utmost stretch of hope, they could find, he would insist on keeping up the search as long as the light lasted, and when the light failed, there would be no more light to come home by. Don't think of worrying; I don't. We'll hear nothing of them for hours."

"It won't be as long as that," she predicted confidently. "My sky-man will probably bring me news before then."

Old Mr. Fanshaw halted his coffee cup half way to his lips, "Your—what?" he questioned. "Oh, I understand." And then he laughed. But his face grew suddenly serious, and he looked intently, curiously, into hers. "My child!" he cried; "it can't be that you are taking that dream of yours seriously. If I thought that, I would have to believe that this queer Arctic climate was doing strange things with those nimble wits of yours. A man alighting on the ice-floe, out of mid air, and telling you that he had just dropped in from Point Barrow; it's like the flight from the moon of Cyrano de Bergerac."

She pressed her finger tips thoughtfully against her eyelids. "I know," she said, "it's perfectly incredible, uncle Jerry, but it's perfectly true for all that."

"Nonsense! Nonsense!" he said explosively. "Don't carry a joke too far, my dear."

"It's anything but a joke," she said slowly, "and if it was a dream—if he, the sky-man, was nothing but a vision, he certainly left me a material souvenir of his visit." Then, with a nod toward the buffet, she spoke to Mr. Fanshaw's big negro valet who was serving their breakfast: "Hand Mr. Fanshaw that queer looking stick, Sam, the one on the buffet. Why—why, what's the matter?" For she had lifted her eyes to the man's face as she finished speaking. It was wooden with fright, and the whites showed all around the pupils of his eyes.

"No, Miss Jeanne," he said, "Scuse me. I wouldn't touch dat stick, not for all de gol' and jewels in de world; not even to oblige him."

"What's that?" Fanshaw exclaimed, whirling upon him. "What do you mean? What, the devil, are you talking about?"

"I seen him, Mr. Fanshaw; I seen him myself, comin' down out of de sky las' night. I was out on deck, suh."

Fanshaw looked quickly from the negro's face to the girl's, as if he suspected a hoax, but the terror in one face and the mystification in the other were obviously genuine.

Then he rose and went over to the buffet, returning to the table with the oddly-shaped, rudely-whittled stick. "Do you mean to say," he demanded, looking up at the girl with a puzzled frown—"do you mean to say that he, the man you dreamed about, made you a present of this stick?"

She laughed. "If that seems a reasonable way of putting it, yes; at least it slipped out of his belt and I found it where he had been sitting. But can you imagine what he used it for?"

"Oh, I know what it is, but that only makes the puzzle all the deeper. It's an Eskimo throwing-stick. They use it to shoot darts with. It lies in the palm of the hand, so, and the dart is put in that groove, though the butt of this one seems curiously misshapen; I can't make it fit my hand. But I can't figure out how the thing got aboard the yacht; it wasn't here yesterday."

"Of course not," she said; "my sky-man brought it."

He ran his fingers through his bushy grey hair perplexedly. Then laid the thing down and seated himself at the table. "At any rate," he said, "we needn't let even a mystery spoil our breakfast. Come, my dear, you've eaten almost nothing. That omelet deserves better treatment."

Obediently she took up her fork, but almost immediately laid it down again, and he saw her eyes brighten with tears. "Of course, if there'd been any news, if there'd been anything to find, we'd have heard."

Silently he reached across the table and patted the hand that lay there on the white cloth.

"Oh, I know I oughtn't to cry," she said, "and I won't; it's your goodness and kindness to me as much as anything else. Ever since he went away you've been like a father to me, and Tom, dear old Tom, like a brother. And then building this ship and coming up here yourself, facing the dangers yourself and letting Tom face them, all for such an impossible, hopeless hope as that message the sea brought to us."

Her voice faltered there, and she bent down abruptly and kissed the hand that was still caressing her own.

"My child," he said, "your father and I were like brothers—nearer to each other than most brothers. He went away, knowing that if his venture failed, if it ended fatally for him, as it probably did, I should regard you as my daughter—as just as much a child of mine as Tom is. If you hadn't been in the case at all, we'd have built this ship and come up here to find Tom Fielding just the same. There, don't cry. Put on that big fur coat of yours and come out with me on deck."

It is safe to say that no craft even remotely resembling the *Aurora* had ever cut the Arctic circle before; but for all that, old Mr. Fanshaw had known what he was about when he ordered the building of her. Captain Corcoran, of the United States Revenue Cutter *Bear*, a man who knew Arctic waters and Arctic ice as well as any who ever sailed, admitted as much when he came aboard at St. Michaels to pay a call. In fact, old Mr. Fanshaw knew what he was about most of the time, as his financial rivals were frequently forced to admit.

His later years of leisure and comparative ease had not dulled the intellectual processes of that keen, shrewd brain of his; and he knew the sea better than he knew most things. In his early rough-and-tumble days he had voyaged much at random about the world, and now that he was old, a fair proportion of his great wealth was invested in ocean carriers.

The news from Captain Fielding,—a strangely pathetic account of his expedition and the loss of his ship, which an Arctic whaler had fished up in a bottle the summer before,—had not reached them in San Francisco until after the passage through Behring Straits was ice-locked for the winter.

Fanshaw had spent the time, therefore, and devoted practically the whole of his personal attention to building and equipping the *Aurora* for the exact purpose to which he meant to put her. Her hull had received the most thoughtful care, and for just one great purpose. In vain the designers at the ship-yard protested that she would be slow, unhandy, wet and laborious in a head-sea. Fanshaw replied, tranquilly, that he knew that as well as they did, but that a hull of that shape could not be crushed in the ice, whatever the milling forces of the pack which beset her might be. It was this milling force of the pack that had destroyed Fielding's ship; that had destroyed also—though Fanshaw did not know it—the *Walrus*. But if the *Aurora* were beset, she would be able to wait till open water came again.

HENRY KITCHELL WEBSTER

She had started out equipped with everything that knowledge and invention could suggest; everything that might prove necessary on her long, precarious voyage. And after that, she had been supplied with all the luxuries that there was room for. Fanshaw had done a good deal of roughing it in his younger days, and he was willing to rough it again should the event make it necessary, but until the necessity should arise, he meant to be as comfortable as possible.

It was altogether likely, they thought when they started out, that they should be able to return from their expedition without wintering north of the straits. In that case, the expedition would be nothing more than a comfortable yachting cruise. And there was no use, Mr. Fanshaw said, in beginning to eat walrus steak the moment one got outside the Golden Gate, just because the cruise was to be in Arctic waters. So the breakfast to which he and Jeanne had just done such scanty justice was as daintily served, and as appetizing a repast as they could have had in the great stone house on Nob Hill that Jeanne had called home ever since her father went away.

It was under this reasonable expectation that the voyage would be productive of few dangers and few discomforts, that the old gentleman had yielded to Jeanne's impassioned plea, and taken her along.

The moment Mr. Fanshaw and Jeanne emerged upon the deck they heard the sound of oars beneath them, and looking over the rail saw one of the boats in which the shore party had set out, pulling up along side the accommodation ladder. Three men were in it, two of the crew and Tom Fanshaw.

"What news, Tom?" his father called out anxiously enough to belie his former tranquil manner. "Have you found anything? I hope there's nothing wrong."

The younger man looked up. He saw his father, but not the girl. "Nothing wrong," he growled, "except this infernal ankle of mine. I've sprained it again, and I did it just when—" He broke the sentence off short there, his eye falling at that moment upon Jeanne.

She paled a little, for she had been quick to perceive that something he had been about to tell would not be told now, or must be told differently. But she waited until his father, together with the two sailors, had got the disabled man up onto the deck and safely installed in an easy chair. Then gravely, but steadily, "Just as what, Tom? What clue had they found just as you had to come away?"

"It was very wonderful," he said, "quite inexplicable. Just as we were about breaking camp this morning, we saw a man coming toward us across the ice. We thought at first that it was Hunter, and we were mighty glad to see him, because he had strayed off somewhere and hadn't camped with us. But we soon saw it wasn't he, wasn't a man anything like him. He was a queer, slouching, shuffling creature, dressed in skins, and he came up in a hesitating way, as if he was afraid of us. He couldn't talk English, nor understand it, apparently. He looked to me like a Portuguese, and I tried him in Spanish—good Filipino Spanish— on the chance. I thought it startled him a little, and he pricked up his ears at it, but he couldn't understand that either. He just kept beckoning and repeating two words—"

"What words, Tom? Out with it!" This from the old gentleman, who had controlled his patience with difficulty during the little silence. But the younger man hesitated and looked into the girl's face, mutely, half-questioningly, before he spoke.

"The words," he said, "seemed to be your father's name—'Captain Fielding'; it sounded like that."

She went quite white, and reeled a little. Then clutched at the shrouds for support. The old gentleman was at her side in an instant, his strong, steadying arm across her shoulders. Tom himself half rose from his chair, only to drop back into it again with a grimace of pain and a little dew of perspiration on his forehead. He looked rather white himself under the tan.

"I suppose,"—the girl said almost voicelessly, "I suppose I mustn't dare—even let myself begin to hope yet, must I, not—yet?"

"I don't know," said Tom. "The fellow seemed half-crazed; seemed, almost, to have lost the power of speech from long disuse of it. But he meant to take us somewhere, that was clear enough from his gestures. If I could only have seen you before I began to blurt the thing out, I'd have spared you the suspense until there was something to tell. I'm sorry, Jeanne."

His contrition seemed to serve as a stronger stimulant than his father's caresses. She went quickly over to him and took one of his hands. "Don't worry, Tom, dear," she said. "Even at the worst, they'll find something, and that's really all we hoped for when we started."

She seated herself on the arm of his chair, steadying herself with one hand upon his shoulder. There was no relationship of blood between these two, but they were like brother and sister, for all that.

"It's queer," she said, at the end of a rather long silence. "I'm sure there was no Portuguese in father's expedition. Except for two or three Swedes and Norwegians, they were all Americans. I know the name of every man who sailed in his ship."

"He might have taken someone on at St. Michaels," suggested the elder Fanshaw.

"Yes," she said a little dubiously, "only he never thought much of southern Europeans as sea-faring men."

There was another silence after that. She rose presently and began sweeping the shore line with a prismatic binocular which was slung across her shoulders. The two men exchanged glances behind her, the elder, one of inquiry, his son, a reluctant negative. No, it would clearly be insane to build any hope on the incident.

At last she let the glass fall from her listless hand and turned to them, her face haggard with the torture of impossible hope. "I wish my sky-man would come,"—she said forlornly, "come whirling down out of the air, with news of them."

"Your sky-man?" said Tom Fanshaw questioningly.

Here was something to talk about at last, and the old gentleman seized the chance it afforded.

"Yes, we've another mystery," he said. "See what you can do toward solving it." With that for an introduction, he plunged into a humorous account of Jeanne's report of her adventure of the night before, of the man who had dropped down from the sky, in the middle of the night, and talked to her awhile, and then flown away again. "She was really out on the ice floe," he said; "so much I concede; but when I assure her that she dreamed the rest, she is skeptical about my explanation."

"But even you can't explain," she protested, "how I could dream about an Eskimo throwing-stick, and then bring it back to the yacht with me when I was wide-awake, and show it to you at the breakfast-table this morning."

"I'll have to admit," said the old gentleman, "that my explanation doesn't adequately account for that."

The expression of the younger man's face was perplexed rather than incredulous.

"But, my boy," cried the elder man, "think of it! He comes down out of the sky and says he just dropped in from Point Barrow; and that's five hundred miles away. That's just as impossible as it would be to materialize an Eskimo throwing-stick out of a dream, every bit."

"No, hardly that," said Tom judicially. "What was his aeroplane like? What was it made of? Did you notice it particularly?"

"Yes," she said; "I helped him fold it up. It was made of bladders and bamboo and catgut, he said."

"And his motor?" cried Tom. "What was his motor like?"

"There was no motor at all," she said; "just wings."

"There you see, Tom," interrupted his father; "absolute moonshine."

But still the younger man shook a doubtful head. "No," he said, "the thing's not impossible—not inconceivable, at least. The big birds can fly that far, and think nothing of it."

The old man snorted, "They're built that way. Think of the immense strength of their wing muscles."

"Not so enormous," said the younger man. "I dissected the wing of an albatross once to see. It's not by main strength they keep afloat in the air; it's by catching the trick of it."

"That's what he said," the girl cried eagerly. "He told me he could fly across the North Pole, from Dawson City to St. Petersburg, and when I asked him if he could keep flying, flying all the time like that, he said the biggest birds didn't fly; they sailed, and he said he sailed, too, and the force of gravity was his keel."

Her story was making its impression on the younger man, at least, even if his father was as impervious to it as he still seemed.

"Well, if you dreamed that," said Tom, "it was a mighty intelligent dream, I'll say that for it."

"But it wasn't a dream at all," she cried. "Didn't I help him take the thing apart and fold it up into a bundle? And didn't he say that he was a tax payer, and that his name was Philip Cayley?"

She was addressing the elder man as she spoke, and as she mentioned the name—it was the first time she had mentioned it to any one—she saw him shoot a startled, inquiring glance at his son. Following it, she met Tom Fanshaw's eyes staring at her in utter amazement.

"Cayley," he said, half under his breath; "Philip Cayley—"

"That was the name," she answered—

"And yet, I'd be willing to swear," he said, "I've never mentioned that name to you in my life."

"No," she said. "Why should you? I know you didn't. I knew I had never heard it before when he told me it was his." She hesitated a moment; then, "Did you ever know a man named Philip Cayley, Tom?"

He let the question go by, unheeded, and, for a long time, gazed

HENRY KITCHELL WEBSTER

silently out over the land. "I suppose," he said at last, "that a coincidence like this, any coincidence, if only it be strange enough, will bring a touch of superstitious fear to anybody. I never had even a touch of it before, in all my life; and I always had a little feeling of contempt for the men who showed it. But now—well, well, I wish poor old Hunter hadn't strayed away last night. I wasn't alarmed about him before, and I've no rational ground for alarm about him now. Only—"

He did not go on until she prompted him with a question. "And has the sky-man, Philip Cayley, anything to do with the coincidence?"

Still it was a little while before he spoke. "I suppose I'd better tell you the story—a part of it, at least; I couldn't tell it all to you." He turned to his father. "You, I think, already know it." Then, with evident reluctance, he began telling the story to Jeanne.

"There was a man named Philip Cayley," he said, "in Hunter's class at the Point, three classes ahead of me, that was. He and Hunter were chums, the 'David and Jonathan,' you know, of their class. I remember what a stroke of luck for them everybody thought it was when they were assigned to service in the same regiment. It seems to me, as I think back to our days at the Point—of course, my memory may be playing me a trick—but it seems to me that even then Cayley was interested in the navigation of the air. Somebody kept a scrap-book of all that the newspapers and magazines reported on the subject, any way; I remember seeing it. I think it was Cayley.

"I lost sight of him and Hunter when they went to the Philippines. It is only justice to Hunter to say that I never heard a word of the thing that happened out there from him. He never seemed to want to talk to me about it, and, of course, I never forced him. Well, I can make a short story of it, any way, though it has to be a nasty one.

"A man came into the Post one day, the head man of one of the neighboring villages out there, a man with white blood in him— Spanish blood. They carried him in, for he couldn't walk. He was in horrible condition. He had been tortured—I won't go into the details of that—and flogged nearly to death. He said that Cayley had done it. He had remonstrated with Cayley, he said, because he feared for his daughter's safety—she was a pretty girl, whiter than her father— and it seems that the man's fears had some justification. It appears that Cayley had come out there, blind drunk, with a couple of troopers, who deserted that same night, and manhandled the old man. The girl joined in her father's accusation, at least she didn't deny anything.

"Cayley was away on scout duty at the time when the man came in—the thing had happened some days prior, just before he started out. It came like a thunderbolt out of a clear sky, for everybody liked Cayley and thought him an exceptionally decent, clean sort of chap, though he and Hunter both were drinking a good deal just then. Poor Hunter was all broken up about it. Everybody believed that he really knew some incriminating facts against Cayley, but he never would speak.

"As for Cayley himself, he made no defense whatever. He denied he did it, and that was all. There wasn't any real corroborative evidence against him, so the court martial dismissed the case as not proved. But he wouldn't testify himself, nor have a single witness called in his behalf, and he resigned from the service then and there, and disappeared, so far as I know, from the world. I heard he had a ranch down somewhere in New Mexico, near Sandoval, I think the place was."

His father saw a quick tightening in the girl's horror-stricken eyes at the sound of the name, which evidently, in some way, helped corroborate the story to her, but he did not question her about it.

"Well, that's all I know," said Tom in conclusion. "The thing about broke Perry Hunter's heart, and he quit the service himself shortly after. It had this effect on him, though. He told me the other night that he had never drunk a drop since he had left the army.

"But you can see how queer it is, can't you? What an odd, nameless feeling of foreboding it gave me when on the night that Perry Hunter disappeared, I learned that a vision, or a man, who called himself Philip Cayley, came flying down out of the midnight sky and talked to you?"

The girl was looking at him in a strange, dazed sort of way. "I can add this much to your story, Tom," she said. "When he was telling me last night, that sky-man, how he lived up there on the wing, I said what a contempt he must have for all the world, for all us wingless ones, to whom the little mountains, seas, and rivers opposed such barriers. And he gave a short, rather bitter sort of laugh, and said if it were true, then he had only conquered for the world the feeling the world had held for him."

There was a silence after that, while the three out there on the *Aurora's* deck looked blankly into each other's faces.

The silence was broken at last, by none of them, but by a hail from the shore. "Ahoy, *Aurora!*" cried the voice.

Mr. Fanshaw answered with a wave of his arm. "That's Donovan," he said to the others; then, "Yes; what is it?" he cried.

"Will you send a dinghy for me, please?"

The boat was despatched at once, and while they waited, Mr. Fanshaw borrowed Jeanne's field-glasses for a look at the man who had hailed them. "He's in a hurry," said the old gentleman. "He looks as if he had news of one sort or another." They all had felt it in the mere timbre of his voice,—something urgent; something ominous.

It seemed an interminable while before the returning boat came alongside the foot of the accommodation ladder. When the new-comer appeared at the head of it, his face had plainly written on it the story of some tragedy.

"What is it?" Jeanne asked, not very steadily. "Oh, please don't try to break it to me! Tell me, just as you do the others."

"It's nothing concerning you, miss, not especially, I mean; nothing to do with your father." Then he turned to Mr. Fanshaw, "I found Mr. Hunter, sir."

"Dead?" The tone in which Donovan had spoken made the question hardly necessary.

"Yes, sir. His body is lodged deep down in one of the ice fissures in the glacier. I could see it perfectly, though I couldn't get down to it."

Tom Fanshaw covered his face with his hands for a moment. Then looked up and asked, steadily: "He slipped, I suppose?"

At the same moment his father asked: "Do you think we shall be able to recover the body?"

Donovan answered this question first.

"We can try, sir, though I've not much hope of our succeeding."

Then, after a moment's hesitation, he turned to the son.

"No, sir, he didn't fall; at least it wasn't the fall that killed him. I found this in a cleft in the ice near by. It must have been driven clean through his throat, sir."

He held out, in a shaking hand, a long, slim ivory dart, sharp almost as steel could be, and stained brown with blood. "He was murdered, sir," Donovan concluded simply.

"Give me the dart," the old gentleman demanded. As he examined it, his fine old face hardened. "Do you see?" he asked, holding it out to his son. "There is no notch in the end for a bow-string, but it will lie very truly in the groove of that throwing-stick that Jeanne brought aboard the yacht this morning."

Then he turned to the girl. "I'm afraid your visitor last night was no vision, my dear, after all."

But the girl was looking and pointing skyward.

V

The Dart

High, high up in the clear opaline air was a broad, golden gleam. Nearer it came, and broader it grew, and as it grew, and as it caught more fully the slanting beams of the low-hanging Arctic sun, it shone with prismatic, iridescent color among the gold, like an archangel's wings. The shining thing towered at last right above the mast-head, but high, high up in the sky.

Then the four watchers uttered, in one breath, a horror-frozen cry, for, as a falcon does, it dropped, hurtling. But not to the destruction they foresaw; once more it darted forward, circled half round the yacht, so close to her rail that they heard the whining scream of the air as those mighty wings cleft through it. And then, as on the night before, his planes upstanding straight, Cayley leaped backward, clear of them, and alighted on the floe beside the yacht.

Old Mr. Fanshaw walked quickly around the deck-house and hailed the new arrival. "Won't you come aboard, sir?" Jeanne heard him call. "I'll send the dinghy for you."

"Thank you," they heard him answer. "There wasn't much room for alighting on the deck or I could have spared you the trouble."

Jeanne stole a glance into Tom Fanshaw's stern, set face, wondering if the tone and the inflection of that voice would impress him as it had her. "Don't you find it hard to believe that he could have done such a thing?" she asked; "a man with a voice like that?"

"I only wish I found it possible to believe he hasn't. Not every villain in this world looks and talks like a thug. If they did, life would be simpler." He paused a moment, then added, "And we know he did the other thing—out there in the Philippines."

Her face paled a little at that, stiffened, somehow, and she did not answer. They sat silent, listening to the receding oars of the dinghy as it made for the ice-floe. Suddenly the girl saw an expression of perplexity come into Tom Fanshaw's face. "When you talked with him, Jeanne, last night, did you tell him our name? Mine and father's, I mean? Did you give him any hint who we were, or that we were people who might know him?"

"No, only my own; and who father was. He asked me about that."

"Ah," he said. "Then that accounts for his coming back."

She had hoped that in some way or other the trend of her answer might be in the sky-man's favor, and was disappointed at seeing that the reverse was true.

She had to repress a sudden impulse of flight when they heard the returning dinghy scrape alongside the accommodation ladder. And even though she resisted it, she shrank back, nevertheless, into a corner behind Tom Fanshaw's chair. The old gentleman was waiting at the head of the ladder, blocking, with the bulk of his body, the new-comer's view of the deck and those who were waiting there until he should have fairly come aboard.

"Mr. Philip Cayley?" he inquired stiffly. "My name is Fanshaw, sir; and I think my son, who sits yonder—" he stepped aside and inclined his head a little in Tom's direction—"is, or was once, an acquaintance of yours." From her place in the background, Jeanne saw a look of perplexity—nothing more than that, she felt sure—come into Philip Cayley's face. The old gentleman's manner was certainly an extraordinary one in which to greet a total stranger, five hundred miles away from human habitation. Cayley seemed to be wondering whether it represented anything more than the individual eccentricity of the old gentleman, or not.

Evidently he recognized Tom Fanshaw at once, and, after an almost imperceptible hesitation, seemed to make up his mind to overlook the singularity of his welcome. "I remember Lieutenant Fanshaw well," he said, smiling and speaking pleasantly enough, though the girl thought she heard an underlying note of hardness in his voice. "You were at the Point while I was there, weren't you? But it's many years since I've seen you."

At that he crossed the deck to where young Fanshaw was sitting, and held out his hand. Tom Fanshaw's hands remained clasped tightly on the two arms of his chair, and the stern lines of his face never relaxed, though he was looking straight into Cayley's eyes. "I remember you at the Point very well," he said, "but, unfortunately, there are some stories of your subsequent career which I remember altogether too well."

The girl did not need the sudden look of incandescent anger she saw in Philip Cayley's face to turn the sudden tide of her sympathy toward him. It was not for this old wrong of his that they had summoned him, as to a bar of justice, to the *Aurora's* deck, but to meet the accusation of the murder of Perry Hunter. Whether he was guilty of that murder, or not, this raking up of an old, unproved offense was a piece of unnecessary brutality. She could not understand how kind-hearted old Tom could have done such a thing. Thinking it over afterward, she was able to understand a little better.

In her own heart she did not believe Cayley guilty. Neither the story Tom had told her, nor the damning array of circumstances which pointed against him had counteracted, as yet, the impression which his singularly charming personality had made upon her during that strange, mysterious hour they had had together upon the ice-floe the night before.

To her, then, his manner of coming aboard the yacht had pointed to innocence rather than to guilt—his self-possession, his smile, his extended hand. But to Tom, who entertained no doubt at all of his guilt, these things were the simple manifestation of effrontery, of an almost inhuman coolness and impudence, and had exasperated him beyond his self-control.

From behind Tom's chair she could see how heavily this blow he dealt had told. For one instant Philip Cayley's sensitive face had shown a look of unspeakable pain. Then it stiffened into a mere mask—icy; disdainful.

It was a moment before he spoke. When he did, it was to her. "I don't know why this gentleman presumes to keep his seat," he said. "If it is as a precaution against a blow, perhaps, he need not let his prudence interfere with his courtesy."

"He has just met with an accident," she said quickly. "He can't stand—No, Tom. Sit still," and her hands upon his shoulders enforced the command.

Cayley bowed ever so slightly. "I suppose," he continued, "that since last night you also have heard the story which this gentleman protests he remembers so much too well?"

"Yes," she said.

At that, he turned to old Mr. Fanshaw: "Will you tell me, sir," he asked, "for what purpose I was invited to come aboard this yacht?"

Tom spoke before his father could answer—spoke with a short, ugly laugh, "You weren't invited. You were, as the police say, 'wanted.'"

"Be quiet, Tom!" his father commanded. "That's not the way to talk—to anybody."

Cayley's lips framed a faint, satirical smile; and again he bowed slowly. But he said nothing, and stood, waiting for the old gentleman to go on.

This Mr. Fanshaw seemed to find it rather difficult to do. At last, however, he appeared to find the words he wanted. "When Miss

HENRY KITCHELL WEBSTER

Fielding gave us an account, this morning, of the strange visitor she had received last night, we were—I was, at least—inclined to think she had been dreaming it without knowing it. To convince me that you were real and not a vision, she showed me a material and highly interesting souvenir of your call. It was an Eskimo throwing-stick, Mr. Cayley, such as the Alaskan and Siberian Indians use to throw darts and harpoons with. It happens that I've had a good deal of experience among those people, and that I know how deadly an implement it is."

He made a little pause there, and then looked up suddenly into Cayley's face. "And I imagine," he continued very slowly, "that you know that as well as I do."

Cayley made no answer at all, but if Mr. Fanshaw hoped to find, with those shrewd eyes of his, any look of guilt or consternation in the pale face that confronted him, he was disappointed.

Suddenly, he turned to his son, "Where is that thing that Donovan brought aboard with him just now?" he asked.

The blood-stained dart lay on the deck beside Tom's chair. He picked it up and held it out toward his father, but the elder man, with a gesture, indicated to Cayley that he was to take it in his hand; then, "Jeanne, my dear," he asked, "will you fetch out from the cabin the stick which dropped from Mr. Cayley's belt last night?"

When she had departed on the errand, he spoke to Cayley, "You will observe that the butt of this dart is not notched, as it would have to be if it were shot from a bow."

He did not look at Cayley's face as he spoke, but at his hands. Could it be possible, he wondered, that those hands could hold the thing with that sinister brown stain upon it—the stain of Perry Hunter's blood—without trembling? They were steady enough, though, so far as he could see.

When Jeanne came out with the stick, he handed that to Cayley also. "You will notice," he said, "that that dart and the groove in this stick were evidently made for each other, Mr. Cayley."

The pupils of Jeanne's eyes dilated as she watched the accused man fit them together, and then balance the stick in his hand, as if trying to discover how it could be put to so deadly a use as Mr. Fanshaw had indicated. He seemed preoccupied by nothing more than a purely intellectual curiosity.

His coolness seemed to anger Mr. Fanshaw, as it had formerly angered his son. For a moment this sudden anger of his rendered him almost inarticulate. Then:

"We don't want a demonstration!" came like the explosions of a quick-fire gun. "And you have no need for trying experiments. You knew how nicely that dart would fit in the groove that was cut for it. You know, altogether too well, what the stain is that discolors it. You know where we found that dart. You're only surprised that it was ever found at all—it and the body of the man it slew."

"Everything you say is perfectly true," said Cayley, very quietly. "I am surprised that the body of that man was ever recovered. I'm a little surprised, also, that you should think, because this stick fell from my belt last night, and this dart, which you found transfixing a man's throat this morning—"

Tom Fanshaw interrupted him. His eyes were blazing with excitement. "It was not from us that you learned that that dart transfixed the murdered man's throat!" he cried.

"I knew it, nevertheless," said Cayley in that quiet voice, not looking toward the man he answered, but still keeping his eyes on old Mr. Fanshaw. "And also a little surprised," he went on, as if he had not been interrupted, "that you should think, because this stick and this dart fit together, that I am, necessarily, a murderer."

"You have admitted it now, at all events," Mr. Fanshaw replied. His voice grew quieter, too, as the intensity of his purpose steadied it. "I suppose that is because, upon this 'No-Man's-Land,' you are outside the pale of law and statute—beyond the jurisdiction of any court. I tell you this: I think we would be justified in giving you a trial and hanging you from that yard there. We will not do it. We will not even take you back to the States to prison. You may live outlaw here and enjoy, undisturbed, your freedom, such as it is, and your thoughts and your conscience, such as they must be. But if ever you try to return to the world of men—"

Cayley interrupted the threat before it was spoken: "I have no wish to return to the world of men," he said. "I wish the world were empty of men, as this part of it is, or as I thought it was. I abandoned mankind once before, but yesterday when I saw men here, I felt a stirring of the blood—the call of what was in my own veins. Last night when I took to the air again, after the hour I had spent on that ice-floe yonder, I thought I wanted to come back to my own kind; wanted, in spite of the past, to be one of them again. Perhaps it is well that I should be rid of that delusion so quickly. I am rid of it, and I am rid of you—bloody, sodden, stupid, blind."

"Yet, with all my horror of you, my disdain of you, I should not expect one of you to do murder, without some sort of motive, some paltry hope of gain, upon the body of a stranger. It is of that that you accuse me—"

"A stranger!" Tom Fanshaw echoed. "Why, when you confess to so much, do you try to lie at the end? You can't think we don't know that the man you murdered was once your friend—or thought he was, God help him! Why try to make *us* believe that Perry Hunter was a stranger to you?"

The girl's wide eyes had never left Cayley's face since the moment of her return to the deck with the throwing-stick. Through it all,—through Fanshaw's hot accusation, and his own reply—through those last words of Tom's, it had never changed. There had been contempt and anger in it, subdued by an iron self-control; no other emotions than those two, until the very end. Until the mention of that name—"Perry Hunter."

But at the sound of that name—just then, the girl saw his face go bloodless, not all at once, slowly, rather. And then after a little while he uttered a great sob; not of grief, but such a sob as both the Fanshaws had heard before, when, in battle or skirmish, a soft-nosed bullet smashes its way through some great, knotted nerve centre. His hands went out in a convulsive gesture, both the stick and the dart which he held, falling from them, the stick at the girl's feet, the dart at his own. Then leaning back against the rail for support, he covered his face with his hands. At last, while they waited silently, he drew himself up straight and looked dazedly into her face.

Suddenly, to the amazement of the other two men, she crossed the deck to where he stood. "I'm perfectly sure, for my part, that you didn't do it; that you are not the murderer of Mr. Hunter. Won't you shake hands?"

He made no move to take hers, and though his eyes were turned upon her, he seemed to be looking through, rather than at her, so intense was his preoccupation.

Seeing that this was so, she laid her hand upon his forearm. "You didn't do it," she repeated, "but you know something about it, don't you? You saw it done, from a long way off—saw the murder, without knowing who its victim was."

"I might have saved him," he murmured brokenly, "if I had not hung aloft there too long, just out of curiosity; if they had been men to me instead of puppets. But when I guessed what their intent was, guessed that it was something sinister, it was done before I could interfere. I saw him going backwards over the brink of a fissure in the ice, tugging at a dart that was in his throat. And when they had gone—his murderers—"

"They?" she cried. "Was there more than one?"

"Yes," he said, "there was a party. There must have been ten or twelve at least. When they had gone I flew down and picked up that stick, which one of them had dropped.—And to think I might have saved him!"

Her hand still rested on his arm. "I'm glad you told me," she said. She felt the arm stiffen suddenly at the sound of Tom Fanshaw's voice.

"Jeanne, take your hand away! Can you touch a man like that? Can you believe the lies—" but there, with a peremptory gesture, his father silenced him.

But even he exclaimed at the girl's next action, for she stooped, picked up the blood-stained dart which lay at Philip Cayley's feet, and handed it to him. "Throw it away, please,"—she said, "overboard, and as far as you can."

Even before the other men cried out at his doing the thing she had asked him to, he hesitated and looked at her in some surprise.

"Do it, please," she commanded; "I ask it seriously."

Tom Fanshaw started out of his chair; then, as an intolerable twinge from his ankle stopped him, he dropped back again. His father moved quickly forward, too, but checked himself, the surprise in his face giving way to curiosity. As a general thing, Jeanne Fielding knew what she was about.

Philip Cayley took the dart and threw it far out into the water.

There was one more surprise in store for the two Fanshaws. When Cayley, without a glance toward either of them, walked out on the upper landing of the accommodation ladder, the girl accompanied him, and, side by side with him, descended the little stairway, at whose foot the dinghy waited.

"You are still determined on that resolution of yours, are you, to abandon us all for the second time—all humankind, I mean? This later accusation against you was so easily disproved."

"Disproved?" he questioned. "That beautiful faith of yours can't be called proof."

"I meant just what I said—disproved. They shall admit it when I go back on deck. Won't you—won't you give us a chance to disbelieve the old story, too?"

"I can never explain that now," he said; "can never lay that phantom, never in the world."

"I am sorry," she said holding out her hand to him. "I wish you'd give us a chance. Good bye."

This time he took the hand, bowed over it and pressed it lightly to his lips. Then, without any other farewell than that, he dropped down to the dinghy and was rowed back to the floe—back to his wings.

When she returned to the deck she found that Mr. Fanshaw had gone around to the other side of it to see the sky-man take to the air.

But Tom sat, rigid, where he was. For the first time that she could remember, he was regarding her with open anger. "I knew," he said, "that you never liked Hunter, though I never could see why you should dislike him; and it didn't take two minutes to see that this man Cayley, with his wings and his romance, had fascinated you. But in spite of that, I thought you had a better sense of justice than you showed just now."

She flushed a little. "My sense of justice seems to be better than yours this morning, Tom," she answered quietly. Then she unslung her binoculars again and, turning her back upon him, gazed out shoreward.

"I am getting worried about our shore party," she remarked, as if by way of discontinuing the quarrel. "If there are ten or twelve men living there, in hiding from us, willing to do unprovoked murder, when they can with impunity—"

"So you believed that part of the story, too, did you?" Tom interrupted.

She did not answer his question at all, but turned her attention shoreward again.

A moment later she closed her binoculars with a snap, and walked around to the other side of the deck, where Mr. Fanshaw, leaning his elbows on the rail, was looking out across the ice-floe.

"Well," he asked briskly, as she came up and laid an affectionate arm across his shoulder, "I suppose you've been telling Tom why you did it—why you made Cayley throw that dart away, I mean; but you'll have to tell me, too. I can't figure it out. You had something in mind, I'm sure."

"I haven't been telling Tom," she said. "He doesn't seem in a very reasonable mood this morning. But I did have something in mind. I was proving that Mr. Cayley couldn't possibly be the man who had committed the murder."

"I suspected it was that," he said.

"It's the stick that proves it, really," she said. "You remember how puzzled you were because the end of it which you held it by wouldn't fit your hand? I discovered why that was when you sent me in to get it a short while ago. It's a left-handed stick. It fits the palm of your left hand perfectly. You'll find that that is so when you try it. And Mr. Cayley is right-handed."

The old man nodded rather dubiously. "Cayley may be ambidextrous, for anything you know," he objected.

She had her rejoinder ready, "But this stick, uncle Jerry, dear, was made for a man who couldn't throw with his right hand, and Mr. Cayley can. He did it perfectly easily, and without suspecting at all why I wanted him to. Don't you see? Isn't it clear?"

"It's quite clear that the brains of this expedition are in that pretty head of yours," he said. "Yes, I think you're right." Then, after a pause, he added, with an enigmatical look at her: "Don't be too hard on Tom, my dear, because you see the circumstances are hard enough on him already."

She made a little gesture of impatience. "They're not half as hard on him as they are on Mr. Cayley."

"Oh, I don't know," the old gentleman answered. "Take it by and large, I should say that Cayley was playing in luck."

VI

Tom's Confession

At intervals during the day those enigmatical words of Mr. Fanshaw's recurred to the girl with the reflection that they wanted serious thinking over, at the first convenient opportunity. But the day wore away and the opportunity did not appear.

It was a hard day for everybody. The news which Tom had brought aboard just after breakfast, of the strange, half-crazed creature who had walked into the camp of the searchers and showed a wish to guide them somewhere,—the man whose language consisted of two words, most suggestive, most tantalizing in their mystery, to those who clustered round him,—this, in itself, would have been enough to awaken, among the people on the yacht, a sense of strange, uneasy expectation, and give a promise of further developments soon.

But the hours had worn away, and not another word had come back from those who had followed this strange guide. And then there was the horror of Donovan's discovery. He had started to accompany Tom back to the yacht, but, finding the two sailors a sufficient escort for him, had lingered behind to make some explorations of his own, with that grim result.

Last of all had come the most incredible thing, suggested by the scene which Cayley reported to Jeanne. The idea that there were ten or a dozen exiles on this remote, unknown land, who, instead of greeting the rescue which the yacht brought them, had gone into hiding at the first sight of it; had murdered one stray member of the rescuing party who fell into their path, and meant, perhaps, to murder the rest should opportunity afford.

Though this strange story added to the feeling of uneasiness among the people who remained on the yacht, it was received with a good deal of incredulity. Tom Fanshaw openly avowed his disbelief in every word of it, and his father, though less outspoken, was almost equally skeptical. He did not share Tom's belief that Cayley had deliberately lied, in order to cover his own guilt in Hunter's murder, but he attributed the strange scene he had reported either to some optical delusion, or to the hallucination of insanity. The fellow might very well be as mad as a hatter, he told Jeanne. His way of life pointed to it. Any sane man who had learned to fly would put his discovery to better use than flapping his wings around the North Pole.

The captain of the yacht—his name was Warner—was on shore in command of the searching party, but the first officer, Mr. Scales, remained on board. His opinion coincided closely with that of the elder Fanshaw. He was in possession of all the data, though they had not told him the story of Philip Cayley's old relation with the murdered man.

"It stands to reason," he said, "that the only party of white men that could be here would be the survivors of the Fielding expedition. We know from the news that young Mr. Fanshaw brought aboard that there is one such survivor here. If there were any considerable number of them left, able-bodied enough to walk across the glacier, we could be sure they'd be here on the shore waiting for us. We could be certain they would have made some attempt to signal us as soon as they sighted us.

"If they weren't white men but Indians—Chucotes—they'd have been quite as glad as white men to get a chance to go back with us as far as St. Michaels. And in the third place, if they were not Chucotes, but some strange, unknown, murderous band of aborigines, there wouldn't have been even one survivor of the Fielding expedition."

"Of course that's not an absolute water-tight line of reasoning, but it seems to me there is a tremendous probability that it's right, and that this flying man has lost his wits."

Gradually everybody on board the yacht, with two exceptions, came around to Mr. Scales's view of the affair. The only exceptions were Jeanne and Tom Fanshaw. Jeanne scouted the theory that Cayley was mad, as indignantly as she did Tom's idea that he was a malicious liar. It might be hard to account for the presence of a party of white refugees on the shore, who didn't seem to want to be rescued, but if Cayley said they were there, then there they were, and a source of great, though undefined, peril they must be to the unsuspecting shore party. And though she won no converts to her belief, still her earnestness added a good deal to the uneasy feeling which mounted steadily, aboard the yacht, for the fate of the party that had gone ashore.

In this uneasiness Tom himself had manifested a share, although he reiterated his belief that the only living person ashore, besides the members of their own party, was the half-crazed stranger who had come into camp just as he had been leaving it.

For all that, he spent a good part of the day sweeping the land, or as much of it as he could see, with a powerful glass. But for all he saw, or anyone else, during the long hours of that day, there might not have been a human being, except those on the yacht, nearer than Point Barrow. There was neither sight nor sound; there was not even a glint of Cayley's bright wings high up in the cloudless Arctic sky.

So utterly deserted did the land appear, so impossible was it to believe that any danger could lurk there, that, after their unsuccessful attempt to recover the body of Hunter, old Mr. Fanshaw and Scales, the first officer, took Jeanne ashore in one of the boats for an exploration of the beach and of the cluster of empty, half-buried huts that stood just back of it. They were gone from the yacht about an hour.

By four o'clock, however, they had decided that, whether or not the sky-man's story might be true, it was high time to send a relief party ashore to find the lost ones. There was a good deal of necessary consultation about who should go. Clearly it would be folly to send a party of three or four on such a mission. They must carry, in the first place, rations sufficient not only for themselves, but for those they expected to find. They must be strong enough, in the second place, to overcome this mysterious, unknown band of refugees, supposing such a band to exist. To form such a party would take practically every able-bodied man remaining on the yacht, and there was, naturally, some demur to this.

But Tom settled the matter. "I can't go ashore on account of this confounded ankle, and Jeanne, of course, will stay here, too. But everybody else can go. Jeanne and I are enough to defend the yacht. Even supposing there was a party of twelve murderous ruffians ashore there, armed with darts and throwing-sticks, they can't get aboard the yacht without putting off in boats. She's as good a shot as I am. We'll keep a brisk lookout, and if we see any piratical expedition setting out to capture us, we will be able to account for the whole lot of them before they can hope to reach the *Aurora's* side."

"That's all right while the light holds out," his father assented somewhat dubiously, "but suppose we don't get back until after dark— it's likely enough we won't?"

"Well, we've a search light, haven't we?" said Tom. "Besides, nobody but Jeanne has the slightest idea that there's anyone within five hundred miles of us, who wishes us harm. There are only ten to go if we two stay here, and considering the amount of rations you will have to carry to be of any service as a relief party, it will be an absurdity to go out with less than ten. Trust us. We'll deliver the yacht, intact, when you get back with them."

At five o'clock accordingly, the relief expedition went ashore, and Tom Fanshaw and the girl were left alone on the yacht.

Two hours later, perhaps, after they had eaten the supper which Jeanne had concocted in the galley, they sat, side by side, in their comfortable deck chairs, gazing out across the ice-floe. The evening was unusually mild, the thermometer showing only a degree or two below freezing, and here in the lee of the deck-house they hardly needed their furs.

They had sat there in silence a long while. Tom's promise that they would keep a brisk lookout against a possible attack on the yacht, had passed utterly from both their minds. It was so still—so dead still; the world about them was so utterly empty as to make any thought of such an attack seem preposterous.

Finally the girl seemed to rouse herself from the train of thought that had preoccupied her mind, straightened up a little and turned for a look into her companion's face. But this little movement of her body failed to rouse him. His eyes did not turn to meet hers, but remained fixed on the far horizon.

A moment later she stretched out a hand and explored for his beneath the great white bear skin that covered him, found it and interlocked her fingers with his. At that, he pulled himself up, with a start, and abruptly withdrew his own from the contact.

She colored a little, and her brows knitted in perplexity. "What an old bear you are, Tom," she said. "What's the matter today? It's not a bit like you to sulk just because we disagree about something. We disagree all the time, but you've never been like this to me before."

"I always told you I was a sullen brute when things went wrong with me, although you never would believe it," he said. "I'm sorry."

"I don't want you to be sorry," she told him; "I just want you to be a few shades more cheerful."

He seemed not to be able to give her what she wished, however, for he lapsed again into his moody abstraction. But after a few minutes more of silence, he turned upon her with a question that astonished her. "What did you do that for, just now?"

At first she was in doubt as to what act of hers he referred to. "Do you mean my hand?" she asked, after looking at him in puzzled curiosity for a moment.

He nodded.

"Why—because I was feeling a little lonesome, I suppose, and sort of tender-hearted, and we'd been about half quarreling all day, and I didn't feel quarrelsome any more, and I thought my big brother's hand would feel—well—grateful and comforting, you know."

She was curious as to why he wanted the explanation, but she gave it to him unhesitatingly, without the faintest touch of coquetry or embarrassment.

"I can't remember back to the time," she continued, "when I didn't do things like that to you, just as you did to me, and neither of us ever wanted an explanation before. Are you trying to make up your mind to disown me, or something?"

He dropped back moodily into his chair without answering her.

After a little perplexed silence, she spoke again. "I didn't know things were going wrong with you. I didn't even suspect it until this morning, when uncle Jerry said—"

"What!" Tom interrupted. "What does the governor know about it? What did he say?"

"Why, nothing, but that you were playing in rather hard luck, he thought, and that I was to be nice to you. Is the world going badly—really badly—really badly?"

"Yes." That curt monosyllable was evidently all the answer he meant to make. At that she gave up all attempt to console him, dropped back in her chair and cuddled a little deeper down under her bear skin, her face, three-quarters away from him, turned toward that part of the sky that was already becoming glorious with the tints of sunset.

"You've never had any doubt at all, have you, that I really deserved the job of being your big brother; that I was that quite as genuinely as if I had been born that way?"

"No," she said; "of course not, Tom, dear. What put such an idea into your head?"

He paled a little, and it was a minute or two before he could command the words he wanted, to his lips. "Because of my hopes, I suppose," he said unsteadily; "because I had hoped, absurdly enough, for the other answer. You asked as a joke a while back if I meant to disown you. Well I do, from that relationship—because, I'm not fit for the job; because—because—I've come to love you in the other way."

She looked at him in perfectly blank astonishment. He would not meet her eyes, his own, their pupils almost parallel, gazed out, unseeing, beyond her.

"But, Tom," she cried, "you can't mean that!—Oh, yes, I know you mean it, but it's only a temporary aberration, it can't be more than that! We've known each other from the time when we were quite small kids—yes, I was a kid as much as you; no politer term would describe us. We've always loved each other, and played together, and spatted and plagued each other, and made up again, and relied on each other to see us through each other's scrapes, and pointed out each other's faults and gloated over each other's whippings. We've got more civilized, of course, now that we've grown up, but the relation is really the same. There can't be any romance about it; no mystery about me for you. You can't possibly love me like that!"

"Can't I?" he said. "Can't I? Will you give me the chance and see if I can't? Love you? I love you so that the touch of a stray lock of your hair drives me half mad! so that the sound of your step makes my heart stop beating; so that the sight of little commonplace objects that happen to have an association with you—things that I don't realize are associated with you at all until they bring up with them a picture that has you in it—make a lump come in my throat! And when you caress me with your hands—!" He flung out his own with an impulsive gesture that finished the sentence; and then clutched them tightly together, for they were trembling.

Slowly her color mounted until she felt her whole face burning. "I didn't know," she said. "You shouldn't have let me go on thinking—"

"I didn't know, myself, until today," he interrupted her stormily; "I didn't know I knew, that is. But when I saw you put your hands on that villain Cayley, I wanted to kill him, and in that same flash I knew why I wanted to."

Turning suddenly to look at her, he saw that she had buried her face in her hands and was crying forlornly. "Oh, I am a brute," he concluded, "to have told you about it in this way."

"What does the way matter? That's not what makes it hard. It's loving you so much, the way I do, and having to hurt you. It's having to lose my brother—the only brother I ever had."

There was a long, miserable silence after that. Finally he said: "Jeanne, if you do love me as much as that—the way you do, not the way I love you, but love me any way—could you—could you—marry me just the same? I'd never have any thought in the world but of making you happy. And I'd always be there; you could count on me, you know."

"Don't!" she interrupted curtly. "Don't talk like that, Tom." She shivered, and drew away from him with a little movement somewhere near akin to disgust.

HENRY KITCHELL WEBSTER

He winced at it, and reddened. Then, in a voice that sounded curiously thick to her, curiously unlike his own, he asked a question: "If I had told you all this a month ago—told you how I felt toward you, and asked you, loving me the way you do, to marry me just the same, would you?— Oh, I suppose you would have refused. But would you have shuddered and shrunk away from me—like that?"

"Did I shudder and shrink away?" she asked. "I didn't know it. I wasn't angry; I'm not now. But—but that was a horrible thing you asked of me."

"Would it have struck you as horrible," he persisted, "if I had asked it a month ago?"

"Perhaps not," she answered thoughtfully. "I've changed a good deal in the last month—since we sailed away from San Francisco and left the world behind us—our world—and came out into this great white empty one. I don't know why that is."

"I know." He was speaking with a sort of brutal intensity that startled her. "I know. It's not in the last month you've changed; it's within the last twenty-four hours; it's since you saw and fell in love with that murderous, lying brute of a Cayley."

"I don't know," she said very quietly, "whether you're trying to kill the love I have for you—the old love—or not, Tom, but unless you're very careful, you'll succeed in doing it. I don't think I want to talk to you any more now, not even sit here beside you. I'm going to take a little walk."

He held himself rigidly still till she had disappeared round the end of the deck-house. Then he bent over and buried his face in his hands!

WHAT THE THING WAS THAT roused him to his present surroundings, he never knew. He was conscious of no sound, but, suddenly, he sat erect and stared about him in amazement. It had grown quite dark. It must be two or three hours since Jeanne had left the chair beside him and announced that she was going to take a little walk.

He spoke her name, not loudly at first, for he thought she must be close by. But the infinite silent spaces seemed to absorb the sound of his voice. There was no sign that any sentient thing, except his very self, had heard the words he uttered. Then he called louder.

It was not until he raised himself, stiffly and clumsily, from his chair that he realized that it was more than dark; that the atmosphere about him was opaque with fog.

He groped for the heavy walking-stick which leaned against the arm of his chair and, with its aid, hobbled slowly along the deck. His damaged ankle was held rigid in a plaster bandage. Though the pain in it was less, he found locomotion difficult.

As he opened the door at the head of the companionway, he called the girl's name again; and this time the absence of any answer frightened him a little, though he tried to reason himself out of his fears. She had gone below, no doubt, to her own state-room, and with the door shut, would hardly hear him. But he had no thought of accepting that explanation without investigating further. Even if she were there and quite safe, he did not want to let another quarter hour go by without finding her and asking her forgiveness. Whatever else might happen in this world, Jeanne Fielding must not be made unhappy. If only he could have perceived that cardinal fact in the universe a little sooner!

The steps were rather difficult to negotiate, but by using both hands to supplement his one good foot, he succeeded in creeping down them, and then in making his way along the corridor to the girl's door.

He knocked faintly at first; then louder, and finally cried out her name again, this time in genuine alarm. He tried the door, found that it was not locked, and opening it and switching on a light, perceived that the state-room was empty.

Standing there, utterly perplexed, unable either to guess at the girl's possible whereabouts, or to construct any plan for finding her, he felt a sudden rush of relief on hearing the soft scrape of a boat against the accommodation ladder outside. It might be Jeanne. It it were not she, it was someone from the shore party, in which case a search for her could be begun in earnest by those whose powers of getting about were unimpaired.

He heard footsteps crossing the deck overhead. No, that could not be Jeanne; it was a heavy tread, a curious, shuffling tread.

He closed the door behind him. Then he limped slowly down the corridor toward the foot of the companionway. The heavy tread was already descending the stairs.

He turned the corner, stopped short and gasped. And that was all. There was no time even for a cry. He had caught one glimpse of a monstrous figure clad in skins, huge in bulk; hairy-faced like a gorilla.

And then, the man or beast had, with beastlike quickness, lifted his arm and struck. And Tom Fanshaw dropped down at his feet, senseless.

VII

The Rosewood Box

On the girl, Tom Fanshaw's passionate, stormy avowal had the effect of a sort of moral earthquake. It left the ground beneath her feet suddenly unstable and treacherous; it threatened to bring down about her ears the whole structure of her life. The very thing she had relied upon for shelter and security against outside troubles and dangers, was, on the instant, fraught with a greater danger than any of them.

Her instinct, when she left him, was simply one of escape. As she had said, the relation between them had always been taken for granted; had always been matter-of-fact. Long before her father's departure on that last voyage of his, ever since she could remember, in fact, she had taken her association with Tom, her affection for him and his for her, completely as a matter of course. They could not have felt any differently toward each other if they had, indeed, been brother and sister.

She was three or four years younger than he, but her girlish precocity had gone far to bridge the disparity in their ages, and now that both had grown to maturity, it had completely ceased to exist. Indeed, since the time when her first party had given her the status of an undeniable grown-up, she had felt like an elder sister of his, rather than a younger one. She had stayed at home, for one thing, while Tom had been away at school, and there, in the intimacy of comradeship to which her father had admitted her, her mind had matured unusually rapidly. She had a wider acquaintance with the world of ideas, at least, at twenty-two than Tom had at twenty-six.

She had teased him out of his youthful absurdities, been proud of him, laughed at him, quarrelled with him, only to make up the quarrel with some cool little, fugitive caress, without one single self-conscious moment regarding him; without a misgiving whether, after all, this relationship, that seemed so firmly established, might prove impossible as a permanent one.

For the first few moments after his avowal she had felt no emotion other than that of astonishment and incredulity. Even when he asked her if she could not marry him, anyway, though the question revolted her, she told the truth in saying that she was not angry.

The anger came later, but it burned into a flame that was all the hotter for its tardiness in kindling. It must have an outlet somewhere, and as such, the promenade up and down the other side of the deck was altogether insufficient.

The sight of a small boat at the foot of the accommodation ladder seemed to offer something better. So, pulling on a pair of fur gauntlets, she dropped into it, cast off the painter, shipped the pair of light oars it contained, and rowed away without any thought of her destination—of any destination whatever; without, even, a very clear idea of what she was doing. She must do something; that was all she knew. Certainly she pulled away from the yacht's side with no idea that she was running into any possible danger.

She had believed Cayley's story. She was the only person on the yacht who had believed it fully. Yet the belief did not translate itself into any bar to her actions.

Profound as was the impression Cayley had made upon her, she had not, as yet, articulated him at all into her real world. He was very vivid, very thrilling; he set her imagination on fire when she saw him and heard his voice. But when he took wing again, he left a strange feeling of unreality behind him. That sense of unreality was all the stronger now that almost the reallest thing in her universe—namely, her relation with Tom Fanshaw—was absorbing the full power both of her mind and of her emotions.

It was half a mile, perhaps, from the yacht to the particular bit of shelving beach toward which she unconsciously propelled the boat. She rowed steadily, without so much as a glance over her shoulder, until she felt the grate of the shingle beneath the bow.

She became aware, not only that she had unconsciously come ashore but also that the yacht was nowhere to be seen. A bank of fog had come rolling in from the eastward, so heavy as to render an object one hundred paces away totally invisible. The clump of empty buildings here on the beach could hardly be half that distance, as she remembered, yet looking round from her seat in the row boat, she could make out no more than their blurred masses against the white ice and sand which surrounded them.

She shivered at first with an instinctive, half-formed fear. This was solitude indeed. But she braced herself and dismissed her fear. Solitude was what she had left the yacht for; and, then, it was a condition she could terminate at will. Through the still air and across that quiet water her voice would carry easily to Tom's ears. She had only to hail and she would hear his voice in answer.

For a moment she thought she would do it. Then she decided the other way. If Tom should miss her, he would certainly call aloud, and she could answer, and use his voice to guide her back to the yacht. It was, of course, impracticable to attempt to row back without some such assistance. She had only a vague idea in what quarter the yacht lay, and the chance of missing it and getting really lost indeed was too great to be taken.

She scrambled out of the boat and pulled it high up on the beach. The fog made the air seem cold, though for the arctic it was a mild night. Two of the abandoned buildings on the beach behind her were mere sheds, windowless, absolutely bare, never having served, evidently, any other purpose than that of storage. But the third, and largest, as she remembered it, offered a shelter that was becoming attractive. There were some rude bunks in it where she could rest comfortably enough; and, unless she was mistaken, Scales had left in the hut a half-burned candle which they had used in exploring its dark interior. She had a box of wax vestas in her pocket. She could go in there and make herself at home, and at the same time keep an alert ear for a hail from the yacht.

She found the candle in the place where she remembered Scales had laid it down, struck a light and wedged the candle into a knot-hole. She turned toward one of the bunks with the idea of stretching out there, and by relaxing her muscles, persuade, perhaps, her overstrung nerves to relax, too.

She had taken a step toward it, indeed, before she saw, through the murk and candle smoke, the thing that lay right before her eyes,—a rather large, brass-bound rosewood box or chest. It had not been here in the afternoon when they had entered the place, for they had searched its bare interior thoroughly in the hope that there might be something which previous investigators had overlooked. This box, six inches high and a foot long, or more, could not have been here then. It was standing now in the most conspicuous place in the room,—in the very middle of the bunk.

The sight of it might well have caused astonishment or alarm in the girl's mind. But it was neither alarm nor astonishment that her next act expressed. She dropped down on her knees beside the rude wooden bunk, drew the chest up close in the tight embrace of her young arms, laid her cheek against the cold polished surface of its blackened wood, and cried.

Every question that might have asked itself—how the thing could have come there, and what its coming might portend to herself or to the other of the *Aurora's* people—was swept away in a sudden rush of filial affection and regret which the sight of it instantly awoke. It had reached her with that sudden poignant stab of memory which inanimate objects, familiar by long association, seem to be more potent to call up than the very persons of the friends with whom they are associated. The sight of her father himself could hardly have had so instantaneous and overwhelming an effect upon her as the sight of this old chest, which was one of the earliest of her associations with him.

It had always stood, until he had taken it with him on that last voyage of his, upon a certain farther corner of his desk in the old library. It was one of those objects of a class that children always love,—smooth, polished, beautiful; beautiful and, at the same time, defying curiosity.

It was quite a masterpiece of cabinet work. No hinges were visible, and the cover fitted so closely upon the box itself that the line which separated them was hard to discover. And there was no trace of keyhole or lock. To those uninitiated into its secret, it defied every attempt to open it.

Somewhere in her mind now, in a comparatively quiet eddy, sheltered from the torrent of memory that was sweeping through it, was a half-amused recollection of what had been, for a long time, her chief ground of superiority over Tom Fanshaw. Her father had taught her the secret of the box. If Tom would turn his back and shut his eyes, she could open it for him in a moment. But the boy, with all his ingenuity, never was able to solve the secret for himself. He had spent whole days over it—long, precious holidays,—but always in vain.

She remembered, too, the day when her father had shown her the mystery, had done it by way of consolation for some terrible childish disappointment she had sustained. He had opened it for her, and then had sat watching her efforts to repeat the operation; correcting her mistakes, pointing with a long, bronze letter-opener, but never touching the box itself nor her own clumsy fingers.

He never had exacted a promise from her that she should guard this mystery; had never even instructed her that she was not to tell. But she remembered, and at the memory she kissed the unresponsive surface of the cover with her cold lips,—remembered just the half-grave, half-amused tone in which he had said, "There is a secret, Jeanne, that we have from all the world,—you and I."

Presently she seated herself on the bunk, took the little chest on her knees and set about opening it. Between the cold and her excitement she found this rather a difficult thing to do, though her mind never, never hesitated over the slightest detail of the necessary formula of procedure. She knew in just what order you pressed in those innocent-looking little ornamental tacks in the brass binding; remembered the right moment to turn the box up on its end to let the just released steel ball roll down its channel to the pocket, where it must lie before the last pressure upon the last spring would prove effective. She no more faltered over it than she would have faltered over her alphabet.

And at last, when her numbed fingers had completed their task, the counter-weighted lid rose slowly by itself, just as it had used to, and revealed to her swimming eyes the contents of the interior.

Up to that moment she had not realized what the finding of the despatch box meant. It had not occurred to her that a full account of her father's expedition, a narrative which would reach, perhaps, to the morning of the last day of all, was lying here, right under her eyes.

But now when the cover opened and she saw beneath it a thick volume, bound in red morocco, she realized that here, under her hand, was the very object, in search of which the *Aurora* had set out upon her perilous voyage.

With the first realization of what the contents of that book must be, a tragedy, and the central figure of it her own father, the man she had loved best in all the world, she found it almost impossible to open the book. She took it out of the despatch box and for a little while sat, dry-eyed, hugging the precious, poignant thing up tight against her breast.

But at last she put the despatch box to one side, brought the candle nearer, so that its light would serve to read by, and began turning the pages of the book.

The first sight of her father's clear, erect, precise handwriting warmed her with a sudden courage. He had not set out upon his voyage of discovery without weighing and expecting the possibilities of failure and death. Well, he had died, but he had not failed. He had added a new coast line to the map of the world. And she knew,—knew as clearly as if his own spirit had stood there beside her talking to her in his old, dearly remembered voice, that next to coming home alive, bringing the fruits of his discovery with him, his last wish in the world must have been that that should happen which had happened now,—that she, his daughter, should hold that very book in her hands and read the story, and know that he had not died in vain.

But even this new inspiration of courage did not make her strong enough to turn back and read the last entry in that tragic journal first. She tried to do it, but the will failed her. So she began at the beginning. Once she had plunged into the fascinating narrative, the whole of the outside world faded away for her. She was oblivious to the fact that the darkness outside was no longer the mere darkness of the fog; oblivious to the rising wind that poured its icy stream through the leaky walls of the hut and made the candle flicker; oblivious, even, to the very sound which she had meant to wait for,—the sound of Tom's voice calling out to her from the yacht, and the sound of other, more alarming, nearer voices.

They all fell on deaf ears as she turned page after page of that precious record of her father's life. It was written, in the main, in the scientific, observant, unimpassioned temper which she knew so well. He chronicled those days of peril, when their ship, crushed in the ice, and only kept from sinking by that very ice which had just destroyed her, was drifting along in the pack, to what seemed certain destruction, as quietly and as explicitly as he did the uneventful voyage through Behring Strait. The man's courage was so deeply elemental in him that he could not be self-conscious about it.

He told of the land, the strange, uncharted shore, whose discovery offered them a respite, at least, from that destruction; told how he got his remaining stores ashore and built the hut, where, in all human probability, he and his companions were to spend the rest of their lives.

Finally she reached the record of the day when he had consigned to the sea the bottle containing the chart of the coast and the account of his plight, together with the course which the relief ship must take, should such a relief ship be sent out, to have any hope at all of reaching them.

"I suppose," his narrative for this day concluded, "there is hardly one chance in ten thousand that my message will ever be picked up, and certainly not one in a million that it will be found in time to bring an effective relief. However, it helps to keep the others cheerful, and that is the main thing."

At the close of the day's entry was a single line which contracted her heart with a sharp spasm of pain. "This is Jeanne's birthday," it said.

She resumed her reading presently, and came to the point where the *Walrus* people entered into the narrative; their plight, their rescue and their welcome by the three men, who by now were the only survivors of the original expedition.

She was reading faster now, with none of those little meditative pauses that had marked her progress through the earlier pages of the journal, for the sinister termination of the narrative began to foreshadow itself darkly, from the moment,—the first moment of the appearance of the *Walrus* people on the scene. Her father's description of the man Roscoe, of the expression that had been plain to read in his face as he had listened to the account of the gold-bearing ledge across the glacier, gave her a shuddering premonition; apparently, her father had experienced the same feeling himself. Day after day Roscoe's name appeared, always accompanied by some little phrase of misgiving.

For just one day this dread seemed to have been lifted from Captain Fielding's spirit. That was the day the sun came back to them, putting an end to their long Arctic night. "It has been a hard winter," he wrote, "and I am glad it is over. The hardest thing about it has been our sleeplessness, from which we have all suffered. Today we have enjoyed a change, having taken a walk along the beach. Even Roscoe seems humanized a little by a return of the frank sunshine, and may, perhaps, develop into a tolerable companion. Tomorrow I have promised, if it is fine, to guide them across the glacier to the gold ledge."

It was the next to the last entry in the journal. She turned the page, paled and pressed her lips tight together when the array of blank pages before her told her that she had reached the end. Then she read the last words her father had ever written.

"Took the *Walrus* people to the ledge today. Have no heart to describe the scene that they enacted there. The man Roscoe certainly means to kill me. If it were not for my conviction that the danger from him is largely personal to myself, that he means me and no other, probably, for his victim, I think I should have him shot as a measure of justifiable prevention. He is not a man, but a great sinister brute—literally sinister, for he is left-handed. I shall walk warily, and hope the crisis may soon be over." Evidently that part of his wish had come true.

The book slipped out of the girl's hands, and she sat, with horror-widened eyes, staring at the candle, until it guttered and went out. Slowly, the outside world began to take its place again around her. She knew that she was shivering, half-frozen, that the icy wind was whining through the cracks in her rude shelter.

She thought she heard someone moving about outside, and that thought brought her quickly to her feet. She made her way to the door of the hut, called out; waited a breathless instant—and cried aloud in sudden terror.

VIII

Apparitions

Roscoe did not pause to investigate the effect of his blow, nor to waste a second one. If the man who had confronted him there in the companionway were dead, so much the better. If he were only half-dead, the job could be finished at any time. He was out of the way for the present at least. Roscoe hurried on, searching state-rooms and passageways and finally the crew's quarters, forward.

When he had satisfied himself that he and his men were in undisputed possession of the yacht, he emerged on deck again by the forward hatchway, and found Captain Planck already there. He directed him to go below with Schwartz, who had been engineer aboard the whaler, and get steam up as promptly as possible. He himself remained on deck, directing the unloading and stowage of those precious golden slabs that the rest of the party were bringing out in boats from the shore.

He paced the deck uneasily, for there was a superstitious streak in his otherwise strong composition which caused him, always, a feeling of alarm when matters went too well with him; when his plans succeeded beyond his hopes for them. He had expected to lose a man or two in getting possession of the yacht, yet they had gone off and left it, apparently, in the sole charge of the one disabled member of their party. And, then, he had not expected that the relief would have set out so soon; he had counted on having to wait twenty-four hours more before the field should clear itself for his operations; and those twenty-four hours would have been fraught with perils.

Now that he was in possession of the yacht,—now that all the gold, except what three or four more boats could carry, was transferred safely to the between-deck space beneath the turtle-back,—now that the smoke was pouring out of the *Aurora's* funnels and the steam rising in her pressure gauges, he fell to wondering just what sort of trap that the devil was baiting for him, with this unbroken train of successes.

When, with the arrival of another boat from the shore, one of the great golden slabs it brought went overboard as they were lifting it up on deck, he astonished the boat's crew by taking the disaster good-naturedly.

"Never mind, boys," he said; "we've got a plenty without that. Come! Look alive with the rest of it."

For now his mind was at ease again. The "hoo-doo," as he would have called it, of a too complete success was broken by this trifling mischance.

In reality, this primitive religion, which was all he had, was satisfied. He had performed a sacrifice, involuntary, as such sacrifices must be, to the envious devil which served him for a god. It occurred to him after it happened that perhaps Miguel would count for a sacrifice, too, for he had not come back. But, then, not even an envious devil of a god could think that Miguel was worth much.

He watched, through the fog, the successive arrival of the other boats, bringing the last of the treasure with them.

"We've got it all, Roscoe, unless you want them barrels of whale oil," a man in the last boat sang out as they came alongside.

"We'll leave them to pay for this nickel-plated ship," Roscoe answered. "Come! Look alive and get aboard. We'll be ready to start as soon as we can get a little daylight."

He looked them over, numbered them as if they had been so many sheep, noted that they were all here, except poor Miguel; Planck and Schwartz were down toiling at the boilers.

"Stay here till I come back," he commanded. "I'm going below to see that everything's stowed all right. When I come back I want to talk to you."

He disappeared down the after hatchway, switched on a light and indulged in a long, satisfied look at the great masses of precious metal which were stacked, according to his directions, in the strong-room.

His purpose in coming down here was threefold. He meant to see that the gold was stowed correctly and he meant to lock the room up, so that its precious contents would not be tampered with, and bring the key away with him. He was not afraid that any of his crew would try to steal it, but he thought the moral effect of having it locked away where it was inaccessible to them, and of his keeping the key in his own possession would be a help in maintaining his prestige as commander. They knew the sea better than he did, just as he knew the nature of gold-bearing rock. It was necessary to do something to bolster up his position as chief of the party and keep it above dispute. He did not want to have to kill any of them yet. The *Aurora* would be short-handed enough as it was.

But there was one more reason for that hurried trip to the strong-room. He wanted to be sure that a certain rosewood box had come

HENRY KITCHELL WEBSTER

aboard along with the treasure and what few stores they were taking away with them.

That little box had occupied much of his leisure since the day when he had murdered the owner of it. He had sometimes wished that when it came into his hands that day he had yielded to his first impulse to shatter it, for the thing had always mocked him—coquetted with him.

He had often seen it lying open on Captain Fielding's table in the tiny walled-off cubby hole of a room they called the Captain's cabin, while the Captain himself was writing up his journal or working upon his charts. He had, during that first winter, frequently thought of trying to open it, should the opportunity offer itself.

After the murder, when he took that little room for his own quarters, he found the box and preserved it with the idea that now, at least, he would get the better of it. He knew what its contents were well enough—Captain Fielding's charts and journal, and he had no curiosity concerning them. But the secret mechanism of the box itself tantalized him, and he meant some day to solve it. Once he had done so, he would kick the thing to pieces and destroy its contents.

There was all there was to it at first, but during the next winter, when the long night kept them prisoners in their narrow quarters, the mystery of that little rosewood box took on an added importance to him and to the others, out of all proportion to any effect which the solution of it could have. One by one, with the exception of the Portuguese, they tried. Hour after hour they labored with it, and invariably they failed.

The rest of them gave it up, and their admitted defeat gave Roscoe another incentive for solving the thing himself, for he meant to leave no stone unturned to convince them that they were fools and weaklings; that he, Roscoe, was the only man among them. Such a conviction was necessary to his leadership.

It was toward the end of that winter that the Portuguese made a suggestion destined to bear fruit. "It's a curse that has sealed up that box," he said. "You can't open it, and if you break it, the curse will kill you."

He evidently believed implicitly in this theory, for no persuasion could induce him to touch the box himself. Gradually the others had shown, by little involuntary acts, shrinkings and glances, that Miguel's belief was infecting them. Sometimes, after a long succession of sleepless, lightless days, Roscoe found himself believing it, too, and regarding that little box as the sealed-up casket of the murder he had done upon the owner of it. The crime was there inside.

To overcome that feeling, he had worked all the harder trying to solve its secret.

His interest now, however, in making sure that the box had really been brought aboard the *Aurora* was not superstitious, but wholly practical. They were leaving most of their stores behind them, as there was no time either to transport them to the *Aurora* or to destroy them. With these stores and with the shelter afforded by the hut and the little clump of surrounding out-buildings, it was probable that some members of the *Aurora's* party, at least, would survive the winter. If a relief ship should arrive the next summer, or even the summer thereafter, it would probably find someone on this desolate shore who could tell the story of the disappearance of the *Aurora* and form a more or less definite surmise as to the cause of it. That rosewood box had Captain Fielding's journal in it,—a journal that had been written up to the very morning when Roscoe had murdered him. Its discovery would go a long way toward bridging the gap which Roscoe meant to leave in their departing trail. In short, if that rosewood box were left behind, Roscoe would always feel that he was in more or less danger of detection. And he didn't mean to have a thing like that hanging over him.

Consequently, when he discovered that the box was not on board, and that his particular injunctions concerning it had been either neglected or disobeyed, he came raging up on deck again, a most formidable figure, which caused his companions, hardened ruffians though they were, to cower and shrink away from him.

In a torrent of furious blasphemy, he demanded to know why that box had not been brought aboard; and the concentrated lees of his rage he emptied at last upon the two men whom he had ordered to do it.

"Now," he concluded, when the torrent had spent itself, "you go ashore, you two. Yes, you, Carlson,—I mean you,—and you, Rose; go ashore now and get it."

Then, after a momentary silence, he raged out the command again, amid a foul flood of abuse.

But still they made no move to obey, and the big Swede, in evident terror, answered him. "I won't get it, Roscoe. If you want that box, you can get it yourself."

"What in hell do you mean?" the leader stormed. But his voice, even as he spoke, lost its confident tang of authority.

Carlson huddled back into place among the other members of the crew, and from their meaning nods and inarticulate growls of assent, it was evident they knew what he meant and why he would not go; that they assented in his refusal. Indeed, if Roscoe had not been lacking in that intuitive feeling for the temper of his followers—the feeling which distinguishes only those leaders who govern otherwise than by terror, he would have perceived that a strange spirit of unrest was distracting the whole party.

He saw it now, at all events, and when he repeated the question, "What in hell do you mean?" it was with an inflection that meant he wanted to be informed.

"You tell him," said Carlson, nodding to his companion, Rose. Evidently it was Rose who had told the story to the other members of the party. He was a squatly built man with a stubborn jaw, and Planck, in the days of his command, had always disliked him as that most undesirable pest that can be found in a forecastle,—a sea lawyer.

"What did you leave the box in the hut for?" he demanded. "He might not have come back if you had left it in the cave."

"Come back!" echoed Roscoe, with a growl.

"That's what I said. We went to the hut to get it, and there was a light inside, and there he sat, just like he used to. And he had the box open—"

"He! Who do you mean?" There was no trace of truculence in Roscoe's voice now. He spoke as though his throat were dry.

"It was Captain Fielding; him to the life. And, yet, it was different from the way he used to be. We couldn't see it very well. Its face was sideways and the light was behind it, and it looked smaller and thinner,—more—more like a woman. (If Rose had had the word 'spiritual' in his vocabulary, he would have used it. In default of it, he gave up trying to express just what he meant.) Anyway, there he sat with the box open beside him, and that red book of his open on his knees. Go back for it? Well, I guess not."

There was a momentary silence after he had finished, and Roscoe could feel, as it stretched itself out to the length of half a minute or so, the chill of their terror enveloping him. To throw it off, he blustered, stormed at and abused them for a pack of liars. But in the end he sprang down into one of the boats, and said he would fetch the box himself. Whether he believed their story, or not, it was the only thing for him to do.

As he pulled shoreward he tried hard to convince himself that he did not believe it; that Rose and Carlson had probably forgotten all about the box, and had trumped up the story to avoid the necessity of going back for it.

He must believe the story was a lie. There was no rational explanation of the thing the two sailors pretended they had seen. The box, not shattered, but lying open, after having defied their ingenuity for four years! And a figure like Captain Fielding, yet strangely smaller, like a woman—there was a touch of undefinable terror about that idea. It did not seem like a lie that Rose and Carlson would be capable of making up. Its very weirdness gave it a horrible resemblance to the truth. He remembered what Miguel—poor, half-crazy Miguel—used to say about it. Miguel in all probability was dead now. Could Miguel, dead, have anything to do,—by way of a vengeance perhaps,—with the thing Rose and Carlson had seen, or had believed they saw?

With an oath, he cast the idea away from him. They had lied, that was all. When he got back to the ship he would have them flogged, both of them. That would teach them, and the others, too, perhaps, that he was not to be trifled with.

He beached his boat, scrambled ashore and set out walking doggedly along in the direction of the hut. The fog was still all but impenetrable, even to his practised vision, but he knew the shore like the palm of his hand, and he trudged on without a pause, until he was within ten paces, perhaps, of his destination.

But there he faltered and stopped, turned about, under an irresistible impulse of fear, and would have fled had not sheer necessity compelled him to stop again. There was a light, a diffused yellow glow, faint but unmistakable, shining out of the windows of the hut.

He knew he could not go back to the *Aurora* without that box; it was necessary both to his future safety and his present command of the situation. His one hold upon those sullen followers of his depended upon his being impervious alike to terror and to defeat. If he were to go back now without accomplishing his purpose, it would only be a question of days before they murdered him. They all hated him, enough for that, he knew.

Yet, even under that necessity, it was three or four minutes before, at the command of his burly will, he began creeping forward on hands and knees toward the lighted window of the hut.

And when he reached a point where he could command its interior, his knees slipped out from under him and he lay prone upon the icy beach, his face buried in his outstretched arms. For those two sailors had told the truth.

Presently he drew himself up and squatted back on his haunches, staring. Human or not, the figure there in the hut seemed unaware of his presence. It was staring at the expiring flame of the candle in profound abstraction. When it stirred, as presently it did, it was with a natural, human motion. And then the candle went out.

In the few seconds of silence which followed, his terror returned upon him with full force. But it went away as suddenly as it had come, and with its recession there surged up in him a wave of brutish anger. It was no ghost that had sat in contemplation over the contents of that box, for it was moving now, with human footsteps,—faltering, uncertain footsteps, at that. And when it appeared, just visible and no more, outside the doorway, it called aloud in a human voice—a woman's voice.

At the sound of it, he drew himself up, towering, before her, and, so, became visible to her,—a monstrous, blurred, uncertain shape.

And she cried out; this time in terror. Then, before he could spring upon her and kill her with his hands, as his brutish instinct of rage urged him to do, he started back suddenly, and himself cried out!

For a faint circle of light, waving, wandering, unearthly, was shining straight down upon both of them through the fog,—out of the sky itself.

Looking up, he saw overhead a single, great luminous eye, and in the reflection of its own light upon the ice, very faintly, the fabric of outstretched wings.

Then from up there, overhead, he heard a voice,—a quiet voice, "I'm here," it said. "Don't be afraid."

Blindly, Roscoe flung up his hands, whirled around and fell; scrambled to his feet again and fled, like a man hag-ridden, down the shore.

As he did so, he heard a ragged volley of shots from the direction of the *Aurora*. This sound of plain human fighting, which he understood and did not fear, helped restore to equilibrium his mind, which a moment before had been tottering to absolute destruction. Once he could get back to his boat and feel the oars under his hands again— once he found himself pulling out toward the yacht, no matter how desperate the odds awaiting him there might be against him, he would, he felt, be himself once more.

He ran on and on down the beach. He had not passed his boat, he knew; but he finally realized that he had passed the place where he had brought the boat ashore.

IX

WAITING FOR DAWN

Cayley wheeled so that he headed up into the wind and dropped, facing the girl and with his back to her retreating assailant. He had to drop almost vertically in order to avoid being blown out into the sea after he struck the ice. Even as it was, he went slithering down the glassy slope toward the water, and only managed to check his impetus by throwing himself flat on his face and clutching at a hummock which chanced to offer him a precarious hold. He had come down "all adrift" as sailors say, and his monstrous wings, powerless for flight but instinct with flapping perversity, cost him a momentary struggle while he was getting them bundled into controllable shape.

All the while he half expected an attack from the man whom his sudden appearance had just put to flight. Whether the man came back or not, would depend on how badly Cayley's portentous intervention had frightened him, but if he came back before the sky-man had got clear of his wings, he would find an antagonist as helpless as the girl herself. Cayley, before he dropped, had weighed it as an even chance that this very thing would happen.

And if it did not, the odds were still rather against his coming out of the manœuver undamaged. Alighting upon an unknown surface at night, in a dense fog and in the teeth of a number seven gale, was not an act which a sane sense of self-preservation would approve of.

But, thanks as much to luck as to skill, he presently found himself upon his feet uninjured. He at once set out, making what haste he could, across the ice toward where he had last seen the girl, shouting up the gale to her at the same time, to know if she were safe. He heard no answer, but presently made her out, dimly, only a pace or two away. His first act then, even before speaking, was to take out his pocket electric bull's-eye and turn it full upon her.

"It's just to make sure you're not hurt,—that I really got down here in time," he apologized. "I wish I might have saved you the terror, but it wasn't until you cried out that I knew—"

"I'm not hurt," she assured him. "I'm a little dazed, that's all.—No, not with fright, with wonder. I hardly had time to be frightened. But

HENRY KITCHELL WEBSTER

I thought you'd gone this morning, that you had abandoned us just as you said you would. And yet, when I cried out just now, for help, it was you that I called to. . . And then you came, out of the sky, just as I was sure you would. For I was certain, with the same certainty one has in dreams. Now, that it's over, I find myself wondering again if you are real. I'm not hurt at all."

Before he could find anything to say in answer, they heard another shot, muffled in the fog, from the direction of the *Aurora*, and in prompt reply to it, another volley.

"Wasn't there firing before?" she asked. "Can anyone be attacking the yacht? There is no one there but Tom, you know, and he's disabled.— Can't we—can't I, get out there any way? The boat I came ashore in is right here."

Without making her any answer, he carried the unwieldy bundle his wings made into the hut and left it there, then returned to her and offered her his hand.

"We'll go down and look for your boat," he said.

Along the water's edge they searched, aided by the little beam from his bull's-eye, the sound of intermittent firing from the yacht urging haste all the while. But it did not take long to force the conviction upon them that the boat was gone. Blown adrift, most likely, was Cayley's explanation.

He felt her trembling. Whether with cold or dread, he did not know, but he took her arm and steadied her with the pressure of his own.

"Come back to the hut," he said. "The situation isn't as bad as you think. I'll tell you when we get to shelter where we can talk."

She turned obediently, and breasted the icy slope with him. Neither spoke again until they were safe in the lee of the hut. Then he said:

"I don't think Fanshaw is alone there on the yacht. The relief party and the first party from the *Aurora* got together sometime this afternoon and started back toward the shore. They should be aboard the yacht by now, though when the fog fell it put an end to my activities. The *Walrus* people have undoubtedly attacked them, but they shouldn't have any trouble in beating them off. They out-number them and they are better armed; in fact, so far as I know, the *Walrus* people aren't armed at all. They knew—your people I mean—that the yacht was likely to be attacked. I told them so myself, and then their pretended guide confessed."

"How did you know about the *Walrus?*" she asked curiously.

"The Portuguese was one of them; he had guided your first party down into a little valley of perpetual fog, under orders to abandon them there. When he saw me sailing about overhead—through the fog, you know,—he broke down and confessed,—and then—well, he made a clean breast of it. He knew nothing of the details of his leader's plans; but the mere fact that he had been delegated to guide the party into a place from which it was to be expected they could never get out, was conclusive as to his intentions at least."

He had spoken rather disconnectedly, his sentences punctuated by the sounds of firing from the yacht. By the time he finished they were almost continuous.

"Why does it sound so much fainter than it did?" she asked. "It's not nearly so loud as that first volley we heard."

"It's a trick of the fog, very likely," he said. "Fog is a frightfully treacherous thing. It deceives men's ears as well as their eyes. There's no judging distance through it. When you cried out just now, I couldn't tell whether you were fifty feet below me or five hundred feet. I was up above it, you see, and I hadn't any way of telling how deep it was.— There! Do you hear?" he went on. "The firing has stopped altogether. Your people are almost certainly safe."

But the girl's mind had not followed him to the new subject. "You were up there in clear air?" she asked, "and the fog was all below you?"

"Like a bluish-grey blanket," he explained, "lit by the stars, and nothing else. It was pouring along like the greatest river you ever saw, the surface of it eddying off in little wisps. The upper air is comparatively still."

"And you couldn't see through it at all?" she questioned—"couldn't see the land any more than you could see the bottom of the ocean through the Water?"

"No more than that," he assented.

She shivered a little and reached out for his arm. "And you came down into that, not knowing what you were to find—not knowing where the land was? I didn't realize you had just risked your life for me."

Cayley had not meant that she should know—not now, at least. In the back of his mind there had been a puzzled wonderment why she had come ashore alone; what curious chain of events could possibly have left her and that hairy monster, Roscoe, face to face upon that wind-swept beach. But the break in her unsteady voice and the way she clung to his arm for support, showed plainly enough that the experience had been an exhausting one to her. She would not have turned limp like this after

HENRY KITCHELL WEBSTER

a mere momentary terror, such as the sight of Roscoe would cause her, however sharp that terror had been.

"Will you let me go inside this hut," he asked, "and see if it is habitable? If it is, you'd better go in and let me make you as comfortable as I can. I don't think you need have any fears about the *Walrus* people. And worrying wouldn't do any good any way. There's nothing we can do but wait for daylight. Nothing can happen anywhere until then."

He had, very distinctly, in mind what might happen then if the *Walrus* people were repulsed from the yacht. Unless they were all destroyed in the attack, they would undoubtedly make trouble as soon as morning revealed the fact that they had two hostages in their hands. But he could fight them off better from the door-way of the hut than from anywhere else. And there was no need of troubling the girl with that consideration, not for the present, at least.

"It's all right in there," she said. "I spent I don't know how many hours there reading before you came. But the candle has burned out."

The open door behind them gave access into a tiny shed, protruding from the corner of the hut and serving, evidently, as a vestibule for it. The inner door, a heavier and stronger affair, opening at right angles to it, gave access to the interior of the hut.

Cayley switched on his bull's-eye and cast a brief glance about the room. There were two or three rude, flimsy-looking doors which undoubtedly opened into small, cabin-like bed-rooms; but the principal part of the hut was taken up by the room in which they found themselves.

It was a dismal looking place enough, fifteen feet square, perhaps, and not more than half as high. In one corner was a heap of smoke-blackened stones, evidently the ruins of a fire-place. There were shelves and cupboards along the walls and a number of narrow bunks.

Cayley set his little bull's-eye on a shelf where they could make the most of its thin pencil of light. He then turned his attention to the door, and after a little struggle succeeded in getting it shut, and, what was more, securely bolted, by means of a heavy wooden bar which dropped into an iron crotch. If they were attacked with the first of the daylight, this place would afford them security until the people from the *Aurora* could come to their rescue. His revolver was a Colt, forty-five, and his belt was full of cartridges. With that weapon, he remembered that he had once been considered the best shot in the Army.

The girl, when he turned to look at her, was seated on the edge of a bunk at the other side of the hut. Her pallor, the traces of tears he could see in her eyes, the pathetic droop to her lips, all emphasized the thing her voice had told him already, namely, that some emotional crisis, which she had been through in those recent hours, had left her quite exhausted.

Without a word, he turned to his bundle which he had deposited in a corner of the room, and fished out from it his sheep-skin sleeping-bag. It was not until he approached her, with it across his arm, that his eye fell upon the rosewood box and the morocco-bound book which lay beside it.

Her eye followed his. "They're father's papers," she said. "I found the box in here. That's why I stayed. I had come ashore—"

"Wait a minute," he interrupted. He took up the book with a gentleness almost reverent, laid it in the little chest and set it down on the floor beside the bunk.

The quality of the act brought the too ready tears to her eyes, but he did not look up at her to surprise them there. "Now," he said, "I'm going to take off these boots of yours, which are wet, but which will serve excellently, nevertheless, for a pillow, and you are to take off that heavy coat and get inside this bag. Have you ever slept in one?"

He was already tugging at one of the boots, and her protest went unheeded—it was only a half-hearted protest after all.

When he had taken off the boots, she submitted, without demur, to his unfastening the frogs on her heavy seal-skin coat and slipping it off her shoulders.

When finally, with some assistance from him, she nestled down inside the great fleece-lined bag, when he had rolled her small boots into a bundle and made a pillow of them for her head, as he had said he would, she exclaimed, half-rebelliously, at the comfort of it all.

"It is so deliciously warm and soft," she said. "I didn't know you were just being a luxurious sybarite when you refused a mattress and a pair of blankets on the yacht. If only you could be warm, too, and comfortable."

"I shall be," he assured her. "I'll make a cushion of that great coat of yours and sit down here at the foot of the bunk. You're not to bother about me. You're to prove the efficacy of the sleeping-bag by going to sleep in it."

"And what will you do all the while sitting there and keeping watch? Would you—would you like to read father's journal? If you would, I'd like to have you, after what you said long ago about the men who risked and lost their lives trying to reach the Pole. I think if you will read that book, you will understand, in spite of your wings. And—well, I'd like to have you understand."

He moved the bull's-eye to another part of the hut, where the light from it would not shine in her eyes, and would illuminate the pages of the book she offered him to read, while he sat, wrapped in her great coat, at the foot of the bunk.

Once as he passed by her in the completion of these arrangements, she withdrew her hand from the bag and held it out to him. "You've been very good to me," she said—"I don't mean by risking your life and plunging down into that bank of fog when you knew I was in danger. A brave man would do that, I suppose,—some brave men, any way. But you've been better than that—"

He told her not to talk, but to go to sleep; and without any more words ensconced himself at her feet, drew his legs up under him, tailor-fashion, and began to read.

She closed her eyes, or half closed them, but under the shadow of her lashes she watched his face. The light that did not shine in hers, illuminated his. It was a beautiful face, but in a wholly masculine way; the first beautiful man's face she thought she had ever seen that had no trace of weakness or effeminacy about it. It had looked bravely into tempests, that face—tempests of the soul, as well as those of the open, cruel sky that he had conquered.

But with all its strength, with all its defiance, it showed a spirit, sensitive, accessible to pain.

Watching him as he read the pages of her father's journal, she was as sure the story Tom had told her about him was false—no; it was not Tom's falsehood: she knew that he believed the story—as sure he was innocent of that imputed treachery and torture as of the murder of the man who had once been his intimate friend, from which her own discovery and her father's journal cleared him.

She could almost follow the tragic narrative that the book contained from the reflections on the skyman's face. His eyes never left the finely written pages, and she was free to watch him as closely as she chose.

For a while every change in his sensitive color, every contraction or widening of his eyelids, every dilation of his finely chiseled nostrils, every move of his half-parted lips, revealed to her something of the spirit of the man who read.

But presently, the warmth, the comfort, the stillness overcame her, and she slept, or, at any rate, dozed, but never deep enough to lose her consciousness of the presence of the man who sat there reading.

When he drew near the end of the narrative, she was again translating the quick succession of his thoughts, in the face, wherein he was unconsciously exhibiting them.

She saw him close the book at last and sit there, as she had sat, with it upon his knees, absorbed, reflective. Suddenly, he took up the book again, opened it and referred to the entry on that last page.

He was thinking now, not dreaming. His mind was on the active present. Before long he stole a look at her. She met his eyes.

"I'm glad father told us that the man was left-handed," she said gravely. "Because the man who killed Mr. Hunter was left-handed, too."

She had spoken the very thing his own mind had been groping for without quite finding, and he started and stared at her. "Why do you say that?" he demanded. "How do you know?"

"It was a left-handed stick. I took it up in my left hand and it fitted; that was when I was fetching it out of the cabin for uncle Jerry."

"Then that was how you knew I hadn't done it?"

"No. I didn't need any proof. I knew already, without that."

"Suppose I had turned out to be left-handed, too?"

"I didn't think of that. But it wouldn't have made any difference to me. When you really have faith in anybody it isn't easily shaken; not by mere circumstances, at least."

"'When you really have faith,'" he repeated. "Yes, I suppose that's so." He pressed his hands against his temples. "But there isn't too much of that divine commodity in the world."

There was a long silence.

X

What the Dawn Brought

The man rose from his seat at the foot of the bunk and, with restless strides, began pacing back and forth in the narrow limits of the little hut. The girl lay still, but her eyes followed him. Her thoughts were keeping step with his.

"There's not much faith in the world, that's true," she said presently. "And yet, that's not exactly the world's fault. When people haven't anything else to walk by, they have to walk by sight—" she hesitated a little there, feeling for the words she wanted. "It was so easy," she went on at last, "to clear you of the thing they thought you did yesterday. Couldn't you give them a chance to believe the truth about the other thing, too? There must be something you could reveal about that old charge that would wash out the stain of it,—something that would make Tom see the falsity of it as clearly as I do."

"No," he said; "that was never possible. It's less possible than ever now."

That involuntary admission told her much. If the thing she suggested were less possible now than it had been before, then, somehow or other, the vindication must have rested in Perry Hunter's hands. But the finality of his voice and the dumb agony she saw in his face, as he paced back and forth beside her, prevented her from following up the admission, or urging him any further.

She lay still and waited.

At last his face cleared. "What gave you that faith of yours in me?" he questioned abruptly. "About the murdered man: how could you be sure, without any proof, that I hadn't done it?"

"Why—I suppose it was your wings," she said thoughtfully. "What you told me, or, rather, what you let me see of the soul of a man who could live in the sky as you do.—It's such a crawling thing to do—to take a man's life out of revenge. One who lives up above the world couldn't stoop to do it—any more than an angel could."

He pondered her words in silence for a while. "You're right," he said at last,—"partly right. I didn't want revenge.—I wouldn't have stooped to take it if I had.—And, yet—well, I didn't stoop to save him, either, and I might have done that; at least it would have come about that way if I hadn't checked my human instinct to go down among them; hadn't stayed aloft too long, watching them as though they were a picture."

He went back to the foot of the bunk and picked up the big morocco-bound book which he had laid down. "That narrative has humbled me some way," he said. "You were quite right. It has made me retract the thing I said, in my ignorance, about the men who risk and lose their lives trying to reach the Pole. Whatever his measure of success or failure was,—the man who lived that story—setting it down on these pages as he lived it—was worth—was worth a whole paradise of angels.—You were right, too, though I didn't know you were until you said it, in telling me that I had a contempt for the world. I did have. I betrayed it this morning, there on the deck of the yacht, with the ignorance and vehemence of a school boy. But this journal of your father's, and your—your beautiful faith in me have shown me what base metal it was made of."

He pulled himself up sharply there and looked at his watch. "It will be daylight in two hours now," he said. "When it comes we'll signal to the yacht, and they'll send for you and take you away—you and this precious find you've made. In the meantime, you must go to sleep. You hardly slept at all while I was reading."

"I hardly dare go to sleep—not really deep asleep. If I did I'm afraid you'd turn out to be all a dream, and I'd find myself back in my state-room on the yacht." She was speaking half in mockery, but there was an undertone of seriousness in her voice. "Think how unlikely it is that all this can have happened," she went on. "You said this morning you were going to leave us, and I watched you go.—How can it be anything but a dream that you were hanging aloft there in the sky, above the fog, ready to come plunging down when I cried out for help?"

"I told you once," he said not very steadily, "that one of us might be dreaming, but that one was not you."

"You will promise, then," she asked, "that if I go to sleep, I'll wake up here and not on the yacht, and that you won't have disappeared?"

"I promise," he said seriously.

He seated himself once more at her feet, switched off the fading light from the bull's-eye and drew the sleeves of her coat across his shoulders. "Good night," he said.

She answered drowsily.

He had meant to indulge in the luxury of a doze himself, for he had not slept since the first light of the day before, and then for only two or three hours. But the train of thought which her last words had set going in his mind were quite enough to banish sleep.

How nearly those wings of his had betrayed him again. How narrowly had he missed throwing away this second opportunity.

When he had taken wing from the ice-floe that morning it had been with the perfectly definite intention of making the long straight flight of five hundred miles to Point Barrow. He remembered now how he had phrased the thought. He wanted to blow the last contamination of humanity out of himself. He was done with men. Even the girl's detaining touch he had brushed off almost fearfully. The feeling he found slipping into his mind regarding her, the force of her challenge to return to the world again drove him, by revulsion, farther than the credulous, unfounded suspicion of the two men.

He meant to go. He would have gone—at any rate have started, had not a small thing checked him,—the most vagrant of nature's caprices,—a shift in the direction of the wind.

In order to steer the course he wanted, he must fly higher, and in gaining that necessary altitude, up a long, easy gradient, he cut a great circle inland. Circling thus he found himself, presently, looking straight down upon the shore party from the yacht.

By that time the exercise of his power of flight had steadied him, as it always did. He was so far above them there, so completely detached from them, that there could be no harm in soaring for a while and watching them. That was the way, at least, that he had explained his having done so at the time. He would not have admitted then that the touch of that girl's hand upon his arm had anything to do with it.

He went on watching them with a quickly enlivened curiosity, when he saw that the man who acted as guide to the score of people from the yacht was clad in skins, as the party of men had been who had murdered Hunter. Of that murder, these people who were following him, of course, knew nothing.

Where in the world Cayley wondered, could he be guiding them. Well, there was no hurry. He would stay and see.

So he hung there, lazily, for two or three hours, in the bright, capricious air. His mind was only about half occupied with the toiling little clump of men below him, who struggled on so slowly, so ludicrously slowly, from one ridge's crest to the next.

Of those other men, his two accusers—the two Fanshaws—he thought very little, either. The importance of their charges, and their insults faded out.

But the girl kept her place. She would always keep her place, he imagined, in his memories. He went over, in minute detail, the hour he had had with her upon the ice-floe; smiled over the effort he had had to make to convince her that she was not dreaming; remembered how she had commented upon the contempt he must have for the world.

Then, more reluctantly, he summoned back the scene just enacted upon the *Aurora's* deck; recalled the touch upon his arm, and the challenge which he had just fled from; recalled, last of all, her declaration of faith in him. "Sodden, stupid, cruel, blind"—Those words did not apply to her, at any rate. He wished that she had wings. And then abruptly dismissed the wish, or tried to.

He had sighted the cup-shaped valley which Roscoe called Fog Lake when the little party, who were making their unconscious way toward it, were still a mile or two away. He himself was slow to perceive that it was their destination. He did not fully realize it, in fact, until he saw them disappear at the edge of it. Even then he waited a while, in expectation of seeing them emerge along another of the slanting ridges which seemed to offer a practicable trail.

When it became evident at last that they were not coming out that way, he wheeled about and set out in the direction of the yacht. He was flying across the glacier on his way seaward, when he encountered the relief expedition, headed by old Mr. Fanshaw and Scales, the first officer. The reflection that in order to send out so numerous a party, they must have left the yacht almost deserted, gave him his first intuitive perception of Roscoe's design.

He hung suspended above their heads for a moment or two, in the grip of a painful conflict of emotion. "Sodden, blind, cruel. . ." He had promised himself he would never breathe their air again. And yet. . .

As he recalled the situation now, his eyes on the relaxed, sleeping body of the girl who lay here, safe, asleep within reach of his hand, he trembled to think how evenly balanced that decision of his had been, that had resulted in his flashing down on the ice beside them and taking a hand in their affair. He had accomplished nothing with the rescuing party. His urgent request that they go back to the yacht, his offer to find the first party and bring it back, his solemn warning of the danger, all fell alike on incredulous, suspicious ears. At the end of it all they had trudged away, uneasily, perhaps, for his earnestness could not have been utterly without effect, but still intent on their original design.

Cayley watched them as they trudged away. Then, with a sudden determination, again took wing and flew, as fast as a long slant down the wind, would carry him, back to Fog Lake. Across its grey, and now darkening, surface he skimmed, this way and that, finally catching the thing he hoped for—the sound of human voices coming up through the fog.

He was under no delusion as to the danger of the thing he contemplated. A dive into water of uncertain depth and bottom was safe in comparison, because water would check the downward rush of the entering body; its buoyancy would offer a means of returning to the air again. The fog had had no more supporting power than the air itself. It was a mask across the face of danger, and that was all. But there were men down there, men he had set out to save; so, with a long, steadying breath or two he allowed himself to go drifting down.

The secret of Fog Lake which had baffled Captain Fielding and the *Walrus* people alike was simple enough, once one knew it. An immense geyser, spouting steam and hot water from somewhere, too far down in the bowels of the earth for nearness to poles or equator to make any difference, filled the deep little valley with warm moist air, which the colder air above constantly condensed and constantly precipitated. The situation was similar to that occasionally found in small lakes, where the warmer and lighter water is at the bottom, held there, and balanced as it were, by the heavier and colder water upon the surface. The sides of the valley were granite, polished to an almost glassy surface by the constant drip of the film of water which trickled down its sides. Of anything like vegetation in this dismal place, there was no sign whatever. The bottom of it, an area of two square miles, perhaps, was scored with deep canals and interlacing ridges.

Before Cayley could make out the figures of the men below him, he heard a sudden cry of terror, and checked his descent. The voice had cried out in a foreign tongue, sounding like Spanish, enough like Spanish, at least, for him to understand.

"The Angel of Death!" it cried. "I will confess—confess everything."

And then as swiftly, in that same sibilant, explosive tongue, the confession poured forth,—a confession now so amply justified by what had happened since.

All the while it went on Cayley hung there, now rising a little, now flying, but always with the portentous shadow of those great dark wings of his spread out above the terrified Portuguese and his only less frightened companions.

They told Cayley afterward that when he had finished speaking—he had made the confession on his knees—he rose, with a face like a blind man or a somnambulist, and, before he could be prevented, walked straight off the edge of the narrow ridge where they were standing. He went down without a cry, without a sound. Whatever his reward was to be, he had gone to it.

When Cayley succeeded in finding a spot where he could alight, and, at the same time, afford some prospect of enabling him to take wing again, he found, grouped around him, a little knot of men, only withheld from flight by the flat impossibility of it, who gazed at him as if they more than half-believed that he was indeed the Destroying Angel which Miguel had declared him.

But Warner, the captain of the yacht and leader of the party, was a man of well-balanced common sense, and he soon recovered from his surprise sufficiently to discuss with the new arrival the best means of trying to find a way out. Without Cayley and his wings such a thing would have been almost impossible. Aided by his ability to fly up through the fog and take occasional observations in the clear air, there was some hope that the thing might be done.

It was done at last. Their progress was slow and infinitely laborious, especially for Cayley, for the air in this deep valley was almost stagnant, and when he rose through it it was by main strength, a strength which the great knotted muscles of his shoulders, back and thighs were barely equal to the exertion of producing.

It was just after sunset when they finally stood on the crest of that little ridge where, hours before, he had seen them, under Miguel's guidance, disappearing into the fog.

Down on the crest of the glacier, still toiling on toward them, he pointed out the relief party. "Go down to them as quickly as you can," he said, "and then make all possible haste back to the yacht."

They left him some ship's biscuit and bacon, and set out down the well-marked trail toward the glacier. He had told himself, as he watched them departing, that now at least his duty toward them was done. He would rest awhile, and then enjoy a long, calm sail across the ice and sea to Point Barrow.

There was no fog in the great valley along whose edge the glacier lay, and he thought when he took wing that he would be able to get a last view of the yacht and make sure that she was still safe, before he started.

So, when he crossed the great line of cliffs which formed the coast, he was both surprised and disappointed to find a dense grey cloud of vapor obliterating everything. It was all quiet enough down there, though. They were all right. There couldn't be any doubt of that.

It made him shudder now, as he sat there at the feet of the girl who slept so quietly,—as he sat there and listened to her slow, steady breathing, it made him shudder to think how nearly, for a second time that day, he had abandoned her. What if that terrified cry of hers had gone unheard? What if Roscoe—

He sat stiffly erect, and rubbed his eyes like one trying to get rid of a nightmare; then, with a long expiration of breath, he settled back again.

If his wings had betrayed him once before, they had made their compensation in that moment when the girl's cry had come up to him, through the fog. Without them he could never have brought help.

She told him she had cried out to him,—to him, Philip Cayley. And his heart went racing madly now as the strange admission came back to his mind, and the declaration of faith that had gone with it. Well, he had his reward. All those lonely years in Sandoval; all the deadly peril that had made up the tale of them; all the heart-hunger, for which he had sought an anæsthetic in the sky, were paid for now and made profitable in these hours he had had with her, and in the memory of them that he would take away with him. It could be nothing more than a memory; that he knew full well. The girl had practically admitted as much when she had urged him to clear his name of the old disgrace that stained it.

He could not take her faith in him and use it for a cloak. The world, as she had said, had to walk by sight. Unless he could convince those two Fanshaws, for instance, of his innocence of the old charge, as the girl had convinced them of his innocence of the later one—unless he could do that,—why, with the coming of morning, with the coming ashore of a boat from the yacht, he must say good bye to her; must let her go out of his life for always.

The yacht would sail away and he would fly back to Point Barrow. However bitter that parting might be, he knew that he would always have something of her that he could keep,—the humanity which her faith had given him. He hoped she would let him tell her so when they should stand on the beach there waiting for the boat to come ashore. He would not tell her any more than that. He did not mean that the parting should give her pain—he wanted to bear all that himself. But he hoped that just once she would give him her hands again and let him kiss them.

Warmed a little, comforted a little with that hope, and oppressed by complete exhaustion, he fell asleep himself. He knew, at least, that he must have done so, when, rousing with a start and springing to his feet, he saw a ray of sunshine splashed golden upon the opposite wall of the hut. It must have been light for hours.

Very silently, very cautiously he unbarred the door and pulled it open. Before opening the outer door, he drew his revolver and spun its cylinder underneath his thumbnail. If the repulsed party from the *Walrus* were camped near by, it would be well to be cautious before reconnoitering.

He pulled the outer door a little way open and glanced slantwise up the beach. The brilliant light dazzled him and made it hard to see; but apparently there was no one there. Stepping outside, he turned his gaze inland, along the foot of the cliff. His mind was entirely preoccupied with the danger of a sudden rush of enemies from near at hand.

That is how it happened that, for quite a minute after he opened the door and stepped outside, he did not cast a single glance seaward. He did not look in that direction, until he saw that Jeanne, awakened by the daylight in the hut, was standing in the doorway. Her own eyes, puzzled, incredulous, only half awake, were gazing out to sea. The expression he saw in her face made him turn, suddenly, and look.

The scene before his eyes was beautiful, with that stupendous beauty that only the Arctic can attain. The harbor and beyond it, far out to sea—clear to the horizon, was filled with great plunging, churning masses of ice, all drenched in color by the low-hanging Arctic sun—violet, rose, pure golden-yellow and emerald-green, and a white whose incandescence fairly stabbed the eye. And as those great moving masses ground together, they flung, high into the air, broad shimmering veils of rose-colored spray.

Of the floe, which they had considered stable as the land itself, there was no longer any sign. There was nothing there, nothing at all to greet their eyes, to seaward, but the savage beauty of the ice.

The yacht had disappeared.

XI

THE AURORA

I tell you, sir, the thing is beyond human possibility. There is no help—no human help in the world. I would swear to that before God. But I think you must know it as well as I do." Captain Warner, standing upon the *Aurora's* bridge, was the speaker.

The two Fanshaws, father and son, their faces grey with despair, turned away and looked over the great masses of loose, churning field-ice, which, filling the sea out to the utmost horizon, confirmed the captain's words.

"How long—" Tom Fanshaw began, then he paused, moistened his lips and rubbed them roughly with his hand.—"How long," he repeated, "shall we have to wait before it opens up?"

"It won't open up again this season—not if I know anything about the Arctic," said the captain.

"It will freeze, though," Mr. Fanshaw said, "freeze into a solid pack that we could cross afoot. How long shall we have to wait for that?"

"It's hard to tell. Generally in this latitude the pack is pretty solid by the first of September. But that warm current which caught Fielding's ship, which caught the *Walrus*—the current which makes, every summer apparently, that long gap of open water which enabled us to reach the land that Fielding reached,—that current would keep loose field-ice floating about for at least another month."

Tom Fanshaw's eyes had almost the light of madness in them. "But she can't live a month!" he cried. "She's alone, unarmed! She has no food; no shelter but those bare huts!"

"The *Walrus* people doubtless left some stores there, if she could find them," said Captain Warner. "But, still, what you say is perfectly true. She can hardly hope to keep alive a week."

"Then," said Tom, in dull, passionate rebellion,—"then, in some way or other, we must go back to her. If you won't go—if you won't take the *Aurora* back, I'll take one of the little boats and go myself!"

"If you want to commit suicide," said Captain Warner, "you could do it less painfully with a revolver. The small boat would not live thirty seconds after we put her over the side. You know that, if you are not mad. As for the *Aurora* herself, if she had not been built the way she is, she would have been crushed hours ago. And if I were to lower the propeller and start the engines, they would simply twist the screw off of her before she had gone a ship's length, and leave us helpless in the event of our ever finding open water. We may never live to find it, but there's a chance that we will. There are more than thirty lives that I am responsible for aboard this yacht, and I mean to live up to that responsibility. If we ever do find open water, then I'll do whatever you say. I will take you to Point Barrow and the yacht can winter there. Then when the pack is solid, if you can find dogs and sledges, you can attempt the journey across the ice. I don't believe it can be done. I don't believe there is a chance in a hundred that any single member of the party that set out would live to reach that shore. That, however, is not my affair.

"Or, if you wish, we can take the yacht back to San Francisco, refit her and come back next summer. I think that with our knowledge of the currents and where the open water is, we might get back to Fielding Bay by the first of July. Then we can find—whatever there is to find."

His own voice faltered there, and there were tears in the deep weather-beaten furrows of his cheeks. "God knows," he concluded, "if there were any possible chance I would take it, but there is none—none in the world, not unless we could fly through the air."

It was only an hour since they had ascertained, beyond the shadow of a doubt, that Jeanne was not aboard the *Aurora*. Until Tom had recovered consciousness, the others had entertained little doubt that she was safely hidden somewhere about the ship.

They had had a grim night of it, as the condition of the *Aurora's* decks, when the dawn first brightened them, testified. When the two parties, which had been re-united by Cayley's efforts, had reached the shore on the previous evening, the yacht was still invisible in the fog, and,—though this they did not know—the *Walrus* people were already in possession of it. Tom was lying unconscious at the foot of the companionway where Roscoe had left him, and Jeanne, oblivious to everything in the world, except the narrative she was reading in her father's journal, was in the abandoned hut on the shore.

That the *Aurora's* people were not surprised by what amounted to an ambush and beaten off on their return to the ship, had been due to two causes, one of which they did not, even yet, suspect.

Cayley's warning, together with the confession of the Portuguese, Miguel, had caused them to steal alongside the *Aurora* as silently as possible. Not a word had been spoken by any of the party, and the sound of the rising wind had drowned the creak of their oars. Half a dozen, well-armed men had stolen aboard over the bows to reconnoiter.

Making out the unfamiliar figures of the *Walrus* people on deck, and knowing that they had a fight on their hands, they had worked their way, unobserved, to a position amidships. Here, under cover of a brisk revolver-fire, they had made it possible for the rest of their party to get aboard.

The *Walrus* people, several of whom were below, came tumbling up on deck at the sound of firing, and their whole party entrenched itself in the after-deck house. They had found arms of various sorts aboard the *Aurora*, and made a spirited resistance before they were finally overpowered.

The *Aurora's* people, under the cool-headed command of Warner and the elder Fanshaw, had proceeded in a brisk, scientific, military style that had spared them many serious casualties. There were a number of flesh wounds when it was over, and one or two of a more serious nature. None of them had been killed.

The *Walrus* people, however, had not surrendered until their plight was wholly desperate. Only five of them were left alive, and two of these were mortally wounded when the struggle ceased.

The uninjured were heavily ironed and locked up in the steerage. All the wounded—friends and foes alike—were turned over to the care of the yacht's surgeon and a couple of volunteer assistants from among the crew.

Altogether, it was two or three hours after the *Aurora's* people had regained undisputed possession of the yacht before it was possible to form any definite idea of what had happened. In the excitement and the necessity of everybody doing two or three things at once, Tom Fanshaw and his serious plight were not discovered, until he himself, having partly regained consciousness, uttered a low moan for help, which was heard by a chance passerby.

The gale, which had been raging all this while, had gone screaming by unheeded, and it was not until dawn that the horrified conquerors of the yacht discovered that there was no land in sight.

It was several hours after that, not, indeed, until the captain had worked out their reckoning from an observation, before they realized that they were one hundred miles away from their anchorage of the previous evening, and that their return was hopeless.

Old Mr. Fanshaw gave his arm to his son, helped him down from the bridge and thence to the now deserted smoking-room, forward.

Tom submitted to be led blindly along, and did not demur when his father halted beside a big leather sofa and told him to lie down upon it. Since that momentary outburst of his upon the bridge, the young man had been unnaturally calm. His muscles, as he lay there now upon the sofa, seemed relaxed; his eyes were fixed, almost dull.

Through a long silence his father sat there watching him, but there was no dawn of a corresponding calmness in his face. It had aged whole years over night. It had been grey and drawn and haggard up there on the bridge when the captain had uttered those hope-destroying words, but now as he sat beside his son there was dawning in his eyes a new look of terror.

"My boy," he said at last unsteadily, "I'm going to ask you to make me a promise, a solemn promise, upon your honor."

The young man did not meet his father's eyes. He made no answer at all, but he paled a little.

The old gentleman tried to say something more, but a great sob escaped his lips before he could speak again. "Don't think that I don't understand, my boy; that I don't know how intolerable the agony is. It's hard enough for me—all I can bear—and I know it's worse for you. I know you loved her. I know you hoped that some day she would become your wife—and—well, I understand.—But, Tom, I saw the look that came into your eyes when Warner, up there on the bridge, said—said that it could be done less painfully with a revolver. That was rhetoric with him. Men shouldn't use rhetoric in times like this.—Tom, I want your word of honor that you won't do it."

"You don't know what you're asking," his son answered brokenly. "If she had died, only that, I could have faced the loss like a man, as you have asked me to do; I could go on living upon my memories of her. But, dad, I've murdered her; that's what it comes to! It was in no idle caprice that she left the yacht last night. I drove her away! . . . Oh, of course, I didn't know that at the time. I began making love to her and I showed her, not the man she had always known, but a hot-headed, hot-blooded brute that she was afraid of; until, at last, she told me that I seemed to be trying to kill even the old love which she had always had for me. . . She left the yacht because she wanted to get away; because she was afraid of me! That's the memory I've got to live on, and I tell you I won't do it!"

The terror died out of his father's face. It was stern, the face of a judge, when Tom finished. "Is there no one in the world but yourself?"

HENRY KITCHELL WEBSTER

he asked. "If what you say is true, if you are responsible for taking my daughter away from me—she was my daughter; was loved like a daughter—because you have done that, you now propose to take my son away, too, and leave me childless. Is that your idea of an atonement? Would it be her idea, do you think? Will it be hers, do you think, if her spirit is waiting anywhere, watching us, conscious of the things we do and of the things we think? Or will she see that it was the act of a coward—of a man who fled his post of duty in the world because it was a hard one to keep?"

His voice changed there, suddenly; the sternness was gone, the tenderness came back. "Tom, my boy, you will see it that way some day for yourself. You are not a coward; but until you see it, I want your bare promise."

Slowly the tears gathered in the boy's eyes, filled them full and overflowed them. Once or twice his pale lips twitched; then, holding out his hand, "I promise," he said.

Then his unsteady lips widened into a sort of grin of agony. "And yesterday at this time," he said, "I was calling Cayley a knave and a murderer—Cayley!"

His composure broke down there completely. He rolled over on his face, buried it in the crook of his arm, his shoulders heaving with smothered sobs.

The old gentleman closed his eyes and waited. He could not watch; he could not go away, and, for a long while, he could not speak. Finally, when he could command his voice, he began again talking quietly of something else.

"It's strange to me," he said, "that we ever recovered possession of this yacht at all, let alone that we were able to recover it without it costing us the life of a single man. This gang must have had a leader, and a clever one. The way he manœuvered his men to keep them out of sight while he drew away first one party and then the other from the yacht, was a piece of masterly strategy. He worked it out perfectly in every detail. He got possession of the yacht without losing a man, without even firing a shot that might give the alarm. And even with the warning we had and with the help of the fog, I don't see how we defeated a man like that. His success must have gone to his head and made him mad."

"He was probably killed in the first volley our people fired when they got aboard," said Tom dully. "He alone could have accounted for half a dozen of you, if he'd ever had a chance—a giant like that."

"A giant!"

"I think he must have been the leader," said Tom. "He was the first man to come aboard, certainly."

"But what makes you call him a giant?"

"Because he literally was. He struck me down with just one blow, and as he raised his arm to strike I saw that his shoulder-cap was above the level of my eyes; and I pass for a tall man."

His father abandoned the subject abruptly, and for a while contrived to talk of other things; of the details of the fight and how different members of the crew had borne themselves.

But his mind was filled with a new terror, and as soon as he could feel that his son was in condition to be left alone, he left him, with a broken word of excuse. He must either set this new terror at rest, or know the worst at once. There had been no one, either among the survivors or the slain of the *Walrus* party, who in any way resembled the monster Tom had described.

An hour later he went back to the bridge to talk again with Captain Warner. He thought that they had sounded the depth of despair that former time when they had talked together there, but in this last hour he had sounded a new abyss beneath it all. He knew now why the yacht had been so easily taken. He knew all the details of the devilish plan which had so nearly succeeded. More than that, he knew the story of the man Roscoe from the time when Captain Planck had taken him aboard the *Walrus*, down to the hour last night when he had sprung into his boat again and pulled shoreward. Captain Planck was dying, and old Mr. Fanshaw's questions had enabled him to enjoy the luxury of a full confession.

So they knew now, those two men who stood there on the bridge, white-lipped, talking over the horror of the thing—they knew that Jeanne was not alone upon that terrible frozen shore. The man Roscoe was there, too.

A sound on the deck below attracted Mr. Fanshaw's attention. Tom, with the aid of a heavy cane, was limping precariously along the deck toward the bridge ladder, and, to their amazement, when he looked up at them, they saw that somehow, his face had cleared. There was a grave look of peace upon it.

"I've thought of something," he said, after he had clambered up beside them,—"I've thought of something that makes it seem possible to go on living, and even hoping."

The two older men exchanged a swift glance. He was not to know about Roscoe. If he had found something to hope for, no matter how illusory, he should be allowed to keep it—to hug it to his breast, in place of the horrible, torturing vision of the human monster which the other two men saw.

"What is it you've thought of, Tom?" his father asked unsteadily.

"It's—it's Cayley. He's there with her; I'm sure he is." He turned away a little from Captain Warner and spoke directly to his father. "I don't know how I know, but it's as if I saw them there together. He has fallen in love with her, I think. I'm quite sure she has with him. I wanted to kill him for that yesterday, but now—" his voice faltered there, but the look in his eyes did not change,—the light of a serene, untroubled hope.—"He's there with her," he went on, "and with God's help he'll keep her alive until we can get back with the relief."

He said no more, and he clutched the rail tight in his gauntleted hands and gazed out north, across the ice.

XII

CAYLEY'S PROMISE

For this small mercy Cayley thanked God. The girl did not understand. She was rubbing those sleepy eyes of hers and putting back, into place, stray locks of hair that were in the way. "The floe must have gone to pieces," she said, "and they've drifted off in the fog without knowing it. I suppose there's no telling when they'll be back; very likely not for hours."

He did not risk trying to answer her. All his will power was directed to keeping the real significance of the yacht's disappearance from showing in his face.

She had turned to him quite casually for an answer, but not getting it, remained looking intently into his eyes. "Mr. Cayley," she asked presently, "were you telling me last night what you really thought was true, or were you just encouraging me—I mean about those men who attacked the yacht? Are you afraid, after all, that our people are not in possession of the *Aurora*, wherever she is?"

"I told you the truth last night. I can't imagine any possibility by which the men who came here on the *Walrus* could get the *Aurora* away from your people, except by stealth."

"But if our people beat them off, why didn't they come ashore? There aren't any of them around, are there?"

"Apparently not," said Cayley. "They may have all been killed before they could get back to shore, or some of them may have been captured. No, I really don't think you need worry about them."

Of course she would have to know sometime. She must know soon, in fact. But Cayley prayed that she might remain ignorant of the horrible, silent menace that lay before her, until he himself should have had time to look it in the face; to plumb the depth of its horror; to see if there were anything that could be built into a hope, or into the mere illusion of a hope.

He knew, all too well, what those great turning, tumbling masses of emerald and golden ice there in the harbor meant. The *Aurora* might be alive somewhere far out in that turbulent sea—might, possibly, still preserve her powers of locomotion, but her spars and funnels would never cut their horizon line again—this horizon that lost itself now before his eyes in rose-drenched haze—never, at least, until the morning of a new Summer.

He must think, think what to do and how to tell her. If only she would give him time. An hour was what he was praying for—an hour in which to gather up his forces for what he knew, intuitively, must be a greater battle than any his soul had ever waged. He did not know what form the struggle was going to take. That was the thing which, in the next hour, he must try to foresee.

He must go away by himself; he knew that. To stand there before her, looking at her, caused a singing in his veins and in his heart, which in other circumstances he would have called joy. The singing made it hard to think. The refrain of the song was, so far as it was translatable into words at all, that they two possessed the world together; that it had been emptied over night of all save themselves. The blind-eyed sisters had caught up two threads out of the warp of life and knotted them together, and until those two threads were sheared across, they would lie side by side.

This was not a thought of his. It bore about the same relation to thought that music does to language. But his nerves were tingling with it; his blood leaping like a March brook.

She had not been looking at him since he had answered her question. All he could see of her face was the rim of one of her perfect ears and a flushed cheek, veiled with that warm, misty bloom which lasts a little while after slumber, and bearing, just perceptibly, the print of one of the creases in the hard pillow upon which she had slept.

She began to speak without turning to him. "You said something last night about my faith. Well, I'm not going to falsify it, not today, at any rate." She turned and faced him, her eyes bright, her color mounting even a little higher. "I'm going to believe that they're safe—uncle Jerry and Tom, and all the rest. I am not going to be afraid for them. And so until they come back, we'll make this day a holiday. Aren't you glad,—just a little glad that it's happened? Because I am, I'm afraid. That's selfish, I know, because they'll be frightfully worried about me, until they come back and find me safe. They don't even know you're here, I suppose. And it was an inexcusable trick of mine, rowing ashore without telling Tom where I was going. But I'm not going to begin to repent until it will do somebody some good. You don't deserve to be made miserable with it."

She drew a long deep breath, flung out her arms wide, and then stretched them skyward. "What a day it is. Was there ever such a day down there in that warm green world that people live in?—Oh, I don't wonder that you love it. I wish I could fly as you do. But since I can't, for this one day you must stay down here upon the earth with me."

Her mention of his wings gave him his first faint perception of the line the struggle would take. His mind flashed for an instant into the position which her own would take when she should know the truth. To her it would not seem that they were castaways together. He was not marooned here on this shore. His ship was waiting to take him anywhere in the world. He was as free as the wind itself—

"I believe living in the sky is what makes you do that," he heard her say,—"makes you drift off into trances that way, perfectly oblivious to the fact that people are asking you questions."

He met her smiling eyes, and a smile came, unbidden, into his own. "You've forgiven me already, I see," he said. "What was the question about?"

"It was about breakfast. Have you anything to eat in that bundle of yours?"

He shook his head, and she drew down her lips in mock dismay.

"Is there anything to eat anywhere?" she questioned, sweeping her arm round in a half circle, landward. "Mustn't we go hunting for a walrus or a snark or something?"

Cayley had to turn away from her as she said that. The remorseless irony of the situation was getting beyond human endurance. The splendor of the day; the girl's holiday humor; her laughing declaration that she would not permit him to fly away; this last gay jest out of the pages of "Alice in Wonderland" about hunting for a walrus.

"God!" he whispered as he turned away—"My God!"

He had his revolver, and besides the six cartridges which the cylinder contained, there were, perhaps, thirty in his belt. For how many days, or weeks, would they avail to keep off starvation?

But his face was composed again when he turned back to her. "There are two things that come before breakfast," he said—"fire and water. There is a line of driftwood down the beach to the westward, there at the foot of the talus. When we get a fire going—" he stopped himself short. "I was going to say that we could melt some ice for drinking water, but until we have some sort of cooking utensil to melt it in, it won't do much good. There must be something of the sort in the hut here."

She shook her head. "They're completely abandoned," she told him. "Our shore party searched them first of all, and afterward uncle Jerry and I searched them through again. There is nothing there at all, but some heaps of rubbish."

"I think I'll take a look myself," said he. "Rubbish is a relative term. What seemed no better than that yesterday afternoon while the yacht was in the harbor, may take on a different meaning this morning."

He disappeared through the doorway, and two minutes later she saw him coming back with a big battered-looking biscuit tin.

"Unless this leaks too fast," he said, "it will serve our purpose admirably."

He observed, without reflecting what the observation meant, that a bountiful supply of fuel was lying in great drifts along the lower slope of the talus. Jeanne accompanied him upon his quest of it, and with small loss of time and no trouble at all they collected an armful. They laid their fire upon a great flat stone in front of the hut, for the outdoor day was too fine to abandon for the dark and damp in the interior, and soon they had the fire blazing cheerfully.

For a while they sat, side by side, upon his great sheepskin, warming their fingers and watching the drip of the melting ice in the biscuit tin.

But presently Cayley got to his feet. "Breakfast!" he said.

"Is there to be anything besides a good big drink of water apiece? If there isn't, I'd rather not think about it until the yacht comes back."

"Unless I'm mistaken, there's an excellent breakfast waiting for us not far from where we got the fire-wood. But I'll go and make sure before I raise your expectations any higher."

He walked away a half-dozen paces without waiting for any reply; then, thinking suddenly of something else, he came swiftly back again.

"Do you know anything about fire-arms?" he asked. "If you're accustomed to shooting, I'll leave my revolver with you.—No," he went on, answering the question which she had not spoken—"no, I don't foresee any danger to you. It's just on general principles."

"I'm a pretty good shot. But if you're going on a hunting expedition for our breakfast and there isn't any foreseeable danger to me in being left alone, it seems reasonable that you should take the gun."

He took the revolver from his belt, however, and held it out to her. "Our breakfast doesn't have to be shot. And as a concession to my feelings,—no, it's nothing more than that—I'd rather you took it."

She did as he asked without further demur, and he went away. When she was left alone, the girl added fresh sticks to the fire, and then, in default of any more active occupation, took up the red-bound book which lay beside her and began once more to peruse its pages. She had by no means exhausted them. In her reading of the night before, she had skipped the pages of scientific description for those parts of the journal which were most purely personal. Even now the whole pages of carefully tabulated data concerning the winds, currents, temperature, and magnetic variations got scant attention. In her present mood the homeliest little adventure, the idlest diversion of a winter's day meant more to her than all her father's discoveries put together. When she saw Cayley coming back toward her across the ice, she put the book down half reluctantly.

Evidently his quest for breakfast had not been in vain; he had a big black and white bird in his hand. "Do you suppose it's fit to eat?" she called out to him. "And how in the world did you manage to kill it without the revolver?"

"Fit to eat! It's a duck. What's more, it's an eider, which means that her coat is worth saving."

"But how did you contrive to kill her?"

"I didn't. She killed herself. She was flying too low last night, I suppose,—going down the gale, and in the fog she went smack into the side of the cliff and broke her neck. That was a very destructive storm for the birds. There must be fifty of them, of one kind and another, lying dead there along the top of the talus, at the foot of the cliff."

"And that's what might have happened, oh, so easily, to you. Yes, it might. I've been realizing that. And I sha'n't forget." Her eyes had brightened and she pressed her hands to them for just one moment; then she straightened up briskly. "Anyway I'll not make a scene about it now," she said. "I'll show a little practical sense and help you with the breakfast."

"No, we're camping out today, and on such occasions the men always do the cooking. Go back to your book while I skin this fowl and dress it." Then as she still hesitated, he went on, "The most beautiful garment I ever saw, anywhere, was on a Chucotte Indian girl. It was made of nothing but the breasts of these eiders. But the process isn't pretty. I'd much rather you went back to your book."

Seeing that he meant it, she did as he asked. A single half page of what was written upon those closely ruled pages was enough to absorb her again completely. The power it had over her seemed to grow rather than to lessen. When Cayley came up with the big bird which was to serve for their breakfast, impaled upon a sharp stick ready to be roasted over the fire, she no more than looked up at him, with a smile very friendly, but half-apologetic, and then went on with her reading. He crouched down near by her, built a little frame-work of sticks above the fire and began his cooking.

It was, perhaps, ten minutes after that when he saw the book drop suddenly from her hands. When he glanced up at her, she was looking seaward—out over those miles of plunging, heaving ice. And, under his eyes, her face turned white as marble. Her bloodless lips were parted. They did not move at all and they looked as if they were frozen. He could not see that she was breathing. Her eyes were turned away from him and he was glad of that. For another moment more, at least, he need not read the look in them. For now, at last, he was sure she understood. He himself fixed his eyes upon the fire and waited.

Since his own look seaward this morning he had had the hour he prayed for. He had not spent it in thinking; in devising phrases of consolation or futile illusions of hope. Anything like consecutive thought had been impossible to him; and not only impossible, unnecessary. He had spent the hour to better purpose, although he could have presented no tangible evidence that this was so. But now at the end of it he felt himself ready. All through it he had been silently mastering his forces. His power of will, his courage, his intuition, his intelligence—they were all there, keyed to their highest tension; ready to do their part.

Without looking at the girl he was aware that she had turned and was gazing intently into his face. He supported her look without meeting it. She would find nothing there now he would not wish her to see. He even stretched out a hand, a steady hand over the fire and twirled the spit with it.

"There's something here," she whispered, "here in this book of father's that—that I want you to read."

It was still open at the page she had been reading when she had dropped it. With his first glance at what was written there he saw how she had come, so suddenly, to understand.

"September 18th.—Field-ice came into the bay last night, just as it has come at about this season in the two preceding years—a dense fog and a whole gale blowing from the east. To me its coming is a relief. It is, in a way, the official beginning of winter. The tantalizing hope of a rescue is now put away on the shelf to wait for another summer. After all, to men in our condition a temporary hopelessness is much more comfortable than hope itself. The long winter night gives an opportunity to revive our belief that with another season of open water, rescue will come.

"I have been very busy lately stocking our larder for the next six months. Fortunately, I have succeeded in killing bears and walruses enough to keep us supplied. I wish I could feel as easy about our fuel. We have swept the beach clear of drift-wood, but shall have barely enough to get through the winter with. For myself, who have no real hope at all, it doesn't greatly matter. I greet the dawn of each of these interminable Arctic days with intense weariness. And I never bid farewell to the sun for another winter without an involuntary *In manus Tuas*."

Cayley read the entry through slowly. "I'm glad it happened this way," he said when he finished, "glad it was your father who told you. All this past hour I've been wondering how I could tell you, how I could make you understand."

The girl had been half-reclining upon the great sheepskin, her weight supported by one hand. While Cayley read, this support failed her, and she sank down, rather slowly, until her head was buried in the arms which were stretched out as if in blind supplication. She was shuddering all over.

As Cayley spoke, he covered those clasped, outstretched hands with one of his own. The touch and the sound of his voice steadied her a little.

"You've known, then, from the first?" The words came brokenly, half-voiced, muffled.

He bent down over her to hear them. "Yes, I knew from the first."

He said no more than that just then, but remained as he was, his hand covering her two, holding them tight, his body bending over hers protectingly.

After a little while she ceased shuddering, and answered the pressure of his hand with a sudden clasp of her two; then drew them away again and sat erect.

Her eyes, when they rose to his face, were still wide with fear,—a deeper-seated fear, really, than her first momentary panic. But now she had it in control and spoke steadily enough.

"There is no chance at all, do you think?"

"For the *Aurora* to come back? No, not this season, at least; no possible chance."

"And—how much ammunition have you, Mr. Cayley?"

"Thirty-one cartridges, besides the ones in the revolver."

HENRY KITCHELL WEBSTER

He would have said something more, but with a little gesture she prevented him. "You've been thinking it out," she said. "You know what it means now, and I—I feel that I don't. I can't quite realize it yet. You must give me a little time to think, too."

He had to assent to that, though he knew, in advance, the direction her thoughts must take, and foresaw the dreadful conclusion of them. And the answer he had to make to that conclusion? Well, he had it ready.

How long that silence lasted, neither of them knew. He sat there beside her, and yet even his eyes allowed her perfect solitude. He mended the fire and attended to his cooking as quietly as before, when the girl was reading.

Finally a little move of hers, preparatory to speech, gave him leave to look at her. In those silent minutes, however long they were, her face had changed. It was grave now, intensely thoughtful, but the color had come back into it. It was alive again.

"When I asked you a while ago if there were any chance, you asked me if I meant a chance for the return of the *Aurora*, and said there was none. That was what I meant then, but it's not what I mean now. Is there any chance at all? I haven't been able to see any myself, and I've been over it all pretty carefully. Do you see any? You—you must tell me the truth, please."

"I haven't been trying to assess the chances. I spent my hour thinking about something else, and I can't answer your question really with a yes or a no."

"Not with a yes, but can't you answer it with a no? Aren't you perfectly sure, in your heart, that there's no chance at all?"

"Not yet," he answered. "There may be a chance, and if there is, we can meet it half way." Then he stretched out his hand. "That red-bound book there is our bible now. Do you remember what your father said? 'We can live like Christians, and we can always hope.' He thought, when he put that bottle, which contained his message, into the sea, that there was hardly one chance in a million of its resulting in an effectual relief. Yet he went on living as a brave man lives, a day at a time. And when he died, he died without fear. Doing that, he not only helped himself, but he helps us in a way that he couldn't possibly have foreseen."

Her eyes filled suddenly with tears, and a smile, of a divine sad tenderness, touched for an instant her mouth. "But that isn't our case, you know. Ours isn't as simple as that."

"What makes the difference?" But he knew the answer.

"Your wings." She said it hardly above a whisper, and as she said it she turned a little paler and her brave lips trembled. But in an instant her will had taken command again. "I am sure you see. It's quite plain," she went on steadily. "If you will spread them, those great wings of yours, and take to the air with them, and fly away, as you are free to do, and leave me here alone, as I really am alone, the only person marooned here—if you'll do that, then I'll follow my father's gospel.—But you won't go away. You can't,—not a man like you, and I know that. I know I mustn't even suggest it."

Her voice sank again and grew unsteady. "While I am starving, you will be starving, too. And while I am freezing, you will freeze." She stopped there with a shudder and a deep, gasping sob; then, "Won't you go?" she cried out. "You said once that one of us might be dreaming, but that one was not I. Can't you believe it's so? Can't you wake up from the dream that is turning into a nightmare, and fly away?—No, you can't! You can't!—There is only one way out of it!"

There was the conclusion he had foreseen, had foreseen long before he could formulate it—the inevitable conclusion that had led him to pray for an hour. And now he thanked God that the answer was ready.

But before he could speak, she turned to him with a sudden transition of mood, which left him gasping. The face she turned upon him now was radiant, flushed with life, fearless. She held out both hands to him. "Come," she said; "that's over. You're to forget it ever happened, and you're to do something for me that I want. Will you? I want this for a holiday, just as I set out to make it when I saw the yacht was gone. The day's as bright as it was then, and we can make the hours pure gold. It all depends on us. Come, will you do that for me?"

Giving him her hands, she had meant him to assist her to rise, but he disregarded the intention and knelt on one knee beside her. "Jeanne,"—he said.

Her color fluttered like a flag at that, and she caught her breath. "Thank you,—Philip."

"We'll have our holiday, Jeanne, but we must have a better understanding first."

"No! No more!—I can't!"

But he went steadily on: "You said there was only one way out, and I knew what you meant. It is a way out,—a way that I can't deny your right to take, if we're talking of rights. During the five years that I spent

HENRY KITCHELL WEBSTER

at Sandoval I always regarded it as a right that I could exercise when I chose. Perhaps that is one of the reasons I never exercised it. But, Jeanne, if you elect to take that way, I shall take it with you."

She struggled away from him, turned and faced him with horror-stricken eyes. "You must not say that! You've no right to threaten me with that! No right!" Then, clutching at his hands again, "You must promise!"

Again she pulled her hands away and covered her face with them. She was trembling uncontrollably.

"It was not a threat," he said steadily. "It was a promise, a promise I have the right to make. I make it again, now, Jeanne,—a solemn promise before God. Whether it's living or dying, I shall go beside you."

"No right—" she repeated in a whisper. "What possible right could you have to make a promise like that—a threat that calls itself a promise?"

"I have the only right there is. Listen. Last night, when you were lying there asleep, I sat thinking, thinking about you, about the love I had for you; about the change which that love had made in me and would go on making after I had lost you. For I faced losing you. I knew that when they sent a boat ashore for you, I should have to let you go without a word. If I could have heard a prophecy then, that today I should be telling you I loved you, telling it with a clear heart and conscience, I should have gone half-mad for joy. It seemed as if the thing could never happen. I am a man with a stain upon me, and yesterday that stain made it impossible to say anything to you but good bye. I meant to say it, and take my way through the air again and live out the rest of my life on what, from your bounty, you had already given me.

"But the coming of a new day has changed all that. It has given me the right to tell you what I have told you, and it gives me the right to make that promise. Isn't that quite plain? Don't you understand?"

She had listened breathless while he talked to her. Now for the space of two deep inhalations she was silent. "It can't be true," she said faintly, "not all that. Not so soon. It was only yesterday—"

"You know truer than that," he interrupted. "You know that hours and days have nothing to do with the thing I'm talking about. Try to remember what I was when I came down out of the air upon that ice-floe. A man who, for five years, had been drugging his soul to death, trying to cast all the humanity out of it. Think what you did for me. Think what you gave me out of yourself. I don't tell you that I love you better than my soul, because—because my soul *is* you—your warmth, your faith, your fragrance. Why, do you know what my feeling has been this morning, the feeling I have tried to fight back out of my heart? Joy, Jeanne! Joy that I was to suffer what you suffered, and live what you lived, whether it was to be for an hour or a day or a month! Whatever it was to bring us, you and I were to share the world together. Do you understand, now, Jeanne, my right to make that promise? Do you see now that it was a promise and not a threat?"

She could not at first make him any answer. The thing his words had revealed to her, coming as it had come, upon the heels of that other revelation, left her mind half dazed. She was not without an answer, but it lay not in her mind nor was it translatable into words. There was a chord there, vibrating in response to the music it had heard, but it could find no expression through her lips.

"I must think," she gasped. "You must let me think."

"No," he said, "I have not asked for an answer. There is nothing that you have to tell me. Nothing that I'm waiting to hear. No decision that you must make. You understand what I said and you know it's true. The supreme fact in my universe is just you. That gives me the right to follow you wherever you go. But you are still free. You can stay here, where Fate has put you, and let me stay here, too, being sure that all the happiness in the world there is for me is to be found here at your side, in helping you. And then if the torture of privation, loneliness and despair become too hard—"

She turned to him then and interrupted. Her words came quietly, unaccompanied by any gesture of her expressive hands. She spoke with the utmost simplicity.

"They won't be too hard, I think,—neither the privation nor the loneliness. There won't be any despair,—not with you, my friend. And— and we will follow my father's gospel."

She saw the blood go ebbing out of his face, and then come back with a surge. He drew in two or three great breaths of the keen, winelike air. Then, in a strangely matter-of-fact fashion, he seated himself beside her.

"That gospel begins with breakfast," he said.

XIII

CAPTAIN FIELDING'S GOSPEL

Side by side, upon that great sheep-skin, they sat, those two people, in the very lap of death. A reasonable estimate of their chances would give them, perhaps, a week to live. With exceptional fortune, that week might stretch itself into a month. The great blue spirit of the Arctic would darken to purple, and to black. The icy hand of the savage polar winter would get its clutch upon them. They had nothing to resist it with. No stores of ammunition or of food. No clothing, except what they wore. No fuel, save what they could contrive to gather along the talus before the winter gales would make further search impossible.

Neither Jeanne nor Cayley was of a sort to face the prospect of that death with resignation. They were young, intensely alive, and with Jeanne, at least, the best and biggest part of life lay, or had lain until yesterday, in a broad open road before her. But a prospect like the one that lay before them brings its own anæsthetic with it. It was so utterly hopeless that it became unreal. The face of the future, into which she had cast just one horrified glance, was so hideous that to the girl, at least, it was like some monster mask of carnival,—too grotesquely horrible to be taken seriously.

That is partly the reason why she succeeded in surprising Cayley by sitting down to breakfast with him in the same mood and spirit which she had shown before when she did not know.

"I'm about half famished," she said as they began their meal, "at least that duck smells perfectly irresistible. It's done to a turn, I think. In a way, it's rather a joke that we should begin our Arctic privations with a roast duck."

"Yes," he said; "it tastes good, even without salt. The man who would complain of the absence of currant jelly—"

"If we were only the 'Swiss Family Robinson' now," she interrupted, "a little jar of it, in perfectly good condition, would come washing ashore."

He had carved the duck dextrously enough with his sheath knife, but for eating it, there was nothing, of course, but their fingers.

"If you'll treat the revelation as confidential," said the girl, "I'll admit that I always like to eat like this, especially when I'm hungry. If anything looks good, I want to take it up in my fingers and pop it into my mouth, without waiting to have it put decorously before me on a plate. I suppose, though," she added, "I shall be entirely reconciled to forks before I get a chance to eat with another. Shall you make me one out of a walrus tusk, or an old tin can, or something?—Why, what are you thinking about?"

"There's something queer about that hut," he replied, "something that gets queerer the more I think about it. Why do you suppose the *Walrus* people abandoned it? Or, rather, do you suppose they did abandon it?"

"I don't see exactly what you mean. Of course, it is abandoned—utterly. We know that."

He shook his head. "I'm not sure. But put the question the other way. Why did they? What possible reason could there have been for such a move?"

"They might have found it unhealthful or unsafe."

The girl answered absently, for half of her mind was exploring for the drift of Cayley's, and did not find it.

"Your father lived here for years," he went on, "and the *Walrus* people must have continued living here for a good while—afterwards. For certainly the place hasn't been abandoned very long."

"Perhaps," she hazarded, "they had given up hope of a rescue, and so didn't care to stay on the beach. They might have found some more convenient place in the interior."

"That's what I supposed," he said, "but the theory won't work—for just this reason. They couldn't have built another house without dismantling this one. There are no trees on this land to furnish timber, and there certainly isn't any hardware store where they could have bought nails, bolts and hinges. But those doors swung on hinges last night and the bolt worked, and, more or less, the walls and roof kept out the gale. For this style of architecture it's in pretty good repair."

The girl was only half convinced.

"That great heap of stones in there," she began, "doesn't look like good repair or recent habitation."

"No it doesn't," he rejoined. "It's been made to look as little that way as possible. It wouldn't have got into that condition otherwise in a hundred years. Come, let's have a look. It's something to hope for, at any rate."

She followed him a little perplexed.

"To hope for?" she repeated questioningly.

He had already entered the hut, and did not at once volunteer any further explanation, but from the shine of excitement she could see in his eyes, it was evident that he contemplated something better than merely holding death at arms' length for a little while.

To the girl's eyes there was little about the interior of the hut to account for such a hope, even though she saw that all of the things he had said about it were true. The flimsy inner doors were still hinged to their frames, and were provided with a miscellaneous assortment of catches. It was marine hardware, all of it, evidently from her father's ship, the *Phœnix*. The bunks and shelves which lined the walls looked perfectly solid and well built. But the general appearance of the room presented a look of disrepair. It was absolutely unfurnished. The great heap of smoke-blackened stones, of various sizes and shapes, and the hole in the roof above them, attested that they had once been a fire-place.

From the forlorn aspect of the room the girl gladly turned her eyes away, and stood looking at Cayley instead. He had been sweeping the walls, roof and floor in a general survey. Now, abruptly, he went over to the heap of stones, picked up one of them, rubbed his thumb over it and scrutinized, with an air of considerable interest, the black smear it left.

"That would account for the drift-wood," he said absently.

At that he might have seen in the girl's face a look of half-amused impatience, but his abstraction was too deep for him to notice it.

He walked over to one of the side walls, pulled open what proved to be a big solid shutter, revealing a glazed window, and, for a long while, stood there, unconscious of the look the girl had turned upon him, unconscious of his present surroundings.

"Yes, something to hope for, certainly." He turned away from the window as he said it, and smiled at her. "A good hope—a good fighting hope that when the relief comes back next summer they'll find you here alive."

"If you say so, I'll believe it," said the girl, "because you told me the truth before. But do you mind telling me why?"

"I should have thought of it sooner. I should have noticed it last night. My guess was right, that's all. This is not an abandoned hut. Don't you see, it's in almost perfect repair? The hinges on this shutter work, although if you look closely you can see that someone gave a tug at them not long ago in an attempt to pull them out. And that patch on the wall was put on within a month. The men who wrecked this place worked hastily and showed no great degree of imagination. They hadn't much time, you see, because they couldn't have begun until they caught their first glimpse of the yacht. They had finished the job before they could send a party ashore."

"But why in the world should they do such a thing?" the girl protested.

He shook his head. "I haven't worked that out yet, not fully, at any rate. After all, it's not the question that concerns us."

"I'm still in a maze about it. What did you mean about the drift Wood?"

"Why, the soot on these stones showed me that. They haven't been burning drift wood in this fireplace. They've been burning coal,—or oil, perhaps. I hadn't thought of that. That's why the drift wood collected again out there on the talus. You remember your father speaks of having used it all? There have been a dozen men living here ever since, and they didn't need it. So they must have had some other sort of fuel."

"You mean they've got a supply somewhere,—hidden?"

He nodded. "Not only a supply of fuel, but of food, too. You remember your father also speaks of having his larder completely stocked for the winter at this time? Well, these fellows weren't expecting any relief. They must have stocked their larder, too.—Of course," he went on a moment later, "I realized vaguely all along that there must be stores somewhere here on the land because men were living here, but on the theory that they had abandoned the beach and were living in some undiscovered part of the mainland, our chance of finding those stores was almost nothing at all. Finding them would be like trying to find Point Barrow in a fog. But you see, if they kept them here in these huts, and then hid them when they caught sight of the yacht, while they may be well hidden, they can't be far away. There wouldn't have been time to move them far; certainly not over the glacier and into the interior there. It must all be hidden somewhere, here on the coast. When we find that hiding place, we shall probably find all the stores we need for the winter."

"Then, I suppose, the next thing for us to do is to go out and find it."

"Not quite the next thing. Unless we have exceptional luck, we can hardly hope to find it for several days; it may take a fortnight, and we must have some temporary security first. In the meantime there is no telling what sort of weather we will have. It's rather late for these beautiful, mild days, I fancy. No, the first thing to do is to rebuild this

HENRY KITCHELL WEBSTER

fireplace and bring in a lot of drift wood and all those birds that were killed last night by flying against the cliff. When we have made this hut habitable against a spell of forty below zero weather, such as we're likely to have at any time, and have accumulated stores of fuel and food for a few days, then we'll begin our search. And if you'll forego the holiday I promised you, I think I had better get to work at once."

She colored suddenly, and spoke with a blunt decisiveness that took him rather aback, though it pleased him at the same time. "Please don't talk that way nor take that attitude. The convention that a woman can't be asked to do anything for herself is all right at a ball, but not here. I want you to give me credit for being an adult human person, fairly strong, and capable of work. We're two castaways here. I am at least, and you're pretending you are—no, I'll take that back. You are just as much as I am. That's the hypothesis we're working on. And you're captain because you know the most. You're to tell me what to do, and I'll obey orders. But I expect you to work me just as hard as you work yourself."

"You're quite right," he assented, holding out his hand. "That's agreed upon. I think I can rebuild this fire-place by myself. Will you go and begin carrying in fire wood, and as many of those ducks and geese and loons as you can find there along the talus?"

She nodded, and turned to leave the hut. "Take the revolver with you," he called after her.

At that she halted abruptly in the doorway. "Why should I have it any more than you?" Then, answering his smile with one of her own, she added, "I suppose a well-trained crew doesn't demand reasons for the captain's orders,—only—"

"There's a perfectly good reason. I'm working in the shelter, and you in the open. Besides that, I'm stronger and I have my sheath knife. If I were attacked by anything, I could give a better account of myself than you could. You'd better take belt and holster and all, and buckle it right around your waist."

It was late in the afternoon before Philip completed his task. Rebuilding the fireplace was a more complicated job than he had imagined it would be. Buried beneath the stones he had found an iron oven and a fire-box, besides a badly battered iron hood and an iron pipe, about three inches in diameter. The stones were evidently to be built up into a table about four feet long, and, roughly, half as high and broad, incasing both the oven and the fire-box. The fire-box was open at the top, and directly above it must hang the hood, much like that over a blacksmith's forge, only in this case, of course, it was intended to radiate as much heat as possible, instead of as little. All the iron had been badly bent and otherwise damaged in the process of tearing it down, and it had cost him a long, laborious hour, or more, pounding it between unhandily shaped stones, to get it into condition to be put up again.

Meanwhile, Jeanne had spent the hours bringing in wood and accumulating, also, a great feathered heap of the victims of last night's fog. At first she had not been able to pick up one of them without the thought that Philip himself might have been lying here this morning, somewhere along the talus, at the foot of the cliff, just as these birds were.

But the steady routine of the job he had assigned her was an efficacious remedy against undesirable thoughts. Those two heaps outside the hut must grow—must be big enough when he completed that job of his indoors to bring, if possible, an exclamation of surprise and pleasure from him.

Incidentally she kept their morning fire burning all day. It would not do to waste a single match out of their scanty store, to light a new one in the hut when Philip's fireplace should be ready for it.

At sometime along the middle of the day they had knocked off for long enough to finish the duck. He had said he did not want to stop for a regular meal until the fireplace was done, and she, in the enthusiasm of the first real manual labor she had ever done in her life, was as unwilling to rest as he. Since luncheon, or what had passed for it, they had hardly exchanged a dozen words. She had sometimes stood for a moment in the doorway of the hut, on her return with a fresh load of wood, and given him a nod of encouragement, and then immediately set out again.

He had told her at luncheon time that he relied on her to stop working before she had over-fatigued herself. As the afternoon wore along a feeling that if she paused at all she would find she was tired enough to quit work altogether for the day, drove her on to work a little faster and more continuously.

When Philip finally had his fireplace rebuilt, in a temporary fashion which he thought would serve till greater leisure should allow him to perfect it, he stepped outside the hut and looked, first down and then up the shore in search for her, and was disappointed at finding her nowhere in sight.

The afternoon was well advanced, and the pitiless, blinding white light of midday was already submitting to refraction by the ice crystals which filled the lower strata of the atmosphere, into the amazing debauch of colors which marks an Arctic evening. The sun had dipped below the crest of coast hills and cliff. Their precipitous sides in the shadow glowed with the blue of pure sapphire; the icy sands of the beach, sloping gradually off to the sea, with the lighter, slightly striated, bluish-green of the turquoise. Out behind the cliffhead, westward, the horizon was lost in golden vapor. The ice was golden, and the little lanes of troubled water between its heaving masses, molten gold.

If Philip could have caught sight of Jeanne anywhere in the picture he would have enjoyed the glory of it as a frame and background to herself; but since she was not there either to enjoy it with him nor to make a part of his enjoyment of it, it struck him only as a good effect of nature's stupidly wasted.

The pile of driftwood here beside the door and the feathered spoil which she had brought in from the talus meant more to him, as the mute evidence of her share in the partnership, and gave him a thrill of keener emotion than all the sunsets in the world.

She must be dreadfully tired, he thought, and with that thought decided to set out to find her. First, however, he transferred the remnants of the fire from the flat stone before the hut to his newly constructed hearth, heaped on more wood and noted, with satisfaction, that his makeshift chimney drew well and did not smoke intolerably. He had discovered an empty cask under a heap of rubbish in the store-room, and this he filled with chunks of ice, and set by the fire to melt.

Five minutes later he was just a wheeling, glinting, sun-bathed speck in the amber air, the thrilling, pringling, winelike air. He had taken to his wings, upon leaving the hut, simply because they offered him the quickest, easiest way of finding Jeanne. But the substitution of the delightful, easy exercise of his power of flight, for the grubby toil at which he had spent the day, the change from the damp, the dark, the confinement of the hut to the full glow of the sunshine and the freedom of the sky's wide spaces, half intoxicated him.

It was an impulse, not a controlled intention, that took him aloft, higher and higher, and then higher still in that sharp spiral, until he lay, panting with the exertion, rocking gently upon his golden wings, a quarter of a mile up the sky.

Yes, it was a potent drug, that strange anæsthetic of the upper air. His surface faculties were not dulled by it. Sight and hearing attuned themselves to a higher pitch than normal. The whole periphery of his body was more acutely alive to every passing sensation; but the depth of him, the inner self, the soul so recently awakened and thrilled to life by a girl's faith, her courage, her tragedy, sank back, under the influence of the old drug, to sleep again.

The old round earth, in its shroud of golden vapor down below, became once more, for him, a remote thing in which he had no part. There it spun, in its endless, futile way, no more to him, with all its load of souls, of griefs and joys and hopes, than a top just freed by the snap of a boy's string.

So he lay there, breathing deep, keeping his place in the unstable sky, with hardly more motion than a skilled swimmer needs to keep afloat.

Suddenly he was flying downward, as fast as gravity and his great wings would take him. Drenched with the sweat of a sudden terror, cleaving the air so fast that the sound of its whining rose to a scream through his taut rigging. Down he slanted, seaward a little, past the end of the great headland. Then, with the sudden exertion of all his strength, upon one lowered wing, the other flashing high like the stroke of a scimitar, in the curve of the shortest possible arc, he shot landward, pounced, checked, and alighted not far from the girl.

She had been seated upon a broken ledge of rock when he had first caught sight of her. She was in the act of getting to her feet when he alighted, not a half dozen paces away.

She had been pale, but her color had come back now in a sudden surge. She was breathing unsteadily and her hands were clasped against her breast. "You—you mustn't fly like that," she said. "If you had been an eagle, the way you wheeled and came rushing down out of the sky would have terrified me. I shut my eyes in order not to see you killed."

He did not answer her at once, and she, looking intently into his face, went on. "You know it was dangerous. You thought yourself that you were going to be killed. I can see the horror of it in your eyes."

Then he got his breath. "You're safe?" he questioned unsteadily. "You were in danger, sudden danger, and in terror at it. That was what frightened me, that sudden knowledge. I came down, fearing I should be too late."

"I had a fright," she admitted; "but I don't see how you could know. I'm very sure I didn't cry out."

"No, I heard nothing, no sound at all. I just knew, and so I came to you as fast as I could. What was it that frightened you?"

"Nothing at all, I imagine. I was sitting here on the ledge, looking at that wonderful sky, and all at once I found I was growing afraid. I didn't know what it was about, at all. I suppose it was just because I was a little tired and had begun to realize that I was a long way from—from home. I had come around the headland, not really to look for more firewood, but in the hope that I might happen to find a clue to where the stores are hidden; and, as I said, suddenly it seemed a long way back and I began to find myself afraid. And then, being afraid, I—well, I thought I saw something moving up there behind the rocks,—something big, bigger than a man, and whitish-yellow."

His eyes followed the direction in which she had pointed, but could make out nothing in the deep, vibrant blue shadows.

"That's likely enough," he told her. "It was probably a bear. If it was, we're in luck. I'll come back by and by and go gunning for him. But first, I'm going to take you—home."

She had used the word before, but in what sense he was not entirely sure; and she had undoubtedly used it not more than half consciously. At any rate, when he said it now she flushed a little, and so did he, and their eyes, meeting, brightened suddenly.

Silently he turned away from her and began furling up his wings, and she helped him, as she had helped him that other time when he had tried to convince her that he was not a dream.

When it was done, they set out slowly, in the deepening twilight, for the hut.

"It's very good of you to walk down here with me," she said, "you who could fly."

XIV

The Red Bound Book

By the time they had rounded the headland, the whole beach before them was enveloped in the sapphire shadow of the cliff, and the little cluster of huts toward which they were trudging was hardly distinguishable. It was not until they had halved the distance that the girl made out the little plume of rose-colored smoke that floated above Philip's newly constructed chimney.

She exclaimed at sight of it, and then suddenly fell silent, abandoning, half told, the account she had been giving him of the little incidents of her day. He tried for a while to keep the conversation going in the same key in which she had left off, commenting humorously upon his deficiencies as mason and stove-fitter. But her new mood was infectious, and before long it imposed silence upon him, too.

It was not until they had come so near that they could see the flickering red of the firelight shining out through the window that the girl turned to him and said, with a shaky laugh: "Isn't it absurd—that a really cheerful sight like that, a house with an open fire blazing upon the hearth, should make one, suddenly, homesick?" Even through the twilight he could see that her eyes were misty with unshed tears.—"Try not to mind," she added; "I'll brace up in a minute. But, somehow, the first sight of it—caught me."

Jeanne was rather tall for a woman,—adoring, fond young men back home had sometimes described her as stately—but to Philip, as she stood before him now, she looked small and strangely childlike. He had an impulse,—an impulse that frightened him a little when he became aware of it—to take her in his arms and pull her up close and comfort her. A tardily checked gesture with both arms and a pair of suddenly opened hands betrayed the impulse to himself, as well as to the girl, and he got the impression that she had started to respond to it; that within those strong arms of his was just where, at that moment, she wanted to be.

But the next instant he laid a hand upon her arm and, with the other, pointed imperatively down the beach toward the hut. "Whether you saw him before, or not," he said, with a short grim laugh, "you can see him now."

HENRY KITCHELL WEBSTER

Looking where he pointed, she saw a big, yellowish-white, ungainly thing come lumbering round the corner of the hut, upon all fours.

"A bear," he said, "and a good big one. You're not to be afraid. This is really unmerited good luck."

"Aren't they dangerous, these polar bears?" she asked.

In his answering laugh she heard the ring of rising excitement. "I won't deny," he said, "that if I had my way about it, I'd have you safely shut up inside the hut there before I tried conclusions with him. Give me the revolver, and take care to keep out of the line of fire. If you see a chance to slip inside the hut, do it. And don't assume that he's dead until I tell you so. These polar bears have no nerves at all. You can't shock them. They don't stop until you have put their locomotor facilities completely out of business."

She was smiling when she handed him the revolver. "Here's luck," she said. "Don't be afraid for me."

Cayley smiled, too. "Keep behind me, but not so far that you're in any danger of getting cut off in case I have to dance around him a little.—There, he's winded us already."

Even at that distance and in the fading light the girl saw the monster bristle and throw up his lolling head with suddenly arrested attention. To her intense astonishment, instead of the snarl she expected, she heard a venomous, voiceless hiss. There was something dreadful about the sound, something which, combined with the weird, insufficient light and the shape of the beast, which loomed ghostly through it, gave her a sensation of dread wholly unrelated to the actual physical danger in which they stood.

Cayley turned for a last look at her. He had slipped his bundled wings from his back and laid them on the ice. He was still smiling, but somewhat ironically. "I'm half afraid he'll run away," he said, "and half afraid he won't."

The next instant all doubt on that head was set at rest. The monster hissed again, and came lumbering toward them, pretty rapidly, across the ice.

Cayley advanced slowly to meet him, but not in a direct line. Instead, he bore off in a curve to the left. The girl understood the manœuver instantly, and, herself, set out landward at a brisk pace, moving in the arc of a circle, parallel to his but larger, in such a way as to keep the bear, Philip and herself, as all three moved in different directions, in a straight line.

They quartered round in this way, the bear swerving in well toward Philip, until all three were in a line, about equidistant from the hut. Philip and the bear, were, perhaps, a dozen paces apart. Without turning, he called over his shoulder to her, "Now run for it—for the hut. I'll keep him amused out here."

At the sound of his voice, the bear rushed him. The girl had never in her life found anything so hard to do as to obey orders now. But she did obey and was running at top speed toward the open door of the hut when she heard Cayley fire for the first time. Just as she reached it, she heard his second shot. When she turned about, panting, to observe the result of it, the two seemed to her to be at horribly close quarters. The bear, reared up on his hind legs, had just lunged forward.

A bear's motions are wonderfully and most deceptively quick. Ungainly to the eye, he can spring and strike with the dazzling swiftness of a leopard. But in this case the man was gifted with superhuman quickness, too. Probably without that power of instantaneous co-ordination of muscular effort he would never have learned to fly. In the course of learning to fly, during those five uninterrupted years at Sandoval, and during those last three months which he had spent almost entirely in the air, he had developed the quality still further.

He sprang back clear of the flashing, scythelike cut of those terrible claws. A little to the girl's surprise and considerably to her alarm, he turned and went sprinting up the beach toward the talus, at full speed, the bear wounded, but not in the least disabled, lumbering after him.

It takes a fast runner to outrun a bear, but Cayley did it. When he reached the foot of the talus, the bear was twenty paces behind him. She saw him stop short, whirl round again and face his pursuer with a shout.

The bear also checked his speed and reared up once more, towering, upon his hind legs. Then Cayley fired twice, the shots coming so closely together as to be hardly distinguishable. One or both of them took instantaneous effect. The great yellowish-white mass tottered forward, and collapsed in a heap only a pace or two from where Philip was standing.

He waved his hand at the girl, and walked back for his wings. When she met him, half way up the beach, he was carefully taking the spent shells out of his revolver, one at a time, and depositing them in his pocket. "No telling how they may prove useful," he commented; then, with a quick look into her face, "I hope you weren't frightened when you saw me run."

"I suppose I shouldn't have been, but I'll have to confess that I was. You weren't trying to get away from him, or you wouldn't have run in that direction. But it looked rather dreadful, just the same. Why did you do it?"

"We were too far down the beach, too near the water's edge before. It was too late to skin him and cut him up tonight, and I was afraid if a storm were to come up before morning, a really big storm, we might lose him. It was a lot easier to get him up the beach before I fired those last two shots than it would have been after. I thought at first of running toward the hut. It occurred to me, only just in time, that there was no use in making an abattoir of your front yard."

"You thought of all that? At such a time?"

"That's the sort of time when one does think of things, isn't it? It's what people call the spice of danger. Nobody likes a risk for its own sake; I don't, at least. But to have your mind work fast and clearly, as it does at such times, that's worth while. But there wasn't any particular danger in this case, once you were safely out of the way."

"What if you had fallen?" she suggested.

"There was a chance of that. If I had, he'd probably have gone over me, and I could have found my feet again as quickly as he."

They had reached the hut, and as he finished speaking, they entered it. Even Philip caught his breath rather suddenly with that first glance about its transformed interior. The drift-wood fire, which glowed upon the hearth, filled the whole room with light, and bathed the walls and rafters with warm colors.

Here was their fortress—against the cold and the dark; a fortress, too, against despair. That rude hearth which he had built today was to be their altar of hope.

The girl stood looking at it a moment in silence, her lips pressed tight together, one outstretched hand groping for the door-jamb behind her, as if she wanted the support of something. Even in this warm firelight she looked a little pale. By an evident effort of will she was breathing very deep and steadily. She did not try to speak.

Cayley understood well enough what it meant. This place that they had come back to for the night was home now, probably the last home she would ever have in the world, if one were to balance the chances fairly. Its warmth and light and comparative comfort did more to enforce a realization of their tragic plight than anything before had done. The thing she was fighting with was a sudden wave of plain terror.

Cayley went out into the little vestibule and closed and bolted the outer door. He contrived to waste a minute or two over the trifling task, in order to give her that moment by herself.

When he came back, closing the inner door behind him as he did so, he found that she had taken off her cap and the heavy fur coat which had cumbered her shoulders all day, and hung them upon a convenient wooden peg in the wall. She was standing near the fireplace now, warming her cold fingers at the blaze.

Cayley started a little at sight of her, for now she was transformed, too. Standing there, silhouetted against the blaze, in her grey cardigan jacket and moleskins, she looked like a young boy. He had discovered before this that there was not a grain of false modesty about her; nevertheless, it pleased him when, with a certain charming frank simplicity, she called his attention to her costume.

"It's a lucky thing," she observed, "that I dressed for a scramble over the ice before coming ashore with uncle Jerry and Mr. Scales. And lucky, too, that I didn't change back when we returned to the *Aurora*. I left it the second time with no other idea than of pulling about for awhile in the dinghy. I'd have done that just the same if I had dressed for dinner that night, as I usually did."

"Yes," he said. "A skirt would have been a pretty serious matter to people in our situation."

"Show me the rest of our house," she commanded presently. "This is the only room I've seen."

The subdivision of the hut was accomplished by an L-shaped partition seven feet or so from the outer wall, around two sides of it. It yielded two tiny, cubical bedrooms (that was the purpose which the wooden bunk in each of them indicated); and a third room of the same width (about seven feet), but running the entire length of the side of the hut nearest the cliff. This room had evidently served for stores and for a kitchen, since part of the re-constructed fire-place projected into it. It was in this last room where the greater part of what the searchers from the *Aurora* had dismissed as "rubbish" was accumulated.

Cayley did as the girl commanded, and showed her every nook and cupboard which the four walls of the hut contained. When they returned to the living room where the fire was, she dropped down on one of the bunks, with a little sigh of fatigue.

"You've been disobeying orders," he said, looking her over with a serious sort of smile. "You've let yourself get too tired. You'll have to make up for it by being exceptionally obedient now."

As he spoke, he shook out the sleeping-bag on the bunk, behind where she was sitting.

"You're to lie down on that," he said, "until I can get supper ready; and directly after supper you're to take this bag into which ever of those bedrooms you would like for yours, and really undress and go to bed."

She heard him through without interruption, but at the end he found her looking at him with a smile of such mocking defiance, that he added, "Well, what's the matter with that plan?"

"I'm to do all the resting, then, while you do all the work. There is a partnership for you. No, my friend, I'll stop when you do, only tonight it's your turn to have the sleeping-bag. Seriously speaking, as a man with a scientific mind, do you believe that I am any tireder at this moment than you are?"

"Yes," he said, "I believe you are. At any rate, you can make yourself comfortable while I get supper. That's a one-man job."

She assented to that after a little demur. That he had rightly guessed the degree of her fatigue was attested by the fact that when he re-entered the hut after dressing the fowl that was to provide their evening meal, he found her cuddled up upon the great sheepskin, fast asleep.

It was not until his rudimentary culinary operations were about completed that, glancing over to where she lay, he found her regarding him with a sleepy smile.

"There's no luxury in the world like being as tired as that," she said, sitting up on the bunk and rubbing her drowsy eyes. "I've been down, down, down, a hundred fathoms deep. I feel as if I had slept a year."

"Come and have some supper," he said. "It's ready now, I think. When you've finished, you'll be ready to do it all over again."

A loose plank from one of the other bunks provided them with a table, while his sheath knife and flask comprised, as before, the whole of their table furniture.

"I thought of something just as I was dropping off to sleep," she said, "a really beautiful idea. I tried to call out and tell you, but I was too sleepy. I hope I haven't lost it. It was something about—oh, I know. Don't you suppose we might find a clue to where the stores are hidden, in father's journal, or in the maps?"

He laid down the drum-stick he had been about to bite into, and gazed at her, partly in astonishment, partly in a sort of amused dismay that the idea had not occurred to him before. "That suggestion," he said, "is worth the whole of my day's work. Of course that's the way to begin our search,—the only way, and tomorrow morning—"

"Tomorrow morning! I thought the worst thing you could possibly say would be after supper. I wanted to let the duck go and begin the search now." She smiled at him. "You'll compromise, won't you, on directly after supper?"

He assented with a laugh. "If you can keep awake, but the first time I catch you nodding—"

"All right," she said, "only let's hurry with the duck." Then, a little later, "It can't be possible, can it, that we're going to eat the whole of it at one meal? It's beginning to look that way."

There was one compensation to the rudeness of their fare and the exiguity of their equipment. Clearing up after dinner was an operation of extreme simplicity.

When it was completed, Philip heaped more wood on the fire, and in the glow of the crackling flames they spread out the maps and began their search.

"Do you know how I came to think of this?" she asked, as she seated herself close beside him and bent her head over the maps. "I was thinking of this morning and of the way you told me.—Oh, how long ago that seems.—And I remembered your saying that father's journal would be our bible. It came to me, suddenly, that there was more to be learned in it than merely faith and courage. It occurred to me that those long pages of scientific observations might tell us just the things that we would need to know to save our lives."

"I believe," said Cayley, "that the journal will be worth more than the maps in this search of ours tonight. Anyway, while you work one I can work the other."

She nodded, picked up the journal and crossed over with it to another of the bunks. There she seated herself, tucked her feet up comfortably under her, tailor-fashion, and, propping her chin upon one palm, began to read. The light coming from behind her made, to Cayley's vision, a misty halo of her hair, and played softly over the cheek and the fingers that were half embedded in it.

The sight of her made it hard for him to stick to his maps. But presently he looked up with a sudden question. "Do you happen to find anything—" he began, and then broke off shortly.

From her face, half-shaded as it was, he could see that what she had been reading just then was no mere description of this land upon which they had been cast away, but something far more personal to the father she had lost here.

"There's something perfectly terrifying," she said, "about father's description of this man Roscoe. Over here near the end, before the sun came back to them, he tells of going out for a walk by himself and of discovering that Roscoe was stalking him, in the hope, he thought, of discovering, in advance of the others, where the gold ledge was. In the twilight, father says, he looked, in his white bear-skins, perfectly enormous and incredible. And Philip—"

She closed the book, holding it tight in both hands, and leaning forward a little as she went on, "and Philip, his description sounds—oh, I suppose it's silly, but it sounds like the thing I thought I saw today when I was alone there on the beach, before you came flying down out of the sky. It didn't look like a bear. It wouldn't have been so dreadful if it had."

"It's possible," he said gravely, "it may have been he whom I frightened off when I came down last night. Certainly there was somebody, and that somebody may still be here on shore, though I supposed he had gone out to join in the attack on the yacht. But it's very strange, if there is any one, that we could have passed a whole day without encountering him."

The girl shivered; then, with a shake of her head as if dismissing the uncanny thought from her mind, said, "You started to ask me about something else, and I interrupted."

It took him a moment to collect his thoughts. "Oh, yes. There's something marked here on this map which I took at first for the location of the hut, but it appears now that it was marked before they built it. I wondered if, in the early pages of the journal, there was a description of any natural formation about here like a cave, or—"

She made as if to open the book, then, suddenly, changed her intention and held it out to him, instead.

"I haven't been playing fair," she said. "I wasn't really looking for anything. I was just reading stories and dreaming over them. It's his handwriting, I think, that makes it so hard to be good. It's—well, almost like hearing his voice. Won't you work the book and the maps and give me something to do—with my hands, I mean?—oh, I know I'm tired, but that doesn't matter."

Cayley's first impulse was to refuse, but it needed only one thoughtful look into her face to convince him that the kindest, as well as the wisest thing was to do as she asked. An uncanny horror of the monstrous Roscoe and the appalling idea that he, and perhaps others of his gang, might be sharing the solitude of this frozen coast with them, was plainly to be read in her eyes, and her own prescription for dispelling it was probably the best that could be thought of.

With a nod of assent, he rose and went into the store-room, returning the next moment with an armful of heavy rope.

"In the old days of wooden ships," he said, "when they wanted to discipline a sailor, they set him to picking oakum. Next to pounding rust off the anchor, it's the dullest job in the world. But we need some for calking up the cracks in our walls. Do you mind?"

"Mind!" she echoed. "Did you think I wanted to do embroidery?"

He showed her how the work was to be done, and in five minutes she was busily engaged at it. She had moved to another bunk, a little further from the fire, and he, with innocent artifice, had contrived that the big soft sleeping-bag should be spread out under her.

Meanwhile he plunged into a systematic search, through journal and maps, for the thing that was to spell either life or death for them.

At the end of an hour he looked up suddenly, an exclamation of triumph on his lips. But at sight of her, it died out in a smile. She had slipped down on the sleeping-bag, her head cradled in the crook of one arm. And she was fast asleep.

XV

Discoveries

The sunlight of another crystalline day had made a path of gold across the floor and half way up the wall, when Philip roused himself from what he had intended to make the merest cat-nap on one of the bunks, and with difficulty rubbed his eyes open. The savour of something good to eat was already in his nostrils.

Jeanne, with her back to him, was bending over the fire, busy with the breakfast. She heard him stirring, and looked around.

"Oh, I'm sorry," she said. "I didn't mean to bang that pan down that way. I meant you to go on sleeping for hours and hours."

Looking fairly at him as he sat there on the bunk she saw his hands clutch tightly over the edge of it; saw the color go ebbing out of his face and then come surging back again. She had seen him do that once before.

"Why—what's the matter, Philip?" she asked.

"It's just the wonder of you," he said slowly; "of waking up to find you here, busy about this home of ours—as if—as if it were all true. I've been very deep asleep."

"You deserved to be. You must have worked nearly all night to accomplish all you have."

Her gesture included the feathered skins of a dozen or more geese and eiders, which hung in a row from a line stretched behind the fireplace, as well as an extremely heterogeneous collection of articles upon the shelves which he had rescued from the rubbish heap in the store-room. There was nothing in that rather pathetic collection which could have been of any value to persons decently equipped for the experience of an Arctic winter which lay before them. The fact that they had a value now, spoke volumes upon the extremity of their plight.

Some battered tin cans, three or four wide-mouthed bottles, a harpoon with a badly frayed line attached to it, an ax-head, a broken handled pick, comprised the greater part of it. Perhaps the most valuable object he had found was a broad-bladed sail-maker's needle. But from the look Jeanne gave them as she glanced along the shelf, it was plain that every object there was a potential treasure.

"But really," she went on after an expressive little silence, "really and truly I have a serious complaint to make against you. You didn't play fair when you went on working, working all those hours, to let me lie asleep."

He rose from the bunk with a laugh. "You'd have had me roaring at you or shaking you up every time I caught you nodding, I suppose; bellowing at you, like a sea captain, to 'look alive with that oakum.'"

But the girl declined to be amused. "Yes," she said, soberly enough, "that's exactly what I would have had you do. That's what you agreed to do yesterday." Seeing that he was still smiling over the notion, she went on: "Philip, can't you contrive to forget that I'm a girl? Can't you treat me like a—like a sort of kid brother, who isn't as strong as you, of course, and doesn't know much, but still is willing and 'likely' and capable of being made a man of? Can't you do that?"

"No," he said rather abruptly, "I can't."

He turned away from her, too, as he said it and, as he went on speaking, stood staring out of the window. "I'll do my best, but I'm—human, and—well, you remember what I told you yesterday. However, I'll try. I'll come as near to it as I can."

The girl's color was as high as his own. "Perhaps," she said not very steadily, "perhaps you didn't know that I might be trying, too."

At that he wheeled round, her name upon his lips, but she herself had turned away by that time, and was bending over the fire.

"You'd better get ready for breakfast," she said, in a tone whose matter-of-fact inflection was a little exaggerated. "It's nearly ready."

He took the biscuit tin, which had served as their reservoir before his discovery of the empty cask, filled it with snow water and started out of the hut with it.

"We'll have to give up even the pretense of keeping clean," he commented, "unless we can find some soap. But this makes a good eye-opener, anyway."

Its efficacy for that purpose was abundantly testified to by his glowing color and the brightness of his eye when he re-entered the hut a few minutes later.

"It's the most beautiful day in the world," he told her. "You ought to go out and have a breath of it yourself."

"I've been," she answered serenely. "I've even indulged in an eye-opener. As a result, I am altogether ready for breakfast. I hope you are."

The meal they sat down to was a sort of condensation and summary of the one they had discussed the night before. It appeared this morning in the form of a stew, but with one important addition. Cayley tasted it, and then set down the tin can in which his portion was served, with an exclamation of surprise.

"Salt! Wherever did you find it?"

"It was caked in the bottom of one of those tin pails. It looked sandy, but it tastes good, doesn't it?"

Certainly it did, in connection, at any rate, with the savour which their hunger lent to it. They did Jeanne's cooking full justice, and somewhat more, and wasted no time about it, either.

When they had finished, and while they still sat face to face across the board plank which had served them for a table, Cayley leaned forward a little and, smiling, asked a question.

"What's the secret, Jeanne? Your eyes have been shining with mystery ever since we sat down here."

She laughed. "You're much too penetrating. I didn't mean you even to dream there was a mystery to penetrate. But—well, it's time to tell you now any way."

She, too, leaned forward a little and shook her head at him with a tantalizing air of triumph.

"You didn't find the thing you were looking for last night in father's journal—the place where they hid the stores, I mean."

"Oh, but I did!" he cried. "I only waited to give you time to eat a necessary and sensible breakfast before I spoke of it. I had it on the tip of my tongue to suggest that we set about finding it in good earnest, when I saw, in your eyes, that you had a mystery of your own."

It was evident from the look in those eyes now that she was both surprised and puzzled.

"You found it last night!" she exclaimed. "Found it in the journal, and then never went to look at it!"

"Why, I found an unmistakable reference to it, and though the exact location wasn't given, it was plain that three or four hours' exploring by daylight would enable us to find it. But even if I hadn't minded leaving you asleep here, unprotected, in the hut, I doubt very much if I could have found it at night.—But what's the mystery you were about to reveal to me?"

"No," she said; "tell me more about your discovery first. What was the reference in the journal?"

He rose and took down from the shelf the big leather-bound volume which was proving itself, with every hour, their greatest treasure.

"It's over here, toward the end," he said, "in that last winter when the *Walrus* came—oh, here we are."

He seated himself on the bunk beside her, and began to read.

"March 10th—We have just spent an arduous and fearful week upon the task of unloading the wreck of the whaler. The weather has been severe—bitterly cold (–10° Fahrenheit being the mildest) and three-quarters of a gale blowing most of the time. The men are inclined to be rebellious over my driving them out to work in such weather, but I dared not wait for it to moderate.

"When the ice opens round the whaler, she will go down like a plummet; and if that event should have happened before we unloaded her of her stores, our plight would have been utterly desperate. Of stores in the ordinarily accepted sense, she had but a scanty supply, and those of a miserably inferior description; but she contained half a cargo of whale oil in barrels, which now that they are landed will settle the problem of fuel for us as long as the last survivor of our company can hope to remain alive. And fuel is, after all, the only necessity which this land itself does not supply us with. Of course we shall have to forego the delights of bear steak when our ammunition gives out, but walruses we can kill with harpoons. And with these and scurvy-grass, which we gather in the valley every summer, there is no danger of actual starvation.

"We hoisted the barrels of blubber out of the whaler's hold with a hand tackle, sledged them ashore along the floe and the crown of the glacier to Moseley's cave, which seemed to be the most convenient place to store them temporarily."

Cayley laid down the book, and turned to the girl.

"That's the place; I'm perfectly sure," he said. "It evidently faces the glacier, but it must be very near the beach, for they wouldn't have hauled those barrels any further than necessary."

"Is that all he says about it?"

"It's all he says directly, but there's a reference just a little further along which made me all the surer I was right. . . Let's see."

He opened the book again and ran his eye down the page. "'—A hundredweight or so of spermaceti and two barrels of sperm oil we took directly to the hut'—here, this is what I was looking for.

"'The knowledge we get by experience often comes too late to be of any great service to us. I made some mistakes in stripping the *Phœnix*, which I should not repeat now. For instance, carrying her pilot house, with infinite labor, up to the cliff-head for an observatory. It is

HENRY KITCHELL WEBSTER

thoroughly impracticable for this purpose. I doubt if I have visited it three times since Mr. Moseley's death—'"

"He was the astronomer and botanist of father's expedition," said the girl.

Cayley read on: "'But now that I have learned my lesson, I have but little to apply the knowledge to. The *Walrus* is, I believe, the most utterly wretched hulk that ever sailed the seas—ill-found, detestably dirty and literally rotting to pieces. We shall, however, get enough planks and timbers out of her to build a shed or two near the hut, for the more convenient storage of our supplies.'"

Again he closed the book. "That's what I was looking for," he said. "You see they brought that stuff down from the cave to these sheds; so the cave would be almost inevitably the first hiding place they would think of when the sight of the *Aurora* drove them to hustle everything out of sight."

"Whereabout on the cliff is the observatory, Philip?"

"I was wondering about that. I've flown across the cliff a number of times, but have never seen anything of it. He may have wrecked it; taken it down and used it for some other purpose."

"No," she said; "he'd hardly have had time for that. There weren't many more pages to write in the journal when he made that entry."

She fell then into a little abstracted silence, which the man did not know how to break. But presently she roused herself and came fully back to the present, back to him.

"Did you succeed in accounting for the thing you asked me about last night, the mark on the map right here where they built the hut afterward?"

"I didn't find anything about it in the journal, but this morning, before breakfast, when I went outside the hut, one glance at the face of the cliff accounted for it fully. The cliff is split right here, from top to bottom, by a deep, narrow fissure. The fissure is full of ice, which I suppose hasn't melted for a thousand years. No summer that they could have in a high latitude like this would ever melt it, certainly."

The girl laughed and rose from her place at the rude table.

"Well," she asked, "are you ready for my discovery now?"

She took down his pocket electric bull's-eye from the shelf behind her, held out a hand to him and, on tip-toe, led him, with a burlesque exaggeration of mystery, out into the store-room. As completely mystified in reality as she playfully pretended to want him to be, Cayley followed.

She went straight across the store-room to the rear wall of the hut, the wall that backed squarely against the sheer surface of the cliff, flashed on the bull's-eye for a second, apparently to make sure that she had chosen the right point in the wall, then, letting go his hand, she stooped and picked up a stick of fire-wood which lay at her feet. With this she struck pretty hard upon the planking. The sound which the blow gave forth was as hollow as a drum.

Cayley started. "A cave!" he exclaimed. "A cave here!—Oh, I see. It's a cold cellar they made by cutting a hole in the ice that filled the fissure. And why do you suppose they boarded it up?"

The girl laughed delightedly. Evidently she had not, as yet, developed the whole of her discovery. She flashed on the light again.

"Look!" she commanded.

In the centre of a little circle of wall which the bull's-eye now illuminated Cayley saw the barrel of a rusty hinge.

"You see," she went on, "it's a door, and they only nailed it up the other day. There's a nail-head somewhere here that's quite bright. I caught the glint of it while I was rummaging before breakfast, and that was what made me look."

Cayley darted back into the living-room, returning almost instantly with the broken-handled pick.

In less than a minute, with a protesting squeak, the rude door swung open, and they saw before them just what Cayley had predicted. A rather high, but narrow cavity, the sides of which were the naked rock of the cliff, but the floor and ceiling solid ice.

Despite the fact that the girl's excitement over the discovery of the cave had, for a moment, carried Cayley along with it, he was not greatly surprised, and not at all cast down when, at the end of five minutes of hasty exploration, it was made evident to them that the ample supply of stores which they sought was not to be found here.

Jeanne herself would not, perhaps, have entertained so high a hope had she learned of the reference to the other cave which Cayley found in the journal before she herself had chanced upon the mouth of this one. As it was, his theory that the stores were to be found in a cave vaguely situated along the glacier, made little impression upon her, she was so sure that they had them right here, under their hands.

When their investigation made it clear that whether he was right or not, certainly she was wrong, she was bitterly disappointed. Cayley was aware of that, even as they stood here, side by side, with no light to see her face by. She said nothing, or very little, but he knew, nevertheless, that for just this moment all the life and courage had gone out of her; knew that the slight figure there, so close beside him, was drooping, trembling a little.

He laid a steady hand upon her shoulder. Almost instantly, under his touch, she turned to him, caught with both hands at the unbuttoned edges of the rough woolen jacket he wore, and, sobbing a little now and then, but otherwise in silence, simply clung to him.

He did not offer, with his arms, to draw her any closer, to turn what was a mere instinctive appeal to the protection of his strength and courage, into an embrace. He kept a hand on each of her shoulders, more by way of support than anything else, and waited a moment before he spoke.

"After all," he said at last, "what we've got here is just so much clear gain, and it will be immensely valuable to us, though it isn't what we expected. The fact that it is their superfluity, the things they hadn't any particular or immediate use for, doesn't make what we've found here any the less valuable to us. That pile of bear skins there will supply what is, at this moment, the most vital of our wants. That big sack appears to contain feathers; and those walrus tusks will serve any number of purposes—forks and spoons for one thing. As to that great lump of spermaceti, it will keep us supplied with candles all through the winter. I can't imagine why they didn't use it themselves, except on the theory that the longer they lived here, the more they grew like beasts; the more content with the beast's habit of life, and the more inert about taking the trouble to provide themselves with such of the comforts and decencies of life as they might have had. So you see, we may find among the things they had no use for, the very ones that will help us most."

He was talking more to avoid the emotional tension of silence than anything else. The thing which was restoring the girl her courage and self-command was the grip of his firm, live hands, the mere physical feel of that magnificent, magnetic, perfectly tuned body of his.

Presently she straightened up and drew away from him. "You're very good to me," she said. "I'll—I'll try not to do things like that very often."

His only comment upon her apology was to keep one hand for a moment longer resting on her shoulder. Then, in a sufficiently matter-of-fact fashion, he spoke: "We haven't exhausted the secret of this treasure house yet. Shall we go a little further?"

The cutting in the ice did not go very far back in the fissure, and they were soon at the end of it, and without having made any new discovery of importance, either. There was a little of cast-off articles of various sorts, chiefly clothing which future privations might make useful to them. There was a great frozen lump of brownish-green vegetation, which they afterward identified as the edible scurvy grass to which Captain Fielding had referred to in his journal.

That was all, or they thought it was, but just as they were about to retrace their steps to the hut, Cayley happened to glance up. The roof of the cave was not very much higher than it had to be to permit him to stand erect in it, something under seven feet; but here at the further end of it he saw a circular, chimney-like hole, about two feet in diameter, leading straight upward through the solid ice in the fissure.

XVI

Footprints

Nature had nothing to do with the formation of it, so much was clear enough. It had been cut out by hand, and evidently with infinite labor.

Flashing his bull's-eye over it did not enable him to see the end of it, but it did reveal a series of notches running straight up the two opposite surfaces. The only purpose they could serve would be to make possible the ascent of the chimney.

Jeanne followed his gaze, and then the two looked at each other, completely puzzled.

"Someone must have made it," she said; "and it must have been frightfully hard to make—a tunnel right up through the ice like that. But what in the world can they have made it for?"

"I've no idea," he confessed, "but it goes somewhere, and I mean to find out where."

"Don't follow it too far," she cautioned. "It would only need one foot slip off one of those icy notches to bring about a dreadfully ugly fall."

"One couldn't fall far down a tube of that diameter, unless he had completely lost his nerve, for there's always a chance to catch one's self. And you're to remember that I'm used to falling. No, I'll be as safe up there as I would on a turnpike.—Yes, really."

With that and a nod of reassurance, he scrambled up into the mouth of the long chimney. He had taken his bull's-eye with him, so the girl was left in the dark. She dropped down on the heap of bear skins to wait for him.

She had no means of measuring the time, and it seemed a perfectly interminable while before she heard Cayley returning down the ice chimney. Had she known how long it really was, she would have been justified in feeling seriously worried about him, but not knowing, she attributed the seeming duration of his delay to the tedium of sitting in the dark, with nothing to do. Even at that, she was conscious of a feeling of relief when she heard him call out to her once more, cheerfully, albeit somewhat hollowly, from the chimney's mouth:

"Jeanne, where are you?"

"Here, just where you left me."

"Here! All the while! You must be half frozen. I've been gone the better part of an hour."

"I didn't know how long it was, and I kept thinking you'd be back any minute. . . But where in the world have you been?"

By the time she asked that question they had groped their way back into the store-room and thence into the living-room of the hut, and by now she was looking at him in the full light of day.

He dropped down, with a rather explosive sigh, upon one of the bunks, and poked tentatively at his thighs and shoulders as if they were numb with fatigue.

"I think by a reasonable estimate," he said, "that chimney is five miles high. I kept going and going and going, till I began to believe that there wasn't any end to it; or that, by some magic or other, I slipped down a yard as often as I went up one. But I did get to the end at last; and I'll give you a thousand guesses as to what I found there."

"The observatory," she hazarded. "Oh! but not really? I did not mean that for an honest guess at all. It was just the first thing that came into my head.—But how could they pull the pilot-house of the *Phœnix* up through that little hole in the ice?"

"Well, to tell the truth, I don't believe they did," he answered with mocking seriousness. "It's more likely that they took it to pieces, and then rigged a boom and tackle up at the cliff-head and hauled it up outside. But when they got it up there they put it together again right across the fissure, and then tunnelled down, or up, the whole depth of the cliff. It must have taken them weeks to do it, and when it was done they had an inside connection between it and the hut, so that they were quite independent of the weather. And it must have been a great place to make observations from."

"*Have* been!" she echoed questioningly. "Isn't it now?"

"No, because it's all snowed and frozen in. It's buried, I don't know how many feet deep by this time, and dark, of course, as a pocket. But everything inside is quite undisturbed. I doubt if a single member of the *Walrus's* crew ever saw it, or even suspected that such a place existed."

"I wish I'd gone with you," she said. "Do you suppose—I could have got up there?"

"Oh, if it were a matter of necessity, yes. I could make fast a line around you, and then I could go ahead as a safeguard in case of slips. But I shouldn't advise you to try it for fun."

She acquiesced regretfully: "I suppose not, if it tired you out like that, you who are so strong and tireless. But it sounds inviting, somehow—the pilothouse of the *Phœnix* perched away up there on the cliff, and all buried in snow. I was there for a few minutes once the day father sailed." After a moment's silence, "you say everything was left apparently undisturbed. What is there up there?"

He unbuttoned his jacket and took from an inner pocket a scrap of paper.

"Being a methodical person," he explained, "I made an inventory. It's really quite a respectable list."

She seated herself beside him on the bunk as if to read the paper.

"I imagine you will need an interpreter," he said. "I've half forgotten what these tracks mean myself. My hands were so stiff with the cold it wasn't very easy to write. But that first word is telescope. And then there are the meteorological instruments, barometers, thermometers, and so on, and the *Phœnix's* compass, sextant, and chronometer, a microscope, a paraffine oven and a big chunk of paraffine, an oil lamp, a five-gallon can about half full of oil, and a small stove. There was a providential treasure for me in the form of a razor, which they used, I suppose, for cutting microscopic sections with. I'm glad they hadn't a microtone to do it properly."

"You didn't find a comb for me, did you?" she asked. "Because, unless you did, or until you do, you won't be allowed to use the razor."

"I suppose I could make you one, or a sort of one. It would be genuine ivory, anyway."

He had come, apparently, to the end of the list.

"Well," she said, "I suppose we might find something to do with almost any one of those things; some of them will be useful, certainly. And it's pleasant, somehow, to think of our little pilot-house, all snowed in, up there on the cliff-head, and of our inside passage leading up to it."

"That's quite true," he said. "I suppose it's all romantic nonsense, but it does give one a certain feeling of security. . . However," he went on, "we're not reduced as yet to anything as intangible as that as a subject for giving thanks. You haven't seen the whole of my list yet. I've saved the best till the last."

He turned the paper over in his hand as he spoke. She did not attempt to read what he had written, but sat there beside him, her hands clasped about one knee, her eyes upon the booted foot which was poised across the other, and waited rather tensely for him to tell her.

"It's not so very much, but it will mean an immense lot to us. What people die of in the Arctic is not so often disease or accident, or even, directly, cold or starvation. They die more often of disgust and weariness and exhaustion. Your father knew that, and he set apart from his general stores some luxuries and delicacies, or things that would seem to be such to men in their plight, to be used against emergency. I'm sure that's why he took them up there and hid them away. Part of them are left. I wish he could have known to whom they were going to be of use.—There's a little cask with brandy in it, a good sized pot nearly full of beef extract, a jar of dried eggs, three tins of condensed milk, a big ten-pound box of Albert biscuit—"

His voice broke off there sharply, but without the downward inflection she would have expected had he reached the end. So she looked quickly and curiously up into his face. As quickly, her eyes sought the bit of paper which still lay open in his hand.

"You didn't finish," she said. "There was something else."

"I thought too late.—Oh! it's nothing, but it caught me—rather, and I thought I would spare you the twinge that finding it had given me. I might better have read it right out. It was a big plum-pudding, in a tin, you know—Cross & Blackwell's. But there it was, waiting, I suppose, to lend some sort of an air of festivity to their next Christmas."

The girl rose from her seat beside him and going over to the window, stood for a while gazing out up the beach.

When she turned back, he saw that her eyes had dimmed a little, but the tone in which she addressed him was steady:

"Well, shall we go to look for our other cave, where the real stores are? There won't be anything heart-rending about that, at all events."

Cayley did not rise when she did, but remained, looking rather thoughtful, just where he was. The girl misinterpreted his hesitation.

"I forgot how tired you must be," she said. "Of course we'll wait."

"No, that's not it. I was only thinking. I believe we *could* live through the winter on what we've got right here—the bear, the birds and what stores we found in the observatory. They wouldn't more than last till the winter was over, but I think with a little good economy they would do that."

"You don't mean not to try to find the other cave?"

"No. It was simply a question of making what we have got safe and shipshape first—spending as much of this fine day as is necessary getting in more wood, the rest of those birds, and skinning and butchering that bear we killed last night, before we go out on an exploring expedition that may prove a wild goose chase."

"I see," she assented thoughtfully. "You mean what Tom would call playing it safe."

"That's a fine day out there," Cayley went on, "but what weather-wisdom I have gained up in this part of the world makes me suspicious that we're about to have a change."

The girl sighed somewhat ruefully. "You are horribly reasonable," she said.

The thought of going back to yesterday's drudgery her muscles were still stiff from, instead of setting out along that sparkling beach with Cayley, in search for their Aladdin's cave, was one that took some courage to face. Nevertheless, her hesitation was only momentary.

"Aye, aye, captain," she said, holding out her hand to him. "What do you want me to do?"

He left her provided with a jack-knife he had in his pocket and the task of skinning and dressing the rest of the birds they had brought in from the talus the day before. Those he had already prepared were to be hung up with these in their cold storage cellar back of the hut.

He himself, with his sheath knife and the axe head he had discovered, fitted into the broken handle of the pick, for a cleaver, set out down the beach to flense the great bear which he had killed the night before. The bear was a colossal specimen, and this fact, together with Cayley's inexperience and lack of proper tools, made the job a long and arduous one. But it was accomplished finally and the four quarters of the huge carcass hung up in the storage cellar, while the immense white pelt, which had been scrubbed with sand and wet wood ashes from their fire-place, was stretched behind it to dry.

Jeanne had been working steadily all day at the task Cayley had assigned her, and by constant repetition had already grown expert at it. The amount she had accomplished surprised him greatly; but she declined to allow him to make a merit either of her application or her skill, and did not take kindly to Cayley's suggestion that she had done what would pass for a day's work.

"When you stop, I will," she told him.

So they effected a compromise. Cayley was to go out and bring in a load or two of firewood, while she cooked supper.

It was just about the same time in the afternoon that it had been yesterday when he set out, a-wing, to find her, and had come flying down out of the sky to drive away the sudden nameless terror which had beset her. That thought led him, now, to visualize some sticks of wood, rather too large to carry, which had been lying on the beach near where he had found her. Thinking that it would be a good time to get them and drag them in, he got a harpoon line, and it was the girl's question what he meant to do with the rope, which caused him to tell her what part of the beach he intended to visit. He asked her then if she cared to come with him, but, after a moment's hesitation, she declined.

"It will be high time for supper before you can get back," she said, "and I'd better stay here and get it ready, that is, unless I can help you."

So he set off alone.

For awhile the occupation of setting their disordered living-room to rights and getting the supper started were sufficient to take the whole of the girl's attention. But later, when it was a question merely of waiting for the pot to boil, and of not watching it so that it would boil sooner, she moved restlessly to the door and stood there, before the hut, gazing down the beach in the direction Cayley had taken. He was already out of sight around the headland.

The gorgeous riot of color in cloud and ice and vapor, which marked the end of the day, had already set in. But this time, perhaps because she was alone, it was not the beauty, but the terror of it that impressed the girl—the heartless cruelty of it.

For one moment the thought of a certain little hill-sheltered meadow, with a sleepy brook meandering across it and the shade of gnarled old oaks dotting its sunny, golden green with patches of deep shadow, of sleek, well-fed cattle and a grassy little lane, which one got into by means of a stile, coming before her all at once, distinct in all its minute, homely detail, gave her mind a sudden wrench that was almost intolerable.

She wished she had gone with Philip, and she gazed with straining eyes toward the narrow bit of slanting beach around the base of the headland which was the place where he must appear. He was not to be expected yet, not for a long time, probably, for his progress, dragging those great sticks he had set out to bring home, must be slow.

And then, even as she looked, she saw him, not moving slowly with his burden, but running,—running at his topmost speed, like a man in fear of something.

Instinctively she moved forward to meet him, and this move of hers enabled him to see her. He slackened his pace instantly, and waved her back toward the hut. She obeyed that imperative gesture of his, without hesitation, but still remained in the doorway, watching him as he rapidly drew nearer.

When he had got near enough so that she could see his face and read, more or less, what she saw there, she again moved forward to meet him, and this time he did not wave her back. When he came within arm's reach of her, he caught her and held her tight in his two hands.

"What is it, Philip?" she asked, searching the depth of his eyes and trying to plumb the horror she saw in them. "What happened out there?"

"Nothing—happened. But I saw something there that made me anxious for your safety. . . It's all right now you're safe. Nothing has happened here, has there, while I have been gone?"

"Nothing. What could have happened, Philip?—It can't be anything that you're afraid to tell me," she went on, for he had not answered her. "There can't be anything you'd be afraid to tell me now—not after yesterday."

"Oh, no; it's not so bad as that, but I saw that I had been wrong to leave you, even for that little while. You see the sight of the place brought back to my mind what you had told me yesterday of the terror you had felt there, and of the thing that you saw in the twilight. And so I looked about, and—Jeanne, it was no baseless terror, no product of the twilight and the fact that you were far from home. There was something there, slipping along from the shelter of one boulder to that of another. I found the tracks in the snow. They weren't more than ten paces away from you when I came down out of the sky."

"Was it the bear?" she asked. "That was what you thought it might have been, at the time." But he could see in her eyes that this was not the answer she expected.

He shook his head; that told her enough.

XVII

The Beast

As Roscoe fled along the beach on the night Cayley descended upon him through the fog, there was no doubt in his mind that he had seen the ghost of the man he had murdered and the shadow of a black avenging spirit hovering over his head.

When he found that his boat had gone adrift and that his only means of getting back to the *Aurora* had gone with it, he dropped down upon the beach, crawled up into the lee of a great rock and had spent the night there, his mind completely torpid with fear.

When the numbness of this terror passed away, as gradually it did, he bent all his thoughts upon the *Aurora* and upon the possibility, not quite inconceivable, that his crew had succeeded in overpowering her people and were now in possession of the yacht. He tried to persuade himself that this was so and that with the coming of the dawn they would send a boat ashore for him.

Of the strange figure he had seen there in the hut, so like and yet so terribly unlike the victim of his murderous lust four years ago—of that, and of the more terrible apparition he had seen coming down out of the sky, he thought, or tried to think nothing at all. It was only a nightmare, only a delusion, natural enough when one considered all the circumstances.

When the fog lifted with the approach of dawn, he discovered what Philip and Jeanne did not become aware of until several hours later, that the *Aurora* had drifted out to sea in the gale. The clean line of the horizon was broken by nothing but the plunging masses of the ice. There was just one chance, he thought, that she might still be comparatively near at hand. Southward and eastward the horizon was unbroken, but the jutting mass of the promontory to the west cut off his view in that direction. It was possible that the gale which had destroyed the floe that formed the harbor, had also broken up the pack ice at the other side of the peninsula, the side from which Cayley, on the wing, had first approached this unknown land. The yacht might be there, riding safely in practically open water.

He got up from the snow nest he had made for himself in the lee of the rock, and cautiously flexed his stiffened muscles, with the idea of setting out at once down the beach and around the headland to learn whether this last hope of his was groundless. Really, in his heart, he had no hope at all, but that fact made it easy to postpone for a little longer the putting of this delusion of a hope he had to the test of reality.

The excuse he made to himself was, that he was ravenously hungry, and that his most sensible course would be to go up the glacier to the cave and cook himself a breakfast before he did anything else.

He was fully persuaded by that time that what he had seen at the hut last night during the storm had been nothing but a hallucination. None the less, he knew that it would be easier to walk past that empty hut in full broad day, than in this tricky, misty, uncertain light of dawn.

He carried out this plan at once, to the point, that is, of going up the glacier to the cave, building a fire there and satisfying his sharp hunger with an enormous meal. But he had not slept at all the night before, and now the warmth and the satisfaction of his appetite made his nerveless hand release the bone he was gnawing, and caused him to roll over beside the fire and to fall asleep.

He slept deeply for a number of hours. Then, arming himself with a throwing-stick and a number of darts, he stepped outside the cave, intent upon his expedition to the other side of the peninsula where there was a possibility of finding the yacht.

The cave was situated some little distance up the glacier, and the shortest, though by far the more difficult, way of reaching his destination lay, not along the beach but up through the interior valley and across the precipitous coast range of hills.

It was not the natural way to go, but the fact that it was actually shorter gave him a sort of excuse for avoiding another visit, just now, to the scene of his discomfiture of the night before. He swore at himself, not so much for taking this course as for the reasons which his common sense alleged against him.

His present route took him close to the gold ledge, and the sight of the inexhaustible, precious, useless metal that remained here brought upon him for the first time, in full force, a sense of his loss, a sense of what that luckless trip ashore from the *Aurora* in search of that rosewood box had cost him.

At an increased pace he descended from the glacier, crossed the valley and scaled the landward side of one of the mountains of the coast range, to a notch where he could command a view of the sea to the westward.

He saw there what, in the bottom of his mind, he had all along been sure he would see—nothing but another barren, bleak horizon.

At that, for a while, his fortitude broke down, and he raved and wept and cursed like one demented. But at last, spent, sobered, conscious once more of a sharp hunger, he climbed a little farther up the mountain to a ledge, where, as his minute knowledge of the country led him to expect, he found a number of loons sitting. He killed one of these birds with a dart, and then, like the brute he was, ate it raw and warm.

By that time it was late in the afternoon. Bravado, combined with a more real belief than he had yet succeeded in retaining, to the effect that all his terror of the night before had resulted from nothing more serious than a nightmare, led him to decide to go home by way of the beach, rather than along the difficult interior trail up which he had come.

The descent from the cliffhead to the beach was nothing to a man of his inhuman strength and activity, though an ordinarily skilled mountaineer might have hesitated before attempting it. Nevertheless, two-thirds of the way down he nearly fell—but for luck he would have fallen, for he caught a glimpse of a lonely figure, a quarter of a mile away, perhaps, seated upon a ledge, bending forward, chin in hand, in an attitude which recalled, and horribly echoed, that of the man he long ago had murdered.

When he had steadied himself a little, he made his way cautiously down to the level of the beach. His emotions were divided about equally between fear and anger, the anger existing because of the fear.

With infinite caution he approached that lonely, unsuspecting figure, slipping from the shelter of one rock to that of one a little nearer.

Three times his left hand drew back the throwing-stick, balanced and aimed along a line that would send its thin ivory dart as swiftly and as surely to that beautiful throat as the one that had found and transfixed Perry Hunter's; and three times his muscles braced themselves for the effort to propel it. But each time, with a breathless oath, he lowered the weapon again, and with the back of his hairy hand wiped the sweat from his forehead.

The act had none of the quality of mercy in it; it was simply the result of a logical dilemma. If the thing he saw before him were a ghost, the ghost of the man he had already murdered, his dart would do no harm. If it were not a ghost; if it were what it looked more and more like as he drew nearer, a living, breathing woman—he licked his lips and wrung them with his hand—if it were a woman, he did not want to kill her.

If he could be sure, could only be sure, he would drop his weapon and make one rush and hold her helpless in those great hands of his.

And with every five paces that lessened the distance between them, that certainty grew upon him. No, she was no immaterial spirit of a man long dead. She was alive; warm. He was near enough now to make out the soft curve of her throat, the retreating and returning color which bathed cheeks and forehead. He could see the faint rise and fall of her breast when she breathed. He laid the throwing-stick upon the ice, drew nerves and muscles taut for his rush.

Then, just then, he saw the thing that made Jeanne close her eyes, the flashing sword-cut of that great golden wing, as the thing it bore turned upon the other.

Roscoe dropped down, as if he had been blasted by the sight of a sworded archangel, in the shelter of his rock. He lay there, prone, hugging his head in his arms. He did not rouse himself, did not succeed in forcing his treacherous nerves and muscles to obey his will until it was quite dark. Then, without a glance behind him, he arose and began scrambling madly up the broken face of the talus, and, reaching the top of it, went on and scaled the cliff itself. It was a feat which even he could hardly have accomplished except under the extremity of terror.

For only so long as was necessary to regain his breath, he lay panting upon the cliff-head. In the dark, rushing along as if the precipitous trail he followed had been a well-worn thoroughfare, he retraced his way down the landward side of the mountain and across the valley. He did not pause until he found himself safe in the cave again beside the glacier.

XVIII

A STATE OF SIEGE

Cayley's discovery of the tracks furnished the last element of the drama which was to play itself out that winter upon this stage which had been so strangely set for it. It was just three days since, flying slowly northward before a mild southerly breeze, the ice pack below him, he had caught his first glimpse of the unknown land where Captain Fielding had met his tragic fate so many years before. Three days since he had witnessed, from aloft, the murder of a man he might have saved, the man to whom, had he saved him, he might have turned for exoneration from a stain upon his name which was now ineradicable.

Three days ago he had thought his world was empty, swept clean of human concern and human affection. Three days ago he had not known that Jeanne Fielding existed.

During those three days there had been hardly an hour which had not produced a revolutionary situation of one sort or another. Even since the disappearance of the yacht, the hours that Cayley and Jeanne had spent together had been a procession of poignant and highly diverse emotions. Happiness and love and dread and despair had alternated with each other, as one revelation after another had changed the face of the world for them.

But this discovery of Cayley's was the last. They did not instantly take in the full meaning of it, indeed, it was not until they had talked out half the night that they comprehended fully what their situation was. And even then, there were mysteries, questions, to which the only answers they could make were strangely fantastic surmises.

But this elemental fact was clear. They had to reckon, not only with cold and hunger and privation and despair, not alone with the savage tenacity of a black Arctic winter, but with human hatred and malice and cruelty as well. Whether their enemy was one or a dozen, they did not know. Yesterday the solitude of this icy land had been one of its terrors, but today that solitude had given place to a more active terror.

As for the identity of the monster who had left the proof of his existence in those tracks which Philip had discovered in the snow, they of course had no certain knowledge; nevertheless, they entertained but little doubt that he was Roscoe himself. The footprints were immense, Cayley said, and their distance apart bespoke the stride of a giant.

If it were Roscoe who had been crouching there behind the boulder, then it seemed to them unlikely that he was here alone; unlikely that he had not at least two or three of his crew with him.

That idea, when it first occurred to them, brought little added terror with it. The person of the monstrous murderous ruffian, who was the chief, dwarfed his subordinates to pygmies. Yet when they came to think over their situation, reasonably, this uncertainty as to the number of their enemy proved a vital element in it. It put an unequivocal veto upon Cayley's first plan, which was to start out at once and take the aggressive against their enemy, before he should have time to move against them.

There was no question, of course, of anything like a truce. What they had seen put down in black and white in Captain Fielding's journal was enough to render an idea like that perfectly fatuous. They must live in mortal peril so long as a single member of the *Walrus* crew remained alive to share their frozen solitude.

But this doubt about the number of their enemy made Cayley's plan for an aggressive campaign impracticable. They had only one weapon between them, namely, Cayley's revolver; it was clear that they could not separate without leaving one of them defenseless. Even though the sky-man, with the advantage of his wings, might be able to discover the whereabouts of the enemy who had lurked behind the boulder upon the beach that day, he would not dare go in pursuit of him for fear of what his possible confederates might do to Jeanne in his absence.

Reluctantly he came to the conclusion that the only thing for them to do was to remain strictly upon the defensive. Jeanne agreed in the conclusion, but she accepted it much less reluctantly. In spite of all they knew of Roscoe, the practical certainty that he had murdered her father, his indubitable murder of Perry Hunter and the diabolical plot he had all but succeeded in carrying out against the *Aurora's* people—in spite of all that, the idea of deliberately seeking him out and killing him in cold blood, before he had made an overt move against them, was highly repugnant to her.

Cayley had no such feeling. To him Roscoe was simply a more dangerous sort of wild beast. To him, at first glance, the idea of merely waiting for their enemy to attack them at his leisure was well nigh intolerable, and seemed hopeless into the bargain. But when he saw that it was the only thing they could do, when he began really to study out the strategic possibilities of the position they held, the outlook brightened considerably.

In the first place, this bit of beach where the hut stood was practically fortified. The cliff behind it was absolutely sheer, and was capped with deep, perpetual snow. Half a mile to the westward was the promontory, and about half a mile up the beach from the hut, to the eastward, the glacier projected its ice masses in a long floe out to seaward. This glacier provided the only practicable means of entrance to the interior valley and the ledge where the gold was.

By means of a large scale map, Cayley pointed out to Jeanne this advantage of their position. "So long as we stick to this bit of beach," he said, "we can't be rushed nor surprised. No one can attack us without either coming down the glacier at one end, or around the promontory at the other. From either direction they've got to approach without cover. Of course if there are a lot of them, we sha'n't have any chance. But it may be there's only one, and it's likely that there are not more than three."

"But at night," said the girl, "—at night there'll be nothing to prevent their coming as close as they please. They may be out there now, not a dozen yards away."

"They're not doing much if they are. We're securely barricaded here, and they can't attempt to break in without giving us fair warning. Unless there are too many of them we should beat them at that game. No; the time to look out for them is when we're outside the hut, out on the beach doing the things we'll have to do—bringing in firewood, looking for more game, and so on."

"Shall we have to do that? Can't we just stay in here, safe?"

"The daylight will answer that question for me," he said. "We must make the most of it. A month from now there'll be but little. We mustn't make prisoners of ourselves until the winter does it for us. There is one thing, though," he added thoughtfully after a little silence, "one thing that I must do at once, and that is to destroy these sheds where they kept their stores. They would furnish a cover—as good a cover as any enemy could ask for. They hinder our view up the beach."

"How long do you suppose it will last?" she asked, in a voice that shook a little. "How long *can* it last? How long can we live like that, even supposing that our watch is effective and that they aren't able to surprise us?" She clasped her hands, with a shudder, and gripped them

HENRY KITCHELL WEBSTER

between her knees.—"Oh, if it would only happen soon," she went on, "whatever it is!"

"What I don't understand," said Cayley, "is why they haven't attacked us already. Why have they waited until we are fortified and secure? Why didn't they attack us yesterday morning when they would have found us helpless?"

"Or yesterday afternoon," she supplemented, "down the beach around the promontory, then, when we know he must have been so near. That's rather horrible all by itself, just the fact that he didn't."

What the girl said was perfectly true. Cayley felt it himself as sharply as she did. Aside from that one element in it, their situation, though terrible, was real, was the sort of situation that a sufficiently determined courage and a sufficiently alert wariness could cope with.

But their immunity from attack during all those hours when the enemy must have been close at hand, and when opportunities for attacking had been so plentiful, had something uncanny about it, and gave to this terrible adventure of theirs something of the quality of horror.

"Of course," said Cayley, "there must be a perfectly valid explanation of it, and it may be one that we can discover for ourselves, if we set about it."

So, as sanely and as logically as possible, dismissing as far as they could the nameless dreadful terror that surrounded the situation, they began to reconstruct the story of the member, or members of the *Walrus's* party who had not been aboard the *Aurora* when the gale drove her out to sea.

"We both slept late that morning," said Cayley. "The yacht was gone when we came out of the hut and first looked seaward. I expected at that time to find part of the *Walrus* party camped near by. I opened the hut door cautiously on that account, and my reason for assuming that none of them was left here, was the idea that they'd have been here on the beach near the hut, if they'd been anywhere. Well, we know now that that assumption was wrong. There was someone here any way. It's probable that with the very first return of the light he discovered the fact that the *Aurora* had been blown out to sea, hours before we did.

"Yet no one came near the hut all day, and I take that to mean that they, or he, avoided it. It would have been an obvious place to come. It's hard to see why they avoided it, unless because they knew that we were here. If they knew, they certainly had plenty of opportunities to attack us, because we were often separated that day. I was in the hut and you were out on the beach gathering fire-wood."

"Surely," said Jeanne, "he couldn't have hoped for a better opportunity to attack me than he had when I was alone there in the twilight, before you came flying down out of the sky; and you said he was quite near. Why do you suppose he didn't? Why do you suppose he waited?"

"And even after I came down," said Cayley, "I was helpless for a minute while I was getting clear of my planes. Yes, that was his chance, and yet he waited. After we had gone, he apparently scaled the cliff, for his tracks led right up to it, and then disappeared. It's not quite so precipitously steep there as it is here, but I would hardly have dreamed that a human being could climb it."

"He's afraid," said Jeanne after a little thoughtful silence, "simply afraid. But if he's the man we think he is, it wouldn't be a human fear. It must be superstitious in some way. It wouldn't be wonderful if he felt that, after the two glimpses he had of you. I remember how I felt at first when you alighted on the floe beside me. He's seen you twice, remember. The first time at night in the fog; the second time in broad day, with the sun on your wings. No, it isn't strange if he thinks of you, not as a man at all, but as a sort of terrible angel keeping guard over me. When I go very long without seeing you, or when I see you in flight, I get to thinking of you in that way myself."

"If that's the way he thinks of me," said Cayley, "we'll try not to disabuse him. A belief like that is an item on our side of the ledger, certainly. And we haven't any such balance in our favor that we can afford to throw an advantage away, even a small one."

Really the balance of advantage between them and their enemy was amazingly even. They had the hut, the enemy the stores. They had Captain Fielding's journal, their enemy the experience and practical knowledge of the country. They were two, with but a single weapon between them. Their enemy, for aught they knew, might be one or a half a dozen; and how armed, they did not know.

Fortunately, no prophetic vision enabled them to anticipate, on that first evening, the length of time that that precarious life and death balance would maintain itself. They had agreed, Philip and Jeanne, that the only thing to do was to wait and to maintain an unwinking vigilance. But both of them thought of the duration of this wait in terms of hours, or, at most, days. Had they foreseen that it would stretch itself out into weeks and months, they might well have despaired.

There were two things that kept them from succumbing to despair. The first was that they never really permitted themselves to hope, to indulge in any thoughts of a summer's day when their horizon should be cut by the spars and funnels of a ship bringing relief. They were simply going to live one day at a time. For everyday that they could snatch out of the hand of death, they would give thanks. It was the only attitude possible for people in their condition.

And the thing that helped them to maintain it was the abundance of necessary routine occupation. They divided their day into watches. Cayley slept from four o'clock in the afternoon until midnight and then kept watch alone, as the girl had done, until eight. During that period they remained inside the hut. The day, from eight until four, they spent out of doors, when the condition of the weather made this possible, either at work or merely tramping up and down for exercise.

At first there was a good deal of work to do. Tearing down the sheds which clustered about the hut, and reducing their frames and planking to fire-wood was an arduous task, but he worked at it until it was done, Jeanne standing sentinel all the time.

When it was done, they were practically secure against surprise, for from their windows, with the aid of a field-glass which Cayley had found in the observatory, they were able to sweep the whole beach absolutely clean, in both directions.

And almost everyday while the light lasted, with Jeanne, armed with the revolver, keeping watch before the hut, Cayley took to his wings and patrolled the beach, from the glacier to the promontory, high up above the level of the crest of the cliff. His flight was always along the same track. He never winged his way inland nor out to sea.

There were two reasons for this. He dared not go so far away from Jeanne that a flash and a swoop would not bring him to her side. The other reason was, that if a superstitious fear of this great man-bird were really what deterred their enemy from attacking them, it was well to let him believe that immunity from this portent could be secured by keeping away from this particular stretch of beach.

As the shortening days sped by and began to get themselves reckoned into weeks, the conviction grew upon Philip and Jeanne that their securest protection lay in his wings, in the terrorizing effect upon their invisible, silent enemy of the majestic winged apparition which was so often seen soaring in mid-sky above the hut and the little stretch of beach surrounding it. Something was protecting them evidently.

Almost every week brought some evidence, not only of the existence but of the nearness of their enemy. They never actually caught sight or sound of him, but sometimes when the wind blew from the right quarter they could make out, with their field-glass, a wrack of brownish smoke, such as would be given off by burning whale oil, drifting down from somewhere along the glacier, and made visible by the dazzling whiteness of that background.

And sometimes they saw tracks in the newly fallen snow, never coming very near the hut, but trespassing a little way, either down from the glacier or up from the headland, upon the stretch of beach they were defending. They never found the tracks of more than a single man, and these were always the same. So that they came to believe, although they could not know, that they had only one man to deal with.

They sometimes speculated on the question whether he was Roscoe or some other member of the *Walrus* crew; really, in fact, they found it impossible to hope that it was any other than he.

They got proof of his identity, or what amounted to it, along toward the end of October. Cayley's keen eyes caught, one day, from up aloft where he was soaring, the glint of something on the beach near the foot of the headland. He circled down in a long swoop, caught it up without alighting and mounted into the air, a trick of aeronautics which made Jeanne, accustomed as she was by now to seeing him in flight, catch her breath a little.

When he descended and alighted beside her a few moments later, he showed her a sheath knife, the haft of which was a rudely carved walrus tusk. The hand of the last user of it had had blood upon it, and its imprint upon the surface of the ivory was plainly to be seen. The lines in the palm were traceable and, lengthwise, along the side of the handle, the print of an immense thumb.

"You see," said Cayley quietly, "he was using this knife left-handed."

The girl paled a little as she handed the weapon back to him, but she spoke quietly enough:

"It's good to know," she said, "almost a relief."

XIX

AN ATTACK

The fact that their enemy was alone and that he was Roscoe himself was responsible for the conviction that Cayley's wings were all that stood between them and an attack. No terror attributable to human causes would have held back that solitary and altogether desperate outcast.

The thing in the situation which caused Cayley the most uneasiness was the fear that sometime, or other, Roscoe would solve the mystery, would see him in the very act of taking to the air. This fear suggested an expedient to him one day as he was flying along near the snow-crested edge of the cliff.

"I don't know why I never thought of it before," he said to Jeanne as he alighted beside her a moment or two afterward; "but I've got it now—the way to prevent Roscoe from ever solving the mystery of your guardian angel. I thought of it when I saw the mound up on the cliff-head that is formed by the observatory. It can't be buried so very deep in the snow because the mound isn't so very big. I'm going up there now to dig it out, enough, at least, so that I can take wing from there."

"You never can dig out enough snow to get a running start up there," she objected.

"I sha'n't have to. I'll just dive off the cliff."

"Philip, you sha'n't!"

"Why not?"

"You know what you told me yourself. That none of the big birds can take to the air without a running start; and about taking pelicans and birds like that up into high buildings and throwing them out of windows, and how they are always killed."

"That's because they've only got instinct instead of intelligence. None of their family had ever been thrown out of windows before, and they didn't know what to do. But I can get my start quite as safely that way as any other. Oh yes, I've done it. Do you imagine, Jeanne dear, that I'd take an unnecessary risk so long as my life is the only possible protection there is for yours?"

He spent the rest of the day tunnelling out from the observatory. He did not dig in the snow; he simply packed it, gradually enlarging the space from a section the size of the pilot house door, to a space at the cliff's edge wide enough for the full spread of his wings.

Jeanne was watching on the beach when he made his first flight from this aerie, and, in spite of her confidence in his powers, she endured a horrible moment or two. For he came hurtling down, head first, at an angle of sixty degrees; and he had traversed two-thirds of the distance to the beach, before his line deflected outward and began curving up toward the horizontal.

When she saw that he was safe, that he had really done the thing he had said he could, she dropped down upon a bear-skin, which was spread before the hut, and shut her eyes, for what she had seen had turned her a bit giddy.

That feeling passed in a moment. She opened her eyes and lay, stretched at full length, upon the bearskin, watching him as he wheeled and dipped, then towered aloft again in that fading violet sky, supremely masterful, majestically dominant of the unstable element he had conquered.

Seeing him thus, even though it was an almost daily experience with her now, always excited in her a mixed emotion, in which she did not know whether joy or pain was predominant. The power, the perfection of grace, the free wide sweep of the performance never failed to thrill her. Whatever he might be to her when his wings were furled, when he labored at their common tasks or walked with her upon the icy beach— whatever he might be then, when he took to the air he became, at once, almost as unreal as he had been on that first night of all when he had descended upon the floe beside her. She had not been exaggerating when she told him that when she saw him in flight he did not seem a man to her at all, but a great winged guardian spirit.

There was a thrill of joy in that feeling, too, although it added to her sense of loneliness. But the pain came with the thought, which she never could dismiss further than the background of her mind, that she had chained that spirit to the earth, she with her human limitations and necessities. She did her best to keep Cayley from suspecting the existence of this feeling. She never referred to it during the long hours they spent in conversation together, and she tried as well as she could to dismiss it utterly from her own thoughts. But this last was impossible. It was always hidden there, somewhere, and when she saw him in flight it was always the thing she was most acutely conscious of. There were times when she could not bear to watch him at all, and it was always a

HENRY KITCHELL WEBSTER

relief when the wings were furled and put away and he was just a man once more, and a comrade.

Comrade, at least, was the word she had settled upon to designate the relation that existed between them. It did not altogether cover the ground, to be sure, but tentatively, and for temporary purposes it was, perhaps, more comfortable than a word or phrase would have been that possessed the merit of greater accuracy. And yet when alone, as she was now, she indulged in speculating how she should frame that more accurate phrase, should necessity arise for doing so.

As if to make up for the kaleidoscopic character of those three first incredible days of her acquaintance with Cayley, days which had changed the meaning and the value of all that had entered into her life before—as if to compensate for that experience, the weeks which had passed since then had slipped away in an almost unbroken routine. There were occasional reminders of Roscoe's existence and a few unimportant discoveries of articles of use, either in the cave or observatory. A furious snow-storm had raged for a week, and had kept them imprisoned in their hut for as long again. These were the only incidents to break the routine.

They still divided their days as they had set out to do upon Cayley's discovery of the tracks of an unknown man in the snow. They kept "watch and watch," as the sailors say, the two of them never sleeping at the same time.

But if the time had gone monotonously, it had slipped away wonderfully fast. She had not been bored nor melancholy, indeed, she and Cayley had both been too busy for that forlorn indulgence. There was an incredible number of things to do, things which would make such a difference to their comfort and security, that what they had to resist was a feverish haste and an attempt to get everything done at once. And she was generally so tired when it came time to call Cayley at midnight for the beginning of his watch, that she slept like a child, until eight o'clock the next morning, when another day's work began.

There was always something delicious about that part of the day. The fact that she and Cayley were together only for those eight hours made it possible to condense their companionship to a rather higher tension than is ordinarily possible for people who are always in each other's company.

But still, she said to herself, as she lay there on the bear skin, gazing up, lazily, at the soaring creature that seemed so unrelated to the man who was the subject of her thoughts, but still, companionship was the word for it. He had not made love to her; he had never repeated the declaration that he had made to her that morning on the beach when she had discovered that the yacht was gone and what its absence meant. Once in a while he had used some caressing little word of endearment in speaking to her, and, more rarely still—much more rarely—had offered her the caress of his hands or of an arm across her shoulders.

But that had happened almost never at all lately. It rather noticeably had *not* happened. Her own expressions of affection were rather impulsively demonstrative, and she had noticed, once or twice, that he had seemed to shrink away from them.

That was the way she reviewed the situation in her own mind. So far, at least, there was no reason for quarreling with the designation "comrade." But she knew perfectly well that she had only reviewed one side of it.

On the other side, to begin with, was the great luminous fact that here, upon this frozen Arctic land alone, and worse than alone, amid privations she would once have thought intolerable, and in daily peril of death, she and Cayley had been unfeignedly and delightedly happy—she and this man whom she never saw until two days before that amazing conjunction of circumstances that had thrown them thus together. They two, strangers as the world reckons such matters, had been living for weeks within the confines of an enforced intimacy, which would have become irksome with any other person, her father excepted, perhaps, that she had ever known. But it was not irksome to them. They began the eight hours they called their day, together, with the high spirits of a pair of children, and they ended them with reluctance, tempered only by the anticipation of another tomorrow.

There was more than comradeship in that, certainly. She and Tom Fanshaw had been comrades and, as she had told him, she loved him very much, but at the thought of spending an Arctic winter with him, she smiled rather wryly.

Was she quite honest, after all, in telling herself that Cayley had not made love to her? He had put nothing of the sort into words, to be sure, and he had sought none, not even the most easily granted, of a lover's privileges, had even, as she had noticed, shrunk away a little from those she had half-unconsciously offered him. Jeanne was a woman, but she was still enough of a girl to wonder a little why he did that.

But this was a digression from the main theme. After all, no matter what he was saying or doing, there was something in his eyes and something in his voice that made love to her everyday. Perhaps it was that something which gave a new exciting deliciousness to each of the shortening days that passed. There was never the cadence of finality about it. It was like a long suspended harmony in music. But she knew all the while that some day, or other, that suspension would be resolved. That first day on the beach when he had told her that he loved her, that her warmth, her faith, her fragrance were, indeed, the very soul of him, he had said she need make no answer, need come to no decision.

He had never asked for her answer since, and yet she knew that some day he would take up that scene where he had left it. It might be on a day when the coming of the relief would open the world to them again, the old world which seemed as if it might be concerned with another planet altogether, it was so far away; or it might be upon a darker day, the last of that precious little string of days that they had stolen, one at a time, out of the palm of death. But on one or the other of those days it would come; she felt sure of that.

She sat up suddenly, erect, upon the bear skin, with the realization that it was nearly dark. Their hours of daylight were getting very scanty now. Today's allowance was gone, although it was not yet three in the afternoon.

She looked aloft for Cayley, but could not see him. Then, the next moment, she heard the whine of the air through his rigging, and he sailed down on a long slant and alighted beside her.

He got clear of his planes with an unaccountable air of haste, and held out both hands to help her rise.

"What do we do with sentinels who go to sleep on duty?" he questioned with a laugh.

"I wasn't asleep," she said contritely, "but it was just about as bad. I was thinking—" She paused there, then added, "about you. What's the sentence of the court?"

Already he had his wings folded up and was handing them to her.

"The sentence is that you shall be frightened with a bear story. There's a big one coming down the beach after you this very moment, and you're to surrender the revolver to me and stay under arrest in the hut until after I have killed him."

She did not need to be told that he was in earnest, in spite of the smile that went with his words. She turned about quickly and looked up the beach, sighting along Cayley's arm as he pointed. Even in the deep twilight she could already make out the shambling figure that was coming along toward them on all fours.

"Why does he move in that queer sort of way?" she whispered.

They had shrunk back into the shadow of the hut, the girl actually inside of the vestibule and Cayley on the door-step.

"He's been wounded. When I was overhead I could make out the blood stains on his side, and he was leaving a track on the ice."

"Wounded in a fight with another bear?"

"No, that's not likely."

She asked no further explanation, but slipped into the hut. The next moment she was back with the field-glasses.

"While you're attending to the bear," she said in a whisper, "I'll just keep watch up the beach for—for any one else."

The past weeks had made one difference in her attitude toward Cayley which she was now aware of, as she contrasted her sensations on seeing Philip step forward, out of the shelter of the hut, to confront the bear, with those she had experienced when he had set out on a similar errand once before. She knew him now, and she had no fear for him. The feeling that thrilled her now was nearer akin to pride than anything else.

Cayley fully justified her confidence. The course the bear was taking would have brought him within twenty yards of their door-step. When he first caught sight of Cayley he stopped, in two minds, apparently, whether to be hunted or to do the hunting himself. Then, as Cayley advanced upon him rather slowly, he decided, hissed at him venomously and reared up.

He was already badly enough wounded to have taken all the fight out of any other sort of animal, but half alive as he was, he cost Cayley four cartridges. Three of those shots Cayley was reasonably sure must have entered a vital spot. The first one took the bear between the eyes as he was rising. The second was fired into his open mouth. The third was probably deflected by the massive fore paw which he was holding across his body, in the attitude of a boxer. The fourth shot, however, penetrated his throat and probably smashed one of the two first vertebrae, for it seemed to bring the monster down all in a heap, where he finally lay still. Cayley could have reached him with his foot.

"Good shooting," said the girl quietly from the little vestibule.

He re-loaded the revolver, letting the empty shells drop unheeded on the ice at his feet. He gave the weapon back to the girl, and bent over the bear.

"I'm less interested in what I did to him," he said, "than in what he got from the enemy who first attacked him."

The light was almost gone, so that all he could see were two or three irregular dark stains upon the white fur. A wound in the flank, which none of Cayley's shots could have accounted for, he explored with practised hand.

Watching him as he did so, the girl could see that he had found something unexpected, something which surprised him greatly. And there was more than surprise. There was alarmed urgency in his voice when he spoke to her. He offered no explanation. Merely told her to go into the hut and make fast the solid wooden shutters over the windows. He would come in and would tell her what it was all about, in a moment.

The girl had hardly finished the task he had given her, when he came in. In his blood stained hand he was holding out something for her inspection.

Conquering a feeling of repugnance, she bent over the hand, cast one glance at the thing it contained and then started up and gazed, wide-eyed, into his face.

"A bullet!" she said. "But—but we thought that Roscoe wasn't armed—not with fire arms, I mean."

Cayley nodded. "But this seems to be pretty good evidence that he is. That's why I sent you into the hut. It occurred to me that he might be following the bear, and that the lighted windows might give him a chance for a shot at one of us. No matter what superstitious fears he has, he could hardly be too much afraid to fire at us from a safe distance, if we happened to offer a fair mark."

"But we must have offered him that a hundred times in the last weeks, that is, if his rifle had anything like a modern range."

"That bullet is certainly a modern piece of ordnance," said Cayley. "It's soft-nosed and steel-jacketed."

He laid it down on a shelf and went into the storeroom to wash the stains of the encounter from his hands.

"After all," he said, "it's only one more mystery, and I don't know that one more can make any great difference. Not in our way of life, certainly."

Both tried to stick to that view of it and, for the present, to dismiss conjecture upon the new topic from their minds, but they did not succeed very well. The idea that forced itself upon them, in spite of their attempts to discredit it, was that Roscoe's acquisition of a modern, long-range weapon with ammunition to match did not date back to the murder of Captain Fielding, nor to the disappearance of the *Aurora*, but that he had found the weapon, by some strange chance, only very recently, perhaps within a day or two. It was a disquieting thought, at best.

It was time for Cayley to turn in and for Jeanne to begin her evening watch alone, but before that happened they paid an extra amount of attention to the security of their doors and windows.

During the first week or two after the establishment of this routine, the girl had found this period of lonely watching difficult and almost intolerable. She had started in terror at noises, some of them imaginary and others insignificant. The timbers of the hut creaked in the frosty air like an old wooden ship. The great ice masses of floe and glacier were always splitting off with reports that varied in intensity from the sound of a pistol shot up to that of the explosion of heavy ordnance.

During the first ten days she had repeatedly roused Cayley on one false alarm after another, but her lately acquired knowledge and experience, together with a better tuned set of nerves, had conquered these fears so completely that she had almost forgotten them.

Consequently, she was irritated and pretty thoroughly disgusted with herself to find the whole pack of these forgotten alarms besetting her again tonight. She started at every sound she heard, and sounds of one sort or another were almost incessant. Half a dozen times she was on the point of waking Philip, but the memory of those former useless invasions of his much needed repose, checked her.

It was a little before eleven o'clock when Cayley came out of a deep sleep to find her bending over him, shaking him by the shoulder and crying out his name.

"Get up quickly!" she said when she saw that he was awake. "Philip, the hut's on fire!"

HENRY KITCHELL WEBSTER

XX

Roscoe

Roscoe had never been able to clear up his doubt as to Jeanne's identity, nor to solve the mystery of Cayley's appearance in the air. The doubt and the mystery tormented him worse than any final conviction could have done. When he thought, as he sometimes did, that the cause of all his terror, the thing which kept him penned up here in the cave and denied him access to more than the furtive edges of the beach, might be just a rather defenseless human couple, a man and a woman, and the woman beautiful, young, alluring—when he thought of all that he would go off into transports of rage, which left even his gigantic body limp and exhausted. If that were the situation, he might have killed the man weeks ago and taken possession of the woman.

What prevented this suspicion from becoming a certainty was the sight he saw, day after day, of the huge golden-winged thing, keeping its majestic guard, in stately circles, over that bit of beach he dared not venture upon.

The only question he had about that was, whether it were really an avenging spirit or an hallucination of his own brain. That these were not the only alternatives, never occurred to him. So, during those weeks, he lived in a sort of hell. Rage and lust and despair and an ineradicable superstitious dread took their turns tearing at him.

The thing that kept him sane was, in itself, a species of insanity, the passion for gold which had led him to murder Captain Fielding. Everyday he tramped up the glacier to the gold ledge and there, while the light lasted, he worked, cutting the precious metal out of the rock, and with infinite labor beating it pure.

As the weeks and months dragged along, this unvaried routine more than compensated for the solitude and the terrors his superstition thrust upon him, and gradually restored him to his old normal, formidable, brutal self. On the day when he made the discovery that was to terminate the long series of golden days which Jeanne and Philip had been enjoying, he was, again, the very man who, during those long years of exile, had dominated crew and captain of the *Walrus* and bent them to his will.

He was returning from the ledge along the crown of the glacier, when, on the day of this discovery, he found that his accustomed path was interrupted by a new fissure in the ice; it had occurred since he had come that way in the morning, and was too broad to leap across. So he was forced to descend by the rougher and more difficult track which lay along the moraine.

Before he had gone three paces along this track his eye made out something, just off his path and a little below it, which caused him at first to utter a snarl of anger, but led him the next moment to give a wild blasphemous yell of joy.

The great fissure which had opened in the ice had done, in an instant, what the party from the *Aurora* had failed to do after hours of hard labor—it had yielded up the body of Perry Hunter, which, during all these months, it had kept imprisoned.

The sight of it was no new thing to Roscoe. He had seen it a score of times, buried deep down in that eternal ice. The sight had cost him no qualms. So long as no ghosts came back to haunt him, he could survey the murdered body of one of his victims with no more emotion than a polar bear would feel in similar circumstances. But that the ice, which had apparently meant to keep it forever, should discharge it thus, gratuitously, into his very path, affronted him; seemed like a piece of insulting mockery on the part of the envious devil which he worshipped for a god.

But that feeling lasted only the period of one brief glance, and then changed to a saturnine joy. For, strapped across the dead man's shoulders, just where he had carried it in life, was a rifle and round his middle a belt full of cartridges.

The next instant Roscoe was bending over the body, jerking savagely at the frozen buckles which resisted his impatient fingers. But they would not be denied. If they were clumsy, the hands were strong.

It was not five minutes later when Roscoe, rifle and ammunition belt in his hands, was hurrying on toward his cave once more. The body lay just where his desecrating hands had left it.

The rifle was uninjured; that he had seen at a glance, though, of course, all the mechanism of its breech was frozen fast. But a half hour's hard work with cleaning rod and rags of what once had been a shirt, sufficed to put it into commission again.

Then, with the rifle over his shoulder, he swaggered out of the cave. With his first glance abroad, he started. His devil was being kind to him today. There could be no doubt of that. Only, was he being too kind? Roscoe wondered a little uneasily. For, shambling along the ice, through the thickening twilight, not a hundred paces away, was a big bear. Roscoe was tired of walrus meat. The thought of a bear steak made his mouth water.

Three years' disuse, however, had made his marksmanship somewhat uncertain. He fired too soon, and though he did not miss, the only effect his shot had was to make the bear turn about and go shambling down the glacier toward the beach, with ungainly haste. Roscoe hurried after him, and fired two more shots. Whether they hit or not, he could not tell. Certainly they did not serve to check the bear's flight. The next moment he had rounded the corner of the cliff and disappeared down the beach in the direction of the hut.

Roscoe hesitated, but only for a moment; then, with an oath, he set out in pursuit. It was not so much the protection which the rifle afforded him that was responsible for this new courage as it was that the mere feel of it in his hands brought him back in touch once more with the everyday matter of fact world, and made his visions and ghosts seem a little unreal.

It was fully dark down here in the shadow of the cliff. The lumbering yellow shape of the bear was indistinguishable against the icy beach. That didn't matter, for he could follow along well enough by the bloody tracks the wounded beast had left.

The last of the twilight was still in the sky, and half his glances were directed thither, looking for something which he told himself could not possibly exist, except in his own fancy, yet fully expected to see nevertheless, the shadow of Cayley's great wings. And at last he saw it impending in the lower air, like a brooding spirit, just above the tiny square of light which marked the location of the hut.

Roscoe abandoned his pursuit of the bear; all thought of it, in fact, was gone from his mind; but he did not, as on a former occasion, drop down prone upon the ground, his face buried in his arms; nor did he turn and flee like one hag-ridden up the beach. He faltered, it is true, and his knees trembled beneath him, and yet, slowly and with many pauses he made his way forward.

He was horribly afraid all the time, but curiosity was all the while overpowering fear. He was not more than two hundred yards away when Cayley alighted beside the girl.

At what he saw then, Roscoe dropped his rifle on the beach, with a whispered oath, and rubbed his eyes. The light which diffused itself from the open window of the hut was not much, but it was enough to reveal the fact that this great man-bird, this golden-winged spirit which had kept him in terror for his own sanity all these months, was taking off his wings and was folding them up into a bundle, in as matter-of-fact a way as if he were furling an umbrella. He stood there now, just an ordinary human figure of a man; the very man, in fact, that he had seen before and would have killed long ago had it not been for his over-mastering terror of the thing with wings.

He presented a fair mark now, and was in easy range, but Roscoe was too thoroughly astonished to seize the opportunity, and in a moment it was gone again. The two figures shrank into the shadow of the hut, and the next moment the light disappeared.

When Cayley fired, for the first time, at the bear, Roscoe thought for a moment he was firing at him, but the venomous hiss with which the wounded beast answered the shot explained the situation. Roscoe squatted down on the beach and set himself to thinking.

In the light of what he had just seen the explanation of the thing which had so puzzled and terrified him became almost ludicrously simple. During the years that had elapsed since any news of the civilized world had come to him, somebody had invented a flying machine, and this fellow happened to have one.

It even occurred to Roscoe that if he could get possession of the apparatus he might be able to use it himself. . . might, after killing the man, and later, the girl, be able to terminate his exile here.

He had no doubt at all, now that the mystery was solved and the terror over, that these two were delivered into his hands. Even without the rifle he would have felt sure of that. With it, the thing was almost too easy. He had only to wait where he was and keep watch until the man should come out of the hut. He could crawl up to within easy range and one shot would settle him.

But before an hour had passed, certain disadvantages about this plan had obtruded themselves upon Roscoe.

The wind was rising and the temperature falling steadily. There was every indication that the first of their big winter storms was about to begin, and, even for one protected as Roscoe was, and inured to cold, his position would soon become untenable. It was a question of time, of course, before he could accomplish his purpose. But he wanted to accomplish it tonight. And the more he thought of it the more he had that desire.

　　　　　　　　　　　HENRY KITCHELL WEBSTER

At last he rose stiffly, picked up his rifle, which he had laid beside him, and cautiously approached the hut.

He was so preoccupied with it, especially as he drew nearer, that he forgot about the bear and stumbled over it in the dark. This gave him a momentary fright and caused him a whispered oath or two.

He picked himself up and examined the great ungainly carcass. Exploring it with his hands, he found the bullet holes made by two of Cayley's three effective shots, one between the eyes and the other in the throat.

This was good shooting. Better marksmanship than he, Roscoe, was capable of. Clearly, it would not do to take any chances. When the decisive moment came, Roscoe must see to it that all the advantages would be on his side. Well, that ought to be easy, since the man had a woman to protect as well as himself.

Leaving the bear he peered stealthily around the three exposed sides of the hut. No light was shining through its well-caulked crannies, and he heard no sounds, either.

Once or twice, from mere habit, he glanced up fearsomely at the star light, and then swore at himself for having done so. No terrifying apparition could appear up there now.

For a moment, an accession of rage against the two who had baffled him and enjoyed immunity from him so long, almost led him to attempt to break into the hut then and there, and settle matters; but his saner common sense told him that the settlement would almost inevitably be against him should he attempt it.

He was still entertaining this notion, however, when a luminous idea occurred to him. Around on the far side of the hut, the west side, which looked towards the headland, was a good-sized heap of fire-wood, which Philip had not been able to find room for inside the hut. Roscoe had with him a flint and steel and a quantity of tow. He never travelled without them.

With infinite precaution against noise he began laying a fire against the windward wall of the hut. Squatting, with his rifle across his knees ready to use in case of an emergency, he methodically whittled a quantity of dry splinters off a few of the sticks, ignited them and carefully nursed the blaze, until, under the rising wind, it grew to the beginning of a fair-sized conflagration. Then, catching up his rifle, he slipped around the other side of the hut, crouching down not more than twenty paces away, and waited.

Already the fire was burning finely and the silhouetted outline of the hut was plain against the glow of it.

His plan was a good one. The people inside the hut would have no choice and, probably, no thought, but of escape. When they rushed out, as they almost certainly would, bewildered and confused, and plainly visible to him against the glow of the fire behind them, it would be easy, from the safe shelter of the darkness, to shoot—*the man*.

Roscoe's hands were trembling a little, but not with fear. He must not fire too soon. That was all. He must wait until the man's body presented a clean mark against the bright illumination of the fire. It would be too easy a shot to miss; and the woman would be left defenseless, without even the inadequate and temporary shelter of a roof and four walls.

It was only, indeed, by the merest hair's-breadth that Roscoe's plan failed to work. The instinct of escape by the nearest way from a burning building is almost irresistible, and it led Philip and Jeanne to the very edge of the destruction, which Roscoe had planned for them.

Cayley had his hand upon the bolt of the great door, whither he had sprung when Jeanne's cry had awakened him, before the saving second thought stayed him and held him frozen where he was. For perhaps five seconds he stood there, while the memory of the unexplained bullet hole he had found in the body of the great bear, and the belated observation that the fire, which was destroying the hut, must have been started outside of it, articulated themselves into a perfectly clear perception of Roscoe's plan.

"The other way! The other way!" he cried, motioning Jeanne back through the store-room. "Into the cave. He is waiting for us outside. That's why he fired the hut. Quick. We must save all we can."

And so it happened that Roscoe waited in vain. He saw the blaze he had kindled reach its fiery climax, and then in spite of the icy gale which was fanning it, die down into an angry, sullen, smouldering glow. But no man appeared to furnish a mark for his waiting rifle, and no woman was delivered defenseless, shelterless, into his brutish hands.

The failure of his plan brought back a moment or two of the old superstitious horror, but his mind was braced against it now and did not readily give way. Somehow, the failure must be accountable—humanly accountable.

At last he solved this mystery too, partly solved it, at least, for he remembered the ice cave back of the hut. His first impulse, when he

HENRY KITCHELL WEBSTER

thought of it, was to attack them there and now, to charge in over the red hot coals of the hut and settle matters once and for all.

He was sane enough to see that the advantage would be all against him. In close quarters he could not do much with a rifle; and he remembered the deadly revolver shooting he had seen upon the body of the bear. Also, he would have to go into the dark, with the firelight behind him. No. It wouldn't do. He must wait. Well, he could afford to wait,—much better than they could.

Reluctantly he rose, turned his broad back to the gale, and began making his laborious way back to the cave.

It was high time. His face was frozen already. The intensity of the cold had already rendered his rifle useless, for the whole mechanism of the breech was frozen fast. His stratagem had failed in its ultimate intention, for nature had laid her great icy hand upon the board and for the present declared the game a draw.

XXI

A Moonlit Day

The midday moon had changed the sombre purple of the snow to silver. The snow lay everywhere, save upon the vertical face of the cliff itself, an unrent, immaculate mantle over all this Arctic world. The valley, the hills, the beach and the frozen sea all lay at peace beneath it, as if asleep or dead.

To Cayley, where he lay, suspended in mid-sky, the moonlight gleaming upon the sensitive fabric of his planes, as it gleams upon the faint ripples on a mill pond in the dead of some June night—to Cayley this white, sleeping, frozen world looked very far away. He was a-wing for the first time since that eternity ago when he had descended upon the beach beside Jeanne to warn her of the approach of the bear.

How long ago that was, by the measure of hours and days and weeks, he did not know. He had no data for an estimate that would be better than a guess. He remembered how desperately they had worked that night, saving what they could from the burning hut and carrying it back into the cave; remembered with what labor he and Jeanne had climbed the ice chimney to the only shelter that now remained to them, the little pilot-house observatory upon the cliff-head; remembered the unremitting labor of uncounted hours while they adjusted their way of life to the conditions imposed by the calamitous loss of the hut.

But after that there were lapses of time which memory did not cover. During that time he knew the utmost fury of the Arctic winter had been raging over them, without cessation. They had been sheltered from it down in the heart of the great drift of snow which the storm had heaped about them. But, even in this security the shock of those successive paroxysms of nature's titanic rage reached down and benumbed them, body and soul.

In some dull, automatic fashion they had contrived to keep alive, to secure a little air to breathe, to eat what would serve to hold off starvation, and to keep from freezing. But the reckoning of the days had lost itself in the unbroken night of mid-winter. Even the months they had spent in the hut, those days of varied, cheerful occupation, the peril with which Roscoe had threatened them, and the unsleeping vigilance they had interposed against him—all of that had come to seem remote and incredible to them.

As for the world of men, of cities and civilization, of busy streets and lights and the sounds of human activity, that was to them almost as if it had never been.

But at last the rage of the storm had spent itself and had become still. The bitterness of the cold relaxed and became milder. Cayley had felt the blood stirring in his veins again, the power of consecutive thought and the ambition to live, coming once more into his possession. He had gone to work, feebly and drowsily at first, but with constantly increasing energy and strength, at the task of opening up, once more, the tunnel through the drift which the great storm had choked.

When he had broken through the outer crust of the drift, and the white radiance of the mid-day moon shone into the black tunnel where he had been working, he stood for a moment drawing deep breaths and gazing over the scene which lay beneath his eyes. He hastened back into the little pilot-house.

Jeanne was dozing upon a heap of bear-skins. He roused her with some difficulty; really waking up had been a hard matter lately, almost as hard as really getting off to sleep. She was still drowsy when he led her along the tunnel to the cliff-head.

"Breathe deep," he told her. "We were half poisoned in there. This air will bring you back to life again, it and the moonlight."

He had been supporting her with his arm about her waist, but now, as she held herself a little straighter and he could feel her lungs expanding with the pure air she breathed, he withdrew the arm and let her stand alone. Even the white moonlight revealed the color that was coming back into her cheeks.

For a while she did not speak at all; then, as if replying to a comment of his, she said:

"Yes, it's beautiful. . . But, Philip, it's dead. Dead."

"Not this air that has ozone sparkling all through it. It is alive enough to make your blood dance. It's doing that now."

He tried to persuade her to take a little exercise along the length of the tunnel, but she demurred to that. Instead, she asked him to bring out some bear-skins and let her sit there at the cliff-head looking out.

"And," she supplemented, "if you want to know what I should like most of all, it would be to have you bring your wings so that I can see you flying again, and a field-glass that I can watch you through."

He felt some hesitation, partly out of a fear of leaving her and partly from a doubt concerning his own strength; but neither of these reasons was one he cared to avow. So he unfurled the bundle that had lain disused so long, spread and tightened and tested it, and at last, with a nod of farewell to the girl, dived off the cliff-head.

Any doubt he may have had concerning his strength disappeared at once. The mere touch of those great wings of his seemed to bring it all back, and hope and joy and confidence along with it.

He made his dive as shallow as possible, and in the sheer exuberance of delight at being once more a-wing, he beat his way aloft again by main strength, towering like a falcon. All his old power was here unimpaired, yet every sensation it brought him was heightened and made thrilling by long disuse. By means of those great, obedient wings of his he played upon the capricious, vagrant air with the superb insolence of mastery. Every trick of flight was at his command, the flashing dive of the piratical frigate bird, the corkscrew spiral of the tern, the plummet-like pounce of the hawk, and, at last, the majestic, soaring drift of the king of them all, the albatross.

So he hung there in mid-sky, and the world, white, frozen, immaculate,—looked far away. The old, godlike serenity, untroubled, untrammeled, unafraid, came back to him. The soul opened its gates, up here, lost its boundaries, and all the spirit of the sky came in, immense, cold, clear as the all-pervading ether. This was Nirvana, though the old Buddhist adepts who had philosophized about it had never conquered the sky, had never bathed in it as Cayley on his wings was bathing now.

The declining moon sank lower, till the refracting ice crystals that filled the air caught its light slantwise and danced with it so that it flickered like a will-o'-the-wisp. The sky deepened from its bright steel-blue to purple. The silver light upon the snow faded, through lavender and lilac, to a purple of its own, only less deep than that of the sky itself. But the stars burned brighter and brighter, until it almost seemed they sang:

> *"Harping in loud and solemn choir*
> *With unexpressive notes. . ."*

The words projected themselves quite unsought into his mind. He spent a moment or two, wondering where they came from, and then it came to him. It was a part of two lines from the "Hymn on the Nativity."

Somehow, the thought of Christmas gave his soul a wrench that brought it back into the world again. They had lost their reckoning of time, and, for anything he knew, this might be Christmas day. Perhaps those stars were caroling their Christmas chimes. Perhaps, down in the world of men, the windows were hung with holly and doorways with mistletoe.

Before his thoughts had advanced as far as that he was flying down toward the cliff-head. He could only guess at the length of time that had elapsed since he left Jeanne, on her heap of skins, there in the mouth of the snow tunnel. It must have been an hour or more, for the moon had been shining when he started, and now almost the last of its twilight had died on the horizon.

A sharp sense of his own delinquency in having left her to her own resources for so long, when she had so few resources to draw upon, increased to a sudden alarm for her safety, when he made out the black mouth of the tunnel and saw that there was no light at the farther end of it. She couldn't have been waiting all this time, out in the cold; and yet his eyes, as he hovered, seeking the exact spot to alight, certainly made out a dark object lying there upon the snow. His heart felt like lead as he dropped close beside it, and scrambled clear of his wings.

It was Jeanne; and for a moment he thought she was dead. She seemed as white and cold as the snow itself. And yet she was not dead; not even frozen. The hands he chafed so frantically were inert, but not rigid; and, as he drew her up in his arms and pressed his head down against her breast, he could hear, very faintly and slowly, the beating of her heart.

He picked her up in his arms and carried her into the pilot-house. The air here was still warmer than that out of doors, but it was no longer exhausted and poisonous.

He laid her down for long enough to light the lamp, to throw off his stiff leather jacket and to get a little brandy out of the keg. This he mixed with a little water and, with the aid of a small ivory spoon, he succeeded in getting a little of it between her lips.

He took off her heavy seal coat, and the woolen jacket she wore under it, and, as well as he could, loosened the other clothing about her waist. Last of all, he gathered her up in his arms again, wrapped the great sheep-skin bag about them both and, with the brandy and water within arm's reach, settled down to attempt to get some of the warmth and vitality of his own body into hers.

She was not fully unconscious now, for the next time he offered her brandy she swallowed it. Her eyelids were fluttering a little, too, and presently she sighed.

He was thrilling all over with a tremendous sense of power. He felt he could have brought her back from the very dead. His arteries seemed to be running with electricity, not blood.

Her lips were moving now, and he bent close to catch the whisper that barely succeeded in passing them.

"Don't—bring me back—Philip. It's—so much—easier to go—this way."

His only reply to that was to hold her a little closer.

She did not resist when he held the drink to her lips again; but, after she had taken two or three sips of it, she said:

"I sha'n't need any more. I'm getting quite beautifully warm again."

He knew it was true. She no longer felt lifeless in his arms, though she still lay there quite relaxed. He knew he could let her go now, safely enough. And yet he held her fast.

"I thought you were dead when I saw you lying there on the snow," he said at last, not very steadily. "If you had been, it would have been my own doing."

She contradicted him with a sharp negative gesture:

"You left me well enough wrapped up to have resisted the cold for any length of time. Besides, if I'd wanted to I could have come back in here. But—but, Philip—Oh, it seems a dreadful thing to confess, now you are here with me—I didn't want to. I just lay down on the snow, thinking I could go to sleep and—and that would be the end—such an easy end!"

She felt him shudder all over as she said it, and she clasped his shoulders and held them tight, in a desire to reassure and comfort him.

"Did you mean to do that. . . Was that why you asked me to fly away for a while?"

"No! No! It was something I saw while you were gone, something that terrified me. Philip, do you remember how many of the people of the *Phœnix* died of what father called the ice madness?"

He nodded gravely.

"Well, what I saw made me think that I was going that way, too. Philip, I was watching the moon go down, and gradually it spread out into three, quite far apart, and then they changed into strange colors, and stranger shapes, and began to dance like witches."

HENRY KITCHELL WEBSTER

He laughed, but the laugh had something very like a sob mixed up in it.

"You poor child! No wonder it frightened you. But that's the orthodox way for the moon to set in the Arctic. It's part of the same refraction that plays such strange tricks with the daylight colors. No, you're a long way from the ice madness, Jeanne."

"But that wasn't all I saw, Philip. It wasn't the worst. I saw a ship against the moon, only it seemed too high above the horizon, somehow. That's the crowning impossibility. And then the moons began to dance, that wicked, witch-like dance of mockery. So I lay down in the snow and hid my face in my arms to. . . to go to sleep. It seemed so easy and, somehow, seemed right, too; not wicked any way."

She felt him shuddering again, and his clasping arms strained her so close they almost hurt.

"Thank God, I came in time!" she heard him whisper.

"But you did come in time," she reminded him, for she could still feel him shuddering with the horror of the thing. "You brought me back, and I'm not even afraid any more." She paused, and there was a little silence. Then she added, "And I'm quite warm now."

His arms slackened for a moment, and then once more they clasped her close.

"I—I—don't want to let you go," he said, and his voice had a note in it which she had never heard before. "Jeanne—Jeanne, dear, can you forgive me—forgive me that it's true? Forgive me for telling you? I have the whole world in my arms when I hold you like this. And life and death and promises, and past deeds, and right and wrong, are all swallowed up, just in the love of you. God forgive me, Jeanne; it's true!" Then he unclasped his arms. "Can you forgive me, too?"

She caught her breath in a great sob. Turning a little, she clasped her own young arms around his neck and held him tight.

It was a long time after that before either of them spoke. Finally, Jeanne asked a question:

"But, why—" her voice broke in an unsteady little laugh, "but why do you ask to be forgiven? You told me the very first day, the day we found the yacht had gone, that you—loved me. That's why I allowed you to stay."

"Yes, but there's an infinity of ways of loving, Jeanne, dear. I had a right to love the soul of you, for that was what had given me my own soul back and my power of loving. But we set out to live through this winter in the hope of a rescue, the hope that when another day came it would bring a ship to take you back into your own real world. I couldn't go back with you, you know, I a man with a stain upon him. Since that was so, I hadn't any right to love you this—other way. I wonder if you understand, even now. I love all of you; from the crown of glory you wear, down to the print your boot has left in the snow. I love your lashes, your wistful lips. The touch of anything that is warm with your hands can thrill me. And as for the hands themselves—oh, I can't make you understand."

"Yes," she said very softly, "I understand, now."

"And yet," he began after awhile, "I haven't any right, when I must give you up some day. . ."

She laid her fingers on his lips.

"We'll not talk of rights," she said. "Not now, not tonight. But there's something more to say. Philip, it wasn't the sight of the ship there against the moon that made me think I wanted it all to end. That was the excuse I made to myself, but it was only an excuse. The real despair came when I saw you flying, saw how gloriously free you were up there, and thought it wasn't love that kept you here beside me, but only pity— Well, a sort of love, perhaps, but not what I wanted, not what I felt for you. I'd seen you draw away when I touched you."

She heard a sound in his throat that might have been a sob, though it seemed meant for a laugh, and she felt his arms tighten about her with a sudden passion that almost hurt. So she said no more, just kissed him and lay still.

It was a good while after that that she made a move to release herself.

"Let me go now," she said, "and I'll get you some supper, or breakfast, or whatever we decide to call it—only you'll have to go down into the ice cave to get some more supplies. We've nothing much left up here."

There were a dozen small employments she might have availed herself of while he was gone, but she found it hard to fix her mind upon any of them. Somehow, in the immensity of that moment, the details of life were hardly important enough to engage her interest.

She dropped down on a heap of bear-skins before the open door, and sat gazing out at the black velvety patch of sky which capped the snow tunnel. Even when she heard Cayley coming back up the ice chimney she did not immediately turn to look at him. It was, in a way, a sort of luxury not to; to think that if she waited she would presently hear his step come nearer, and feel his hands upon her shoulders.

XXII

A Sortie

B ut that did not happen, and a sudden instinct that something must have gone wrong reached her, with almost the force of a spoken word.

"What is it? What's happened, Philip?" she asked, as she turned.

He did not answer at once. He was bending over the hole formed by the top of the ice chimney and rather deliberately replacing the wooden cover upon it. When he did straighten up at last, and she saw his face, she knew her instinct had not lied to her.

"It's rather a queer thing for us to have forgotten," he said, "after all those weeks when we lived in terror of him, and after the last thing he did to us. But we had forgotten him—Roscoe, you know—and now he has stolen a march on us."

She looked at him in a sort of wonder.

"It is true," she said, "we had forgotten. Those days when we lived in the hut seemed almost as far away from us up here as the rest of the world seemed then. . ." She made a little pause there, then roused herself. "What is it that he has done, Philip?"

"He has found our stores down below here. He has taken everything— made a perfectly clean sweep."

There was a little silence after that. Before she spoke again she came over to him and kissed him. There was a grave sort of smile on her face when she said:

"Well, is there anything we must do?"

"Oh, yes," he said. "That move of his doesn't end the game. It only begins a new one. Really, I think, the odds are more in our favor this time than they were before, only this time we shall have to move quickly. I would have followed him up at once, without coming back here, only I didn't have. . ." He stopped rather short.

"Of course," she said, "you hadn't the revolver."

"That wasn't what I wanted; I wanted my wings. Now I've got back to them I must start at once."

She uttered a little cry of protest at that.

"Can't you—can't you wait a little—a few hours? Life has only just begun for me—for us—with what you told me just now."

He let a moment go by in thoughtful silence, before he answered.

"No," he said, at last, "it's got to be settled now, before another moonrise. The light is all in his favor, the darkness in mine. If I can find him now, I think I can kill him. Now I think it over, it seems to me likely he doesn't suspect we are alive at all. The *Walrus* people never discovered the ice chimney nor the pilot-house. That's perfectly clear. If they had they would have rifled it long ago.

"When Roscoe got about after the storm and came to explore the ruins of the hut he found no signs of human habitation at all. He doesn't know of any other shelter for us, so he must certainly think of us as frozen to death in a snow drift somewhere. He won't be on his guard at all. So you see you are not to be afraid for me. He has, probably, got a fire, and, of course, that'll help me. I shall have the dark sky for a background and he the white snow."

"Yes," she said breathlessly, "I can see that."

"You are to be the garrison of the fort," he went on. "Until I come back you must keep watch every moment. I don't think he knows about the ice chimney or the pilot-house, but he may, and we must not run any chances. You must be alert every second. If he comes up here you will be able to see him before he sees you, and you must shoot him with no more compunction than you would if he were a bear, or any other monster. But I don't think he'll come.

"When I—finish, I'll come back to you. I don't think I shall be gone very long. You aren't to be afraid for me, and you can trust me to be careful. I know I have your life in my hands as well as my own. Your part is harder than mine; I quite understand that. You must be keeping watch every second. If he eludes me and comes here, you must shoot him, without word or warning. Shoot to kill."

"But I sha'n't have the revolver!"

There was an electric moment of silence between them, while she gazed into his face, horrified at the meaning she read there.

"You didn't mean that! Philip, Philip—you *can't* mean that. And leave you to face that monster unarmed."

"I shall have the only weapon that will be of any service to me, my knife. It's got to be done at close quarters. I couldn't possibly shoot him from the air. But if I can alight near him and come up within striking distance he will have no chance with me, not with all his strength."

"No," she said resolutely, "I won't let you go. Not that way."

HENRY KITCHELL WEBSTER

"Listen, Jeanne. If I can find him, I can kill him. Do you know what the movements of ordinary men, even unusually quick men, look like to me? Like the motions of marionettes. The only chance Roscoe has against me is of picking me off at long range with his rifle. He could do that whether I had the revolver or not. And if he did, if he killed me and I had the revolver, then,—well, then he would come here and find you—defenseless. Don't you see? I couldn't take the revolver. I should be unnerved with terror from the moment I left you."

With a sob she clasped her arms about his neck and held him tight. Then, in tragic submission, they dropped away.

Without saying anything more, Cayley blew out the candle, opened the door into the tunnel and took up his furled wings. With trembling hands she helped him spread them and draw them taut.

As he adjusted the straps across his shoulders, he felt her hands again, upon his head, felt them clasp behind his neck.

"Good bye," she said.

He was trembling all over, as her hands were, but it was not with fear.

"I shall come back safe," he said. "Nothing can harm me tonight."

He pulled her up close in his enfolding arms and kissed her mouth. In an instant he turned and dived off the cliff-head into the night.

He headed up into the wind, and hung for a moment soaring upon a fairly steady current of air, that poured along parallel to the cliff.

He was still tingling with excitement, with triumph, with a sort of joy which he hardly yet dared contemplate, over that wonderful last hour of his with Jeanne.

But now that he was out of her presence this excitement expressed itself, as it commonly did with him, in a sort of exaggerated coolness. When he told her that nothing could harm him tonight he was not guilty of a mere lover's exaggeration. It was quite true that with body and mind tuned, as they were now, to their very highest pitch—with every faculty at the uttermost reach of its powers, ready and waiting to be called upon—nothing was likely to be able to harm him.

His original plan had been to follow Roscoe up the beach to the cave, in the hope of overtaking him, laden with their stores, and settling matters, out of hand, then and there.

But a moment later he rejected that plan for a better one. He towered in a sharp spiral up five hundred feet higher, into that velvet, spangled sky, swept across the crest of the cliff, and sailing thwart-wise to the breeze which he found on that side, he went glancing down the valley toward the glacier, with the velocity almost of an arrow.

The snow mantle which covered the world beneath was glazed with an icy crust, and in the starlight it glowed with the milky, iridescent gray of an enormous pearl.

From the glacier where ice pinnacles pierced the snow, there glinted tiny twinkling lights of sapphire.

When he reached the glacier he checked his speed a little, and slanted down to an altitude of not more than two or three hundred feet above the crest. He hardly expected a glimpse of Roscoe so soon, having no reason to think he would be here, but he began scanning the earth's surface closely with the idea of accustoming his eyes to the light and the distance. Yet it was not his eyes, but his sensitive nostrils which gave him his first hint of the probable where-abouts of the man he was looking for.

The frozen air which he had been drawing deep into his lungs was odorless, save for the faintly acrid suggestion of ozone about it—a thing, by the way, which he was puzzled to account for, unless it presaged some titanic electrical display in the sky.

But the odor which now invaded his fastidious nostrils automatically checked his flight. He tilted back his planes and his momentum sent him towering almost vertically aloft. He did not analyze it—not that first instant, but his sensation was the same one that makes a dog suddenly throw up its head and snarl, bristling.

In a moment he knew that it was smoke, the smoke of no clean, sparkling wood fire, but of smouldering bones and the flesh of some animal.

Slowly he began to descend in the sweeping circles of a great spiral, constantly searching with an eagerness, which amounted almost to an agony, for the point of angry red which would tell him where his enemy was to be found. He had no doubt at all that his enemy was there. The man who had laid that fire was likely to be sleeping beside it.

He was within twenty feet of the level of the ice before his little mirror of concave silver caught the gleam of red that he was looking for.

He threw his head back sharply and gazed at it. He could not see the fire itself—that must be hidden behind the great rock which almost blocked the entrance to what must be the cave.

The gleam he had caught in his mirror had been reflected in turn from the gleaming surface of a mass of ice a little farther out.

HENRY KITCHELL WEBSTER

He slanted away again, searching now for a level place to alight, found it within a hundred yards of the cave-mouth, circled once completely round, to make sure that he could not be surprised in the act of getting clear of his wings, and a moment later came down soundlessly, except with a faint slither of his planes, upon the ice.

He bounded almost instantly to his feet, slipped his knife out of his belt and held the haft of it between his teeth while he furled his planes. That done, he deposited the bundle in the angle of a projecting rock, and stealthily made his way toward the cave-mouth.

The plan which most naturally suggested itself of bearing away from it a little and attempting to get a glimpse into the interior from a safe distance first, he rejected in favor of a more audacious, but probably not more dangerous one.

He skirted the rock, which partially blocked the mouth of the cave, as closely as possible, intent on rounding the corner and appearing suddenly within what he hoped might be almost striking distance of the man he sought.

Of course he did not know where Roscoe was; could not even be sure that he was in the cave at all, though he felt very little doubt of that. But he reflected that while Roscoe's position might surprise him—his position would surprise Roscoe even more. He was sure that he was quicker than Roscoe, and better able to seize the advantage in an unforeseen situation.

At the very edge of the shelter afforded by the rock he paused for an instant; then, with every nerve tuned to the highest pitch—with every muscle in a state of supple relaxation, yet instantly ready for any demand that might be made upon it—he stepped round the corner and into the mouth of the cave.

Probably no apparition of the monster he expected to find there— no sight of him towering expectant, armed, anticipating all that Cayley hoped to do, and ready to frustrate it, could have been so terrifying to Philip as the thing he actually saw, which was—nothing. At least, so far as a first glance into the cave would reveal, his enemy was not there.

For a full minute Cayley stood motionless, staring into the smoky, wavering shadow. He was not consciously looking at what was before his eyes—certainly not cataloging the details which went to make up the picture.

He seemed to be taking it in through some extra sense, or, perhaps, through all his senses at once. But he did not need to explore the remoter recesses of the cave to make sure that Roscoe was not there. The place cried aloud that it was empty.

Cayley shuddered, not with fear, and yet with a sensation stronger than disgust. It was as if a leopard had been standing over the deserted lair of a hyena. A wild beast's lair it was and not a human habitation.

The floor was littered with feathers and half-gnawed bones. The rocky walls dripped with the oily soot of his horrible cooking. The foul air of the place was actually iridescent. But the real horror of it lay in the fact that Roscoe was not there.

Cayley's reasoning faculties attacked that blind, irrational horror with all their force. From the condition of the fire it was evident that Roscoe had been gone several hours. It was almost certain that he would return soon. Cayley's arrival in his absence really gave him an immense advantage. A man always comes unwarily into the place he calls home. If Roscoe came back now he would have no chance at all against Cayley's quick spring and the flash of the long knife-blade.

Certainly it was reasonable to expect that Roscoe would wait for another moonrise before setting out on any serious sort of expedition, and, if that assumption were correct, he might be returning to the cave at any moment.

Cayley tried hard to force himself to accept this line of reasoning—to use it to combat the shuddering horror which Roscoe's mere absence caused him.

He strode a few paces forward into the cave, then turned about and faced the entrance, with the idea of selecting a good strategical position in which to wait for Roscoe's return.

He realized almost immediately, however, that quite without reference to the inexplicable terror which Roscoe's absence seemed to cause him, he would be unable to wait for his return here in the cave. The stench of the place was already turning him sick, and the poisonous exhaustion of the air making his eyes roll in his head.

He strode abruptly back to the cave-mouth. As he did so, however, his eye alighted on something that made him pause—something so strangely out of keeping with its surroundings that it caused him—or he thought that was the reason—a sense of recognition, almost of familiarity.

The thing which so evidently did not belong to Roscoe that it seemed almost to belong to Philip himself, was a gold locket. It lay on a flat bit of rock, which seemed to serve Roscoe's purpose as a table. The objects which surrounded it—an irregular piece of raw walrus hide, an over-

HENRY KITCHELL WEBSTER

turned bottle of whale oil, with a smudgy wick in it, a sailmaker's needle and some ravelings of canvas, together with some scraps of food—all spoke so loud of Roscoe and made such a contrast with this bit of jewelry that Cayley's action in stooping to pick it up was automatic.

He held it in his hand a moment as if he did not know quite what to do with it, then put it in his pocket and went out of the cave. Only during the moment when it had first caught his eye had it really commanded his attention at all. By the time he got outside of the cave he had forgotten it.

Two or three breaths of the clean air outside of the cave were all he needed to revive him, physically. But to his surprise they did not suffice to rid him of the feeling which he regarded as superstitious, namely, the impulse to fly back to Jeanne as fast as wing could carry him.

He had every reason to believe that she was safe, he told himself. She was armed with a heavy revolver, was a good shot and had plenty of nerve. She was in a place, the only avenue of access to which would give her a tremendous advantage over any invader. So that, even supposing the worst—supposing that Roscoe's absence were taken to mean that he had gone to make an attack on the pilot-house, there could hardly be a doubt that Jeanne would kill him.

His reasoning was all based on the assumption that the pilot-house was inaccessible to any wingless creature except by way of the ice chimney. Even now, when his fear for the girl was amounting to a superstition of almost irresistible intensity, it did not occur to him to question that.

He steadied himself as best he could and crouched down in the shelter of the big rock to await Roscoe's return.

He had hardly settled himself here when he saw something that made him shake his head impatiently, and swear a little. It was the winking glow of an aurora borealis, off to the north.

Struggling as he was with a fear which his reason offered him no foundation for, he was in no mood to appreciate one of those infernal, inexplicable exhibitions that a succession of those long Arctic nights had made him all too familiar with. No familiarity could lessen the wonder of it.

He hoped that this one might pass off without amounting to anything; but it was not long before a slender, flickering, greenish-white flash across the sky convinced him that he was in for it. He remembered having read, in Captain Fielding's journal, how the members of his own crew, and more particularly the *Walrus* people, had been frightened to the verge of terror by them, and how the Portuguese had always fallen on his knees and begun jabbering his prayers when one of these phenomena took place. He had believed them, Captain Fielding thought, to be veritably the fires of hell.

Cayley and Jeanne had often watched these auroras, from beginning to end, with delight; but it had always been a strange, piquant sort of pleasure that had a spice of terror in it.

But tonight, as he crouched there alone on the beach, waiting for the man who did not come, the wild, freakish, indefinably menacing quality of those strange lights affected him powerfully. The way they leaped in long arcs, clear across the sky—and vanished; the way their brilliant streamers could flaunt themselves from zenith to horizon with all the colors of the sunset, and still leave the earth as dark as it was after they had rolled up and disappeared; the horrible, winking, shuddering ghostliness of them, made it difficult to think of them as part of the order of nature,—turned them into a sort of malevolent miracle. It was never possible to tell how long they would last. Sometimes they rolled up and left the sky unvexed at the end of a few brief minutes; sometimes they kept up their witches' dance all night.

The one he saw brightening now was developing itself into a stupendous spectacle. The long, greenish pencils of light, rippling, flickering, fading, flashing out again, gradually established themselves in an immense double devil's rainbow clear across the sky. The streamers, which began presently to pour out from both sides of it, ran a gamut of color from angry purple up to a flaming orange. The horizon, all the northern half of it, was banked with what looked like luminous sulphur-colored clouds, shot with occasional gleams of bright magenta.

Cayley gazed at the spectacle unwillingly, but still he gazed. And, somehow, though he fought the feeling desperately, it began to assume a personal significance to him,—a significance of mockery. The whole sky was quivering with vast, silent laughter. Was it because he, with his fancied cleverness and daring in finding Roscoe's lair and waiting for his return to it, was really doing precisely the thing that Roscoe would have had him do? Were those sky-witches laughing over what was happening up at the pilot-house while he sat here and waited?

No intelligence, no sane power of consecutive reasoning can resist this sort of thing indefinitely, and at last Cayley's power of resistance came to an end.

He sprang to his feet, at last, dripping with sweat, in spite of the cold, caught up his bundled wings, unfurled them and took the air with a rush. Once he had jerked himself aloft to a height a little above the crest of the cliff, it was hardly more than a matter of seconds before he came opposite the dome-like mound of snow which covered the pilot-house.

There was no light shining out of the tunnel entrance. But that was as he had expected it to be. He made it out easily enough; and in another moment had alighted there.

"Jeanne!" he called.

It was not the exertion of flight, but a sudden intolerable apprehension that made him breathless. The word had halted a little in his throat. Exactly as he uttered it he saw down the tunnel, and in the pilot-house itself, a tiny spark of fire, and heard the click of steel against flint.

What the spark illuminated were the fingers of a gigantic, hairy hand.

"Jeanne!" he called again, and now his voice came clear enough, "Wait a minute and I'll make a light for you."

XXIII

In the Pilot House

C ayley had been right in assuming, as he did in his conversation with
Jeanne, upon the subject that Roscoe and the other people of the
Walrus had never noticed the ice chimney, nor suspected the existence of
the pilot-house upon the cliff-head. Also, he had followed correctly the
track of Roscoe's mind in the deduction that the two latest castaways upon
this land—that is, Philip and Jeanne—must have perished in the great
storm which began on the night when he fired the hut, and continued for
so many weeks that he, like them, lost all trace of the reckoning.

During the storm he had lived in the cave, much as Philip and
Jeanne had lived in the pilot-house on the cliff; he had, that is to say, in
some purely automatic fashion, kept on existing. The mere momentum
of a mature man's vitality makes it hard for him to die. But when the
storm abated and milder weather came, he bestirred himself, as Cayley
did, and set about digging a tunnel of his own through the great drift
which had blocked the entrance to his cave.

On the whole, the long weeks he had been hibernating, for that is
what his state amounted to, had had a beneficial effect upon him. He
was not only sane again, but had ceased altogether to be self-conscious
about his state of mind.

That period of weeks when he had permitted himself to be terrorized
by the ghost of a murdered man and an old rose-wood box, and what he
had taken to be an avenging angel from heaven, had no more connection
with his present self than the half-remembered delirium of a man who
has once been sick.

The next time the moon came up, after he had completed the tunnel
from the cave, he set out down the beach toward the ruins of the hut.

It was not mere curiosity which attracted him, nor any lurking fear,
but simply the hope of making some salvage from the wreckage of the
hut, or possibly, from the bodies of his two victims, in case he was lucky
enough to find them there. He had no doubt at all that they were dead.

His pleasure over the quantity and condition of the stores he found
in the ice cave compensated for his disappointment over not finding the
bodies of his two latest victims.

Evidently they had not even attempted to use such shelter as the ice-chamber afforded, for it showed no marks of human habitation at all. They had probably wandered outside and died in one of the near-by drifts. Perhaps he would find them some day. For the present, however, the stores occupied his whole attention.

Very methodically he set to work, carrying them off to his own cave, working without fatigue and without intermission—working so long as the moonlight lasted.

He was just setting out with his last load when, glancing sky-ward to see how long the light would hold, he caught a glimpse of Cayley on the wing. The sight occasioned him no return—not even momentary—of the old terror. He cursed a little because he had not his rifle with him; the sky-man soaring slowly and not very high, presented a mark he could almost certainly have hit.

It was surprising, of course, to see him alive, but Roscoe, in his present state, never thought of looking to supernatural means to account for the fact. Indeed, he was hardly more than a moment in approximating the true explanation. There might well be, he supposed, up somewhere in the face of the cliff a cave, or shelter, of which he knew nothing, and easily accessible to anyone who happened to possess a flying-machine.

Skirting the cliff and keeping well in its shadow, he made his way with his last load, back to his cave. Here he spent a few minutes cleaning his rifle, making sure that the mechanism of the breech was working perfectly, and filling its magazine full of cartridges.

The moon was just setting, but the sky was still bright enough to give him a good hope of making out Cayley's winged figure against it.

He did not follow the old track down the beach, but made straight out over the rough masses of ice which covered the bay. It was dark enough to do away with the danger that the sky-man might see him first.

He was in better humor than he had been at any time since the coming of the *Aurora*. He was out hunting, and confidently expected to succeed in bagging his prey. Of those human passions which incite men to do murder, he felt, for the moment, none whatever. He expected a certain pleasure in getting the winged man squarely on the sight of his rifle and bringing him down, hurtling, from the sky, with one clean shot.

He expected he would come. He was almost certain to return to his shelter, wherever it was, before the last of the light had faded from the sky.

Roscoe squatted down in the lee of the great hummock of ice, surveyed the heavens with keen, practised eyes, munched on a strip of dried walrus-meat which he had brought with him, and waited very contentedly.

He had not long to wait. Long before the moon-twilight had gone out of the sky he saw in it, silhouetted against it, the sight from which he had once fled with such mad terror—the broad expanse of the sky-man's wings.

He was coming along almost directly above the spot where Roscoe waited and within easy range. Roscoe had raised his rifle and was sighting deliberately along the barrel before the idea occurred to him, which caused him to lower it again rather suddenly, and swear at himself a little, under his breath, as a man will who has nearly made a bad mistake.

What a fool he would have been, to be sure, if he had killed the sky-man before learning from him the location of this unknown shelter of his; for, if the man was living, there was a pretty good chance that the woman was too. There would be plenty of chances to kill the man after he had discovered the location of their nesting-place.

So, instead of firing, he scrambled up to the top of the nearest ice hummock and from there watched Cayley's flight to his landing place.

He laughed aloud when he saw that it was not in the side of the cliff, as he had feared, but quite at the crest of it—where it was as accessible to a man who could climb a bit as to one with wings.

He did not move from his attitude of strained attention, on the summit of a little ice hill, until he saw a faint glow of golden light diffusing itself from the mouth of the tunnel that led to the pilot-house. Then, with that queer shuffling gait of his, which was neither walk nor run, he began making his way inshore, over the ice, towards the foot of the cliff.

Cayley's tunnel was not at right angles to the crest, but bore off diagonally westward. Roscoe had noted this fact, and he figured it out that from the top of the promontory, which formed the western boundary of their strip of beach, he should be able to command a view straight into the tunnel. Also, there was at this point a precipitous trail up the cliff. No one but Roscoe would have called it a trail, but that was the way it existed in his mind.

He had not climbed it since the day when the sight of Philip coming down from the sky had prevented his attack upon Jeanne. It was a hard climb, even for him. But it was worth the trouble.

There was a sheltered hollow where, except in the severest weather, one could pass a number of hours quite comfortably. Cayley had slept there once, on the night of his first meeting Jeanne on the ice-floe.

His calculation of the angle of the tunnel proved to be correct, for from his newly-gained coign of vantage, he could see straight into the pilot-house, and make out clearly enough two figures there.

Once more he was tempted to fire, and might have yielded to the temptation had not the light been put out before he had fairly got his eyes adjusted to the distance.

It is to be remembered, always, that he knew nothing whatever of the ice chimney, and suspected no connection between the hut and the pilot-house, except by the air. For anything he knew to the contrary, Jeanne might be able to fly, as well as Philip, or he to carry her with him upon his flights. Consequently, he did not suspect, when he saw Cayley take to flight again, that this action had any reference to himself; nor that the woman who was left alone would be on her guard against him.

The moment he glimpsed the shadow of Cayley's wings against the stars he began making his way, cautiously, over the crusted snow, toward the pilot-house. The distance was not great—not more than half a mile—but progress over that glazed precipitous surface was necessarily slow. He had no chance to stand erect, and most of the way he had literally to crawl, often cutting little holes in the crust with his knife to dig his fingers and toes into.

But he was tireless as well as persistent, and at last he drew himself over the crown of Cayley's tunnel, let himself down, and dropped, with cat-like lightness for so heavy a man, just outside the pilot-house door.

The door was closed, but there was a light shining out through a crack beneath it. It was a glass door, but something had been hung over the glass so that he could not see into the interior.

Both Jeanne and Philip had made the mistake of assuming that the only way of access to the pilot-house, except to Philip with his wings, was the ice chimney. It was a natural mistake enough—one that almost any but a practised mountaineer would have made.

Furthermore, they had no reason—either of them—for anticipating an attack on the pilot-house while Philip was gone. They had been living here, now, for weeks, in unbroken security. So, though the girl obeyed Philip's injunction literally and scrupulously, she did it without the slightest sense of personal danger, and indeed she would hardly have had room for such an emotion even if there had been a much more reasonable ground for it.

An acute terror for Philip, who had gone out to find their monstrous enemy and try to kill him, would in any case have dominated both thought and feeling. And this terror was all the sharper because of what had passed between them the hour before—the coming of the full, complete, wonderful understanding and the sweeping away of the last barrier there had been between them.

Probably no human being, not even the sanest and most commonplace, is inaccessible to that fear of Nemesis—the fear that merely being too happy, finding life too complete—is sufficient to suggest.

Only an hour ago the thing had happened which made life perfect for her; and now Philip was gone and she left alone.

For a while after he left she had kept the pilot-house door open, and, bundled in her furs, had sat near it, her ears strained for the sound of a cry or the report of a rifle.

But the torture of that situation was too great. Philip might be gone for hours; and at this rate she would be fairly beside herself long before his return. So, resolutely, she made a light, shut the pilot-house door upon the world, took up her father's journal and tried to read.

But even this fascinating narrative lacked the power to command her attention tonight. She rose half a dozen times from the rude bench on which she sat, to make some trifling alteration in the room.

One thing she did had reference to the possibility of Roscoe's attempting an attack on the pilot-house—this was to remove the wooden cover from the chimney-mouth. If Roscoe should succeed in eluding Philip, or in killing him, she wanted ample warning. The rising wind rattled the pilot-house door, and wailed in the chimney; but she knew she would be able to detect the sound of the monster's laborious ascent long before he could reach the top.

She was sitting beside the oil-stove, in one of the farther corners of the room. The chimney hole was in the corresponding corner. The revolver lay on the table in the middle of the room, a few paces behind her. The pilot-house door was directly in line with it, and almost exactly behind her back. The door was hinged to swing inward.

When it burst open she attributed the fact to no other agency than the wind. She laid down the red-bound book upon the bench beside her and rose, rather deliberately, before she turned round.

As she did so Roscoe sprang forward to the table and seized the revolver. Her failure to turn immediately had given him the second he needed to take in the strategical possibilities of the room.

His rifle was a clumsy weapon in close quarters. So, as he sprang forward, he dropped it and made for the revolver instead. It only needed a glance at the girl to convince him that she was unarmed. Quite deliberately, he broke open the breech of the revolver and satisfied himself that it was loaded. Then he looked up again, blinking at the girl.

She had not moved since she had caught her first glimpse of him. In her mind was the thought that Philip must be dead, and the hope that Roscoe would kill her quickly—before she could realize that fact—before this strange, blessed numbness which had frozen her in the instant of her first glimpse of him,—should have lost its anæsthetic power.

With that in mind, she kept her eyes upon the revolver, which those vast, hairy hands of his were manipulating.

She had uttered no cry at all. She turned dead-white and her eyes were wide, but there was no terror in them. Roscoe on his part stood staring at her.

It was no wonder that Carlson and Rose had mistaken her for the ghost of the man their leader murdered. She looked like her father as a woman may resemble a man, and her whiteness, her fineness, her delicacy all increased rather than diminished the credibility of the idea that she was in fact his spirit.

It was this thought that for a moment held Roscoe staring blankly at her. But he conquered it and forced his eyes upon the details of her.

He saw that her fine hands were trembling a little; he marked the faint rise and fall of her breast, as she breathed, and then his greedy eyes ran over her, from head to heel, and back again.

The hand which held the revolver dropped nerveless at his side. He swallowed hard, and wrung his cruel lips with his other great hand. It was then that the girl looked up into his face. It was then she uttered her first cry.

For she saw that he did not mean to kill her.

That was a horror she had never foreseen, never, during all the months in the hut, when the shadow of this monster had been a part of their daily life. The worst that had ever occurred to her was that he might kill them both. She understood now why Philip had shuddered; why she had seen that look of horror in his eyes, when he said that if Roscoe killed him—when he had the revolver—he would come back here and find her defenseless. She understood now, to the full; it needed only one look into the monster's face to understand.

The shock of this new idea brought an instantaneous change in her. A moment ago her mind had been absolutely lifeless. She had been incapable either of thinking or of acting. Now she was intensely alive; her body keyed and ready for sudden action; while her mind, with the vividness of sudden summer lightning, took in the situation and assessed her chances—her chances, not of escaping with her life, but of foiling the loathly intent which she could read in the monster's face.

Already her eyes had brightened and the color come back to her cheeks; and, at that, Roscoe moved restlessly to one side, as if he meant to come round the table.

Suddenly Jeanne's eyes detached themselves from his face. A look of sudden alarm came into them, and she raised her hand to her throat, as though she were choking. She was looking past Roscoe, and straight down the snow-tunnel.

"Philip!" she cried, "take care; he's here."

The snow-tunnel was empty, and for aught she knew, her lover's body might be lying mangled in the monster's cave. She had thought of that before she tried the trick. But, even if that were so, that cry of hers might lead the monster to steal one uneasy glance at the door behind him; and even that would give her time enough. If he had not killed Philip, but simply eluded him, he would turn instantly.

That was what he did. He sprang round with a suddenness which bespoke a perfectly genuine, commonsense alarm. And then he found himself in darkness.

He understood at once that he had been tricked. Without wasting the time to turn back and look at Jeanne, he sprang toward the pilot-house door. He thought she meant to attempt to rush by him, gain the snow-tunnel and throw herself over the crest of the cliff. He had not misread the sudden loathing he had seen in her eyes when they met his face.

In the open doorway he wheeled round, triumphantly. She had not got ahead of him that time. He laughed aloud into the darkness, and then spoke to her, with a vile, jocular familiarity.

But he got no answer, in words or otherwise. There was no outcry, no stifled sobbing. Nothing at all but the sigh and whine of the wind.

It was not perfectly dark. The faint blue flame of the oil-burner began slowly to bring out the objects in the room, as his eyes adjusted themselves more to the darkness.

The man, who the moment before had laughed out the vile, triumphant taunt, now began to tremble and sweat. For the girl was not there.

He stood where he was for a little while, drawing deep breaths to steady himself. She must be there—must be hiding somewhere in the shadows. She could not have got out. There was no way out.

He moved forward, groping in the dark, but stopped when he felt the pressure of the table across his thighs. He could do nothing without a light. He would re-light the candle, first of all, and then he would find her.

He took a bit of flint, a nail and a rope of tow from his pocket. He struck a spark, but it failed to kindle the tow.

It was at that instant that Philip alighted.

Philip's stratagem was a perfectly rudimentary one, and it was an instinct rather than a conscious plan that suggested it. His mind did not pause to draw even the most grimly obvious inference from the fact that it was Roscoe's hand which held the flint and steel here in the pilot-house.

He knew that the next thing to do was to kill him; and he fully expected to do it—though almost equally to be killed himself in the process.

His calling Jeanne's name the second time, telling her to wait and that he would make the light for her, would enable him, probably, to get within striking distance of Roscoe, before Roscoe attacked him. The man would think he had him at his mercy.

Philip sprang clear of his planes, left them as they were there at the tunnel-mouth, and walked steadily up toward the pilot-house door.

Roscoe, on hearing his voice the first time, had dropped the articles which encumbered his hands and groped on the table for the revolver. Before he could put his hand on it Cayley spoke the second time.

At that, wanting no weapon, confident that he needed none, his great hands aching for the feel of the sky-man's flesh within their grasp, he moved a step nearer the door and waited.

He saw Philip cross the threshold, unseeing—suspecting, apparently, nothing; saw him, at last, within hands' reach.

Just as he touched him he uttered a sobbing oath, and his great hands faltered, for Philip's knife had struck through, clean to the hilt, and just below the heart.

The effect of the shock was only momentary. With a yell of rage he sprang upon Cayley, crowded him back against the wall, tore at him blindly, like a wild beast, and finally getting Philip's right fore-arm fairly in the grip of both hands, he snapped it like a pipestem.

In a moment Cayley got round behind him and with the crook of his good arm round Roscoe's neck, he succeeded in forcing him to release his grip and in throwing him heavily.

As he lay, his body projected through the doorway, out into the tunnel.

Philip left him huddled there, and went back to the table. He found Roscoe's flint and steel beneath his hand; but it was a full minute before he could summon his courage to strike a light, for the inferences from Roscoe's presence here in the pilot-house began to crowd upon him now, grim and horrible. But he struck a spark at last, lighted the candle and looked about.

The reaction of relief turned him, for a moment, giddy, as the glance about the room convinced him that what he feared worst had not happened. But another thought occurred to him, almost at once, when he saw that the cover had been removed from the top of the ice chimney.

In his mind, of course, that represented the way Roscoe had come. What if Jeanne, unable for some reason to defend herself, had chosen, as the lesser evil, to fling herself over the cliff from the tunnel-mouth?

The moment he thought of that he went out into the tunnel, stepping across Roscoe's body to do so. He went to the edge and looked over, but it was too dark to see. The light of the aurora which still blazed in the sky, dazzled his eyes, without lighting the surface of the world below.

He must go down there, in order to be sure. He had not stopped to furl his planes when he alighted, and they had wedged themselves sideways into the tunnel, still extended and so ready for flight in an emergency.

He righted them and slipped his arms through the loops that awaited them. He stood for a moment, testing the right wing tentatively. There was a play about it that he did not understand. So far as he could see nothing was broken. The fact that it was his own arm did not occur to him.

He was just turning to dive off the cliff-head when, suddenly, he saw the great form of the man he had supposed to be dead, rise and rush upon him.

Philip's knife had, indeed, inflicted a mortal wound, but a man of Roscoe's physique lets go of life slowly. He was bleeding to death, internally, but the process was, probably, retarded by his huddled position, as he lay there in the tunnel.

So he had lain still and awaited his chance. Cayley was standing quite at the edge of the cliff, and the man's momentum carried him over. His clutching hands grasped Cayley's shoulders, and they went down together, over six hundred feet of empty space.

For Cayley the space was all too little. As they went over he thought that he and his gigantic enemy were going down to death together. Instinctively, and much quicker than a man can think, he swept his great fan-tail forward and flung himself back in an attempt to correct the balance destroyed by the great weight that was clinging to his shoulders.

They were, of course, bound to go down. Neither his strength nor the area of his planes was sufficient to support them both in the air. But in the position into which he had flung himself they would go down a little more slowly. He would gain, perhaps, a precious second more.

But he did not waste even an infinitesimal moment in any struggle against the force of gravity.

Twice, with all his might, he sent his left fist crashing against the face, the staring, horrible face, that confronted his own. But still that convulsive, dying grasp held fast.

They were no more than a bare two hundred feet above the ice. With a supreme effort, an effort whose suddenness availed it better than its strength, he wrenched himself free and the great weight dropped off. Another effort, the instantaneous exertion of every ounce of force he possessed, corrected the sudden change of balance and prevented him from falling, like the great, inert mass he had just cast off.

Trembling, exhausted, he managed to blunder around in a half-circle, slanted down inland and stumbled to a landing on the beach, not fifty yards from the ice-clad ruins of the hut.

As he did so, the thought was in his mind that during his struggle in the air, with Roscoe, he had heard a cry, which neither he nor his antagonist had uttered.

The perception came to him as a memory, and in memory it seemed to be Jeanne's voice.

Now, unless his wits were wandering, he heard it again, and it called his name. He was half incredulous of its reality, even as he answered it. But the next moment, before he could extricate himself from his planes, or even attempt to get to his feet, he felt the pressure of her body, as she knelt over him.

XXIV

SIGNALS

There were a good many days after that—not days at all, really, but an interminable period of night—which were broken for Jeanne by no ray of hope whatever. She kept Philip and herself alive, from day to day, and this occupation left her hardly time enough to think whether there was anything to hope for or not.

Philip had fainted within a moment after she had reached his side there on the ice, after the fight with Roscoe. He had recovered almost immediately, and had walked along with her, steadily enough, as far as the ice cave; but here he collapsed in good earnest. His injuries would not have been dangerous if he could have been put directly into a hospital, or even if they could have commanded medical and surgical skill of the simplest sort. Situated as they were, however, it was no wonder that within a few hours he became a very sick man.

It was impossible, of course, for him to get back into the pilot-house. Jeanne mounted thither and dismantled the place as well as she could, throwing or carrying down such articles as she thought might be of use. With the skins they had accumulated during the winter she contrived a sort of shelter, in the half-burned storeroom behind what had been the hut. There she took what care she could of her invalid.

Much of the time Philip was delirious; sometimes violently so, and yet she often had to leave him. When she did so, it was with no certainty at all that she would find him alive upon her return.

Occasionally during that interminable time, when all reckoning of time itself was lost, she found herself recalling passages from her father's journal, with an infinitely better understanding of them and of the man himself than she had ever commanded before. She was living his gospel now, in all earnest—without real hope, yet equally without despair. Living life one hour, one problem, one act at a time.

She had little leisure and less energy for reflection. As a rule, when there was nothing that needed immediately to be done, she would drop down on the bear-skins beside Philip, and snatch a morsel of sleep. But, even at that, she sometimes wondered at the change which had come over her—at the things which she could do quite simply and effortlessly now.

She had once asked Philip, half playfully, if he could not treat her like a kid brother, and make a man of her. Well, that was what he was doing now, unconsciously and involuntarily—just by lying there helpless—just by depending utterly upon her for every hour of life he had.

In one of his brief periods of lucidity Philip had told her what he had done during his brief and disastrous absence from the pilot-house. How he had found Roscoe's cave, and waited there for his return.

At the risk of forcing his fluttering mind back into delirium, she had pressed him for as exact a description as he could compass, of the location of this cave. During his next comparatively quiet sleep she set out to find it. Philip's description of the place had not been reassuring, and he had done even fuller justice to its horrors during the wanderings of his delirium; and yet she had faced the situation with hardly a shudder.

She set out, equipped with flint and steel and candles, and found the place without difficulty, and had explored the grisly lair where the man-monster had lived, to the utmost, hardly conscious of its loathsomeness—not conscious at all, in fact, except as she thought of the effect the sight of such a place would once have had upon her.

This she was sure of: If she and Philip ever came alive through this winter, ever went back together to the world of men, there would be an entirely new joy for her in living, a joy springing from a feeling of independence, from a certainty that whatever situation she might be confronted with she would be equal to it.

At last the conviction was forced upon her that Philip was actually on the road to recovery. His delirium became less violent and occurred at longer intervals. The frightful condition of his wounds began visibly to improve. Instinctively, she resisted this conviction as long as she could, refusing almost passionately to begin to hope—for the return of hope brought an almost intolerable pain with it. Without hope there had been no fear, no apprehension—just as in a frozen limb there is no pain. But, as the possibility of his recovery became plainer, the slenderness of the thread by which his life was hanging became plainer, too. A thousand chances which she could not guard against might cut the thread and destroy the hope new-born.

The greatest and most terrible of these was the caprice of nature herself. Until Philip should grow strong enough to struggle, with her help, up that endless ice-chimney to the pilot-house, they must live utterly at the mercy of the weather. The rude shelter which she had contrived for him would not avail ten hours against one of the terrific

Arctic storms which might be expected at any time. But the vast black sky stayed clear, and the stars twinkled through it, kindly. Their friendly light did not, as she expected, turn to mockery. And Philip steadily grew stronger, and her daily prayer for another day's grace was daily granted.

He was able, at last, after a long sleep and a really hearty meal of sustaining food—which she hardly dared give him—to get up and walk out of their shelter to the star-vaulted beach. Fifty paces or so was all he was equal to; but at the end of the little promenade he expressed a disinclination to go back to the stuffy little shed which had been the scene of his long illness. The clean, wide, boundless air was bringing back the zest for life to him. So Jeanne brought out from the hut a great bundle of furs and made a nest of them on the beach, and there he lay back and she sat down beside him.

"Do you remember, Jeanne," he said, "the first time we sat out like this, there on the ice-floe beside the *Aurora*, and I told you how I had learned to fly?"

She locked her hand into his before she answered.

"I couldn't believe that night that I wasn't dreaming," she said softly.

"Nor I, either," he told her; "and, somehow, I can't believe it now—not fully;—not this part of it, anyway."

He had lifted the hand that was locked into his and pressed it to his lips before he spoke. There was a silence after that. Then, with a little effort, the girl spoke.

"Philip, do you remember my saying what a contempt you must have for the world that didn't know how to fly? Do you remember that, and the answer you made to it?"

He nodded.

"Philip, is that still there? Your contempt, I mean, for the world?"

"I don't believe," he said, "that you can even ask that seriously—you, who gave me first my soul back again and then, in these last weeks, my life. For it's been your life that has lived in me these last days—they must be a good many—just as it was your warmth and faith and fragrance that gave me back my soul, long ago." He paused a moment; then, when he went on his voice had a somewhat different quality. "But the other contempt, Jeanne, that still exists, or would exist if I gave it the chance, the world's contempt for me. Not even your faith could shake that."

She had been half-reclining beside him, but now she sat erect purposefully, like one who has taken a resolution.

"I'm not so sure of that," she said, in a rather matter-of-fact tone, though there was an undercurrent of excitement in it. "Philip, I have been trying to solve a puzzle since you were ill. I hoped I could solve it by myself. If I were intelligent enough I'm sure I could; but I'll have to ask you to help me. It's a string of letters written around a picture, in a locket."

"A locket of yours?" he asked, surprised.

"Never mind about that just now." She spoke hastily and the undercurrent of excitement was growing stronger in her voice.

"Do you want me to try it now?" he asked. "If you'll make a light and show me the thing I'll see what I can do."

"Perhaps you won't need that," she said. "I can remember the letters. They are divided up into words, but I'm sure they are not any foreign language; they are in a code of some sort."

She did not turn to look at him, but she felt him stir a little, with suddenly aroused attention, and heard his breath come a little quicker.

"The first letter was all by itself," she said, trying to keep her voice steady. "It was N—. And then, in one word, came the letters p-b-j-n-e-q."

"That means 'A coward,'" he said. His voice was unsteady, and he clutched suddenly at her hand. She could feel that his was trembling, so she took it in both of hers and held it tight.

"It's a code," he said, "a boyish code of my own. I remember that for a long time after I invented it I believed it to be utterly insoluble; yet it was childishly simple. It consists simply of splitting the alphabet in two and using the last half for the first, and *vice versa*. It must have occurred to hundreds of boys, at one time and another, and yet—" His voice faltered. "Yet, it's a little odd that you should have stumbled upon another example of it."

"The next word was o-r-g-e-n-l-r-q."

"That means 'betrayed,'" he said, almost instantly. "Was—was there any more?"

"One little word, three letters, 'u-v-z.' But I know already what they mean, Philip." There was a momentary silence, then she repeated the whole phrase—'A coward betrayed him.'" She was trembling all over now, herself. "I knew," she said, "I knew it was something like that." Then she dropped down beside him and clasped him tight in her arms. "Philip, that was written around your picture, an old picture of you it must have been, which fell out of your pocket when I was undressing you that night after your fight with Roscoe. I recognized the locket it was enclosed in as Mr. Hunter's. I had often seen it on his watch fob, and it's engraved with his initials."

"It fell out of my pocket," said Philip, incredulously.

"Yes," she said, "that puzzled me, too, for a while; and finally I figured it out. You must have found it—"

"That night in Roscoe's cave, when I was waiting for him. I had forgotten it until this moment."

"I knew it must be like that"; she said, "something like that. And wasn't it. . ." she began—

"Hunter's code as well as mine? Yes. We made it up together when we were boys," he said, "and we used it occasionally even after we left the Point. We wrote in it, both of us, as easily as in English; and read it the same way."

Her young arms still held him fast.

"Philip, he must have been sorry a long time—almost since it happened. It's an old, old picture of you, dear, and the ink of the letters is faded. He's carried it with him ever since, as a reminder of the wrong he did you, and of his cowardice in letting you suffer under it."

"I suppose it was that from the first."

"I don't believe he ever meant. . ." She let the sentence break off there, and there was a long, long silence.

"I suppose that's true," he said at last. "I suppose I might have saved him then, just as I might have saved him later, from Roscoe's dart. I can think of a hundred ways that it might have happened—the accusation against me, I mean—without his having any part in it." Then he said rather abruptly, "Fanshaw told you the story, didn't he?"

She assented. "Most of it, that is. Perhaps not quite all he knew."

"I don't know it all myself," he told her, "that is, I have filled it in with guesses. I knew about the girl. Hunter was half mad about her, and she, I suppose, was in love with him. Anyway, he came to me one night— the last time I ever talked with him—raging with excitement. The girl's father had found out about him and meant, she said, to kill him, and perhaps her, too. Anyhow, she had forbidden Hunter's seeing her again. We took a drink or two, together, before I started, and I suppose he must have drunk himself half mad after that; for he started out right on my trail and did what you know. I have always supposed, until just now, that he had used my name as his own with her, to screen himself from possible trouble. But that may not have been the case. He may simply have spoken of me as his friend.

"The girl was in love with him, and it would be natural for her to give her father my name instead of Hunter's, and make the accusation against me. I suppose he thought that I could, probably, clear myself easily enough, without involving him, and that the whole row might blow over without doing any irreparable damage to either of us. And then, when it didn't blow over—when it got worse and meant ruin for somebody—the fact that he hadn't spoken at first would have made it ten times harder to speak at last. I might have helped him. He sent word to me once, when I was under arrest, to ask if I would see him, and I refused. I was very. . ." His speech was punctuated now by longer and longer pauses, but still Jeanne waited.—"Very sure of the correctness of my own attitude then. Correct is, perhaps, the exact word for it. I wouldn't turn a hand to save a man—a man who had been my friend, too—from living out the rest of his life in hell." He shuddered a little at that and she quickly laid her hand upon his lips.

"That was long ago," she said. "You can see now what a god, perhaps, would have seen and done then. And, if you did wrong, then it's you who have suffered for it—you who have paid the penalty. You have paid for the thing you left undone as well as for the thing he did. But we must not talk about it any more, now. You're not strong enough. I ought not to have spoken of it at all, but, somehow, I couldn't wait any longer."

"Just this much more, Jeanne, and then we will let it go: You see now, don't you, dear, why I said I never could go back to the world, never clear myself of the old charge at Hunter's expense—Perry Hunter's expense—now that he is dead; and don't you see that that's as impossible now as it was when I first said it?"

It was with half a laugh and half a sob that she kissed him.

"Oh, my dear," she said, "what does the world matter. This is the world here. You and I. The space of this great bear-skin we are lying on. The past can't come between us, and what else is there that matters? Come, it's time for you to take another nap. Are you warm enough out here, or shall we go back to the hut?"

"I'm warm, soul and body, thanks to you," he said.

But it was Jeanne who went to sleep. Somehow, since that last explanation a wonderful great, soft calm seemed to envelop her. She slept there like a child beside him, his hand still half-clasped in hers.

It was Philip's voice that wakened her. How long afterwards she did not know. He was sitting erect on the great bear-skin, and all she could see of him was the dim silhouette of his back against the sky.

"What is it?" she asked drowsily. "Is anything the matter?"

"No; it's just a rather odd-looking aurora over there in the south."

But for her drowsiness she would have noted the strange ring of excitement in his voice. As it happened, she took the words literally, settled back with a contented little sigh and let herself fall back again into the slumber she had hardly aroused from.

"You're all right, aren't you?" she contrived to ask, but she did not hear the answer.

The next thing she knew she was sitting up erect beside him. Again it was his voice that had aroused her, but this time the summons was imperative. He had caught at her hand and was holding it in a trembling grip that almost hurt her. She released that hand, only to throw an arm around his shoulders, and then she gave him the other.

"Philip, dear," she said quietly, "what makes you shake like that? What has happened, dear? Try to tell me."

He could hardly command his voice to answer.

"It's that aurora, over there," he said. "No, it's gone now. It may come back. It's right over there in the south—straight in front of you."

"But, my dear—my dear—" she persisted, "why should an aurora. . . Is it because of the one we saw the night you killed Roscoe? Is it that old nightmare that it brings back?" She was speaking quietly, her voice caressing him just as her hands were. She was like a mother trying to reassure a frightened child.

"No, it's not that," he said unsteadily. "I don't know—I think I may be going mad, perhaps. I know I wasn't dreaming. I thought so at first, but I know I'm not now." Then she felt his body stiffen, he dropped her hand and pointed out to the southern horizon.

"There," he said, "look there!" What she saw was simply a pencil of white light, pointing straight from the horizon to the zenith, and reaching an altitude of perhaps twenty degrees. Compared with the stupendous electrical displays that they were used to seeing in that winter sky, it was utterly insignificant, and from it she turned to search his face, in sudden alarm.

"No, no—look—*look!*" he commanded, his excitement mounting higher with each word.

She obeyed reluctantly, but at what she saw her body became suddenly rigid and she stared as one might stare who sees a spirit. For the faint pencil of white light swung on a pivot, dipped clear to the horizon, rose again and completed its circuit to the other side.

She sat there beside him, breathless, almost lifeless with suspense while that pencil traced its course back and forth from horizon to horizon, stopping sometimes on the zenith, to turn back upon itself—sometimes continuing through unchecked. At last her breath burst from her in a great sob. She turned and clung to him wildly.

"Philip," she said, "it can't be that—it can't—it can't!"

"Tell me—tell me what it looks like—what you think you see?"

She stayed just where she was, clinging to him, cowering to him, as if something terrified her, her face pressed down against his shoulder.

"Signals," she gasped out. "From a light—from a search-light."

He drew a long, deep breath or two, and his good arm tightened about her.

"Well," he said, his voice breaking in a shaky laugh, "if we are mad, we are mad together, Jeanne, dear, and with the same madness; and if we are dreaming, we are living in the same dream. Did you read what it said? Oh, no, of course you couldn't—but I did. It's the old army wig-wag, and it has been saying all sorts of things. Spelling out your name most of the time. What it just said was, *Courage. They are coming.*"

XXV

Unwinged

For a while she stayed just where she was, her head cradled against his shoulder, but, presently, she stood erect once more, pulled off one of her heavy gauntlets, and with her bare palm pressed the tears out of her eyes.

"You aren't strong enough yet to be used as the support for a really good cry." Her voice was shaky and her speech uneven. There were still some little half-suppressed sobs in it. But she turned her face again towards the southern horizon. "If that's the army wig-wag I ought to be able to read it. Tom taught it to me years ago. Perhaps—perhaps it is he who is signaling now."

"Was there a search-light on the *Aurora?*" Philip asked, "I didn't notice when I saw her." He tried to make the question sound casual, but his own voice was hardly steadier than hers.

"Oh, yes," she said. "It was one of the things we laughed at uncle Jerry for insisting upon, but he insisted just the same. It's a very powerful light. Philip," she said suddenly, after a little silence, "is it not plain impossible, that that we see over there? You know you said, and father said in his journal, that there was no possibility of a relief in the winter. Philip—Philip, isn't it madness—is it the ice madness?"

"If it is," he told her, with a laugh that was steadier now, "if it is, it has taken us both the same way. But, really, there is nothing impossible about it. Of course, the *Aurora* is not steaming along toward us through open water. If she is out there she is frozen into the pack, and she is moving with it. It was in the dead of winter that the *Walrus* came here and the *Phœnix*, too, for that matter, and if the *Aurora* was beset before she got too far away and frozen up in the pack, the drift would gradually bring her back here very slowly—only three or four miles a day." He felt her droop a little at that.

"How far are they away now, Philip?" she asked.

"I don't know," he told her. "For a guess I should say forty or fifty miles."

"Two weeks!" she computed, thoughtfully. "Philip, do you think we can stand it as long as that? Won't we just—just go mad with the agony of waiting for them?"

"We sha'n't have long to wait," he assured her. "Remember, they said they were coming. They didn't mean they were coming with the drift. They have set out afoot—some of them—over the ice. And, I don't believe it's Fanshaw who's sending those signals. He's probably been out on the ice for days. It's very rough and their progress would be slow,—not so very much faster than that of the ship."

"Oh, if he had your wings!" she whispered.

Cayley got to his feet. "We must build a fire," he said, "out here—the biggest fire we can possibly contrive, to guide them by."

"And to give them a hope, too," she said, "they can hardly have any—not of finding us alive, I mean."

How they ever succeeded in doing it they were both rather at a loss, afterwards, to understand. Neither Cayley, nor even Jeanne, thought of his illness. That was forgotten, except so far as the fact that he had only one good arm obtruded itself. Jeanne was as weak as he, and the source of her weakness was the same as his. Both had a tendency to laugh shakily at nothing at all. Both found it hard to command their voices. Both found themselves wandering about blindly, in spite of the intensity of their desire to get the fire blazing as soon as possible. But at last they got it blazing with the better part of their precious store of fuel. Then, as best they could, they settled down on their great bear-skin before the fire, to wait. How long they waited neither of them knew, though it seemed an eternity. Sometimes they tried to talk, but their voices had a disconcerting way of breaking.

"We must do something," Philip said, at last, "must try to get our old routine going, somehow. It may be hours—days, before they get here."

"I suppose," said Jeanne, "we could cook a meal, even if we couldn't eat it."

But before he could answer they heard a rifle-shot ring out in the still air.

"No," he cried, "the long wait is over. Thank God they are here. Fire, Jeanne! Fire the revolver! Let them know they are in time." His lips trembled and tears glistened in his eyes.

It was lying under her hand. There were only three cartridges left, but she fired them all into the air. Then, almost before the echo from the cliff behind them had died away, they heard a dim hail in a human voice—a voice that broke sharply as if the shout had ended in a sob.

"It's Tom," she said.

"Call out! It's your voice he'll want to hear." But it was a moment before she could command it. She called his name twice, and then a third time, with a different inflection, for a long, leaping flicker of firelight had revealed a little knot of figures rounding one of the great ice-crags that covered the frozen harbor. One figure, a little in advance of the others, dashed forward at a run. Jeanne sprang to meet him.

For a little while Cayley stood hesitating before the fire, just where Jeanne, in her impulsive rush toward their rescuers, had left him, then, slowly, he followed her.

The details of that last encounter with Tom Fanshaw on the *Aurora's* deck crowded back into his memory, but he met them squarely and defeated them.

What had happened since that last encounter must, he knew, change the attitude of the Fanshaws toward him. They owed the girl's life to him, and however little they might relish taking it at his hands, still they must take it, gladly, and Jeanne's happiness involved their taking him with her.

He was still quite clear that he never could tell them the story which Jeanne's discovery of the locket had forced him to tell her, so few hours ago. Not knowing it all, still believing him stained with that old disgrace, they must dislike him—regard him for a long time anyway—with profound suspicion. Well, for Jeanne's sake he must treat that suspicion as if it did not exist—or existing, as if it were powerless to hurt him. It would be nearly powerless, when it came to that. The warmth of the girl's faith would compensate for it all.

The party on the ice was moving landward again. Even at Philip's slow pace, the distance between them was narrowing. Jeanne and young Fanshaw were coming on ahead. He saw her stop suddenly and throw an arm around the man's neck. She was laughing and crying all at once, and there were tears in the man's eyes, too. Philip expected that. He knew that Fanshaw loved her. His memory of that fact was all that redeemed his memory of their encounter on the *Aurora's* deck.

But, what he did not expect, was to see Fanshaw suddenly release himself from the girl's embrace and come straight toward him. That was not the most surprising thing—not that, nor the hand which Fanshaw was holding out to him. It was the look in the young man's face, as the light from the great blazing beacon on the beach illuminated it.

There was a powerful emotion working there, but no sign of any conflict, no resistance, no reluctance. It was the face of a man humble in the presence of a miracle. He stripped off his gauntlet and gripped Cayley's hand. It was a moment before he could speak.

"It's only just now," he said, "now that I see you here together, that I find it hard to believe. Because I've known all along that you were here with her, keeping her alive until we could get back to her. I've been the only one who has had any hope at all, and with me it's been a certainty rather than a hope. It's as if I had seen you here, together. I've seen you so a thousand times, but now, that I do actually, with my own eyes, it's hard to. . ." his voice broke there. There was a moment of silence, then he went on, "You must try to forgive us, Cayley—me, in particular, for I'm the one who needs it most. We know the truth of that old story now. No, it wasn't Jeanne who told, it was poor Hunter himself, in a letter. He had written it long ago, and it was among his papers. I want you to read it sometime. I think, perhaps, when you do you will be able to forgive him, too."

"That's done already," said Philip. "No, not long ago—within the last few hours. Come, shall we go back to the fire? I suppose we had better wait for another moonrise before we try to get to the *Aurora*."

It was six months later, a blazing, blue July day, when the gunboat *Yorktown* lifted North Head, the northern portal of the Golden Gate. Tom Fanshaw and his father had gone to the bridge, but Philip and Jeanne, the other two passengers, remained, unmoved by the announcement, seated as far aft as possible, the ensign, limp in the following breeze, fluttering just over their heads.

The great floe which for so many months had held the *Aurora* fast imprisoned, had broken up under the unrelenting warmth of the June sun and had set the ship free at last, to plod her slow way southward. True to old Mr. Fanshaw's predictions, she had weathered the Arctic winter and the grip of the Arctic ice in safety. The wounded survivors of the *Walrus* party had died and one of their own crew. Otherwise, the sun and the open water found them as well as they had left them—better off, if one is to take an account of the gold—the incredible amount of gold which they had found in the strong room. That, by Mr. Fanshaw's reckoning, belonged to Jeanne, was the fruit of her father's discovery. Sometime, perhaps, they would realize the importance of it, but, there upon the Arctic sea they were far enough away from the world and its standards to make it seem trivial, almost unreal. If they had had to lighten the ship they would have pitched it over first.

The *Aurora* was doing very well for her, grinding out eight knots an hour, which was about the best she was capable of, when, off St. Lawrence Island, she sighted the gleaming white man-of-war, with the stars and stripes snapping at her rail. At that sight old Mr. Fanshaw's impatience took fire, and it became irresistible when he learned that she was bound for San Francisco, as they were.

What international consideration had taken her into those waters is no concern of ours. Her business was done and she was homeward bound, as her long pennant, streaming out astern, attested. So the *Aurora* hailed her. Mr. Fanshaw went on board and when he returned it was with the astonished captain's invitation to himself and the others in his party, Jeanne, Philip and Tom, to go back to San Francisco in the gun-boat. They left the *Aurora* to follow along at her own gait, in Captain Warner's charge—left gold and all—taking with them only some civilized clothes, and two precious articles which Jeanne would not leave behind—her father's journal, in its rosewood box, and Cayley's wings.

As for the civilized clothes, when the two lovers, so equipped, encountered each other for the first time in the ward-room of the man-of-war, just before their first dinner on board of her, they had gazed at each other almost incredulously. Now, as they sat here on deck, the last golden hours of that golden voyage slipping away, Philip reverted to that moment, to his feeling at first sight of her.

"Clothes aren't mere externals. They really strike in a little way, at least. It was not just that you looked different that night in the ward-room, you were different, a little—really not quite the same person who walked back beside me across the ice to the *Aurora*."

"Do you like her—this new person?" Jeanne asked. She drawled over the question a little, as if her lips caressed it, in the speaking. Cayley laughed like a boy.

"I even like being a little afraid of her," he said.

They had been talking lazily, as it had been their wont to do lately. There was a certain luxury in taking their happiness for granted—in slipping along the surface of life for a while and evading the emotional deeps in themselves, which they knew were there. That was natural, after the series of tremendous experiences which that long Arctic night had provided them with. They seldom spoke of that time. It was with difficulty that Tom and his father could get any account of it.

When Jeanne went on speaking now it was in the same tone of lazy enjoyment, which she had employed before.

"I'm afraid of myself," she said, "and that isn't a joke. I've been in terror all the voyage for fear I'd do something dreadful—stretch out at full length on the deck, after dinner, or something of that sort. In a long skirt I feel as I remember I used to when I was about ten years old and I was allowed to dress up in my mother's clothes. And Philip, now that we are nearly home—nearly back to the world—I am afraid of it, really afraid—afraid I'll hate it, the people—I don't mean friends, just people—and being polite and behaving respectably, and having nothing really particular to do." As she finished, her voice had a deeper note in it, and, looking quickly up at her, Philip saw that she was in earnest.

"I suppose we shall feel that," he said, "but we can come back gradually. We can build us a bungalow, somewhere up on a mountain side where we can be quite by ourselves—with no servants, or anything, I mean—and then we can take humanity in small doses, a little at a time."

"You will have your wings," she supplemented, "and you can go towering up, far up in the sunshine, to where the air is as cold as that you flew down through the night you first came to me—so high that the world will look deserted, even though it isn't—and you can believe it empty, just as once it was. Only—only—then you'll have to come back to me." She saw he meant to speak, but she forestalled him. "Philip, haven't you a little fear all of your own? Won't you wish that you could fly unhampered? I don't mean always, but sometimes. Won't you regret the days when the world was really empty of me and everybody else—regret that night when you came flashing down upon the ice-floe beside me?"

This time she would have let him answer her, but they were interrupted just then by a footfall close by on the deck, and, looking up they saw one of the junior officers standing close beside them. He was a dark-haired, dark-eyed, good-looking youngster, whose frank adoration of Jeanne ever since they had come aboard had amused the Fanshaws and secretly pleased and touched Philip, although he pretended to be amused, too.

They both rose and lounged back against the rail as he came up.

"Glad to be nearly home, Mr. Caldwell?" said Jeanne. "You navy people regard any port in the States as home, don't you?"

"Oh, I'd be glad enough of a month's shore-leave," he said, "if it weren't this particular voyage. I mean—I mean if it didn't mean that we are going to lose you."

She gave him a friendly little smile, but made no other answer. He turned to Philip.

"I'll have to confess," he said, "to the rudest sort of inquisitive curiosity about the strange-looking bundle you brought aboard with you from the *Aurora*. It looks like some primitive Eskimo's attempt to build a flying-machine."

"It is something like that," said Philip. "If you'll have it brought up here on deck I'll open it out for you."

The young fellow's pleasure was almost boyish. "I'll have it brought at once," he said.

The breeze was straight behind them and just about strong enough to compensate for the speed of the vessel, and the air on deck was quite still. With the boy's puzzled assistance Philip spread his wings for the first time since that night when he had dived off the cliff-head to go in pursuit of Roscoe. The recollection was almost painfully vivid, and, as he looked into Jeanne's face, he saw the same memory mirrored there.

But young Caldwell soon brought them back to the present. He was no longer embarrassed, shy, deferential. Aerial navigation was, apparently, a subject he knew all about. He criticized the shape of the planes, the material they were made of, the curve of this, the dip of that—all in the tone of an expert—and by way of summing up, he said—

"It's rather pitiful, isn't it? In a way any primitive thing always affects me—like old locomotives they have in museums. Somebody, probably, believed once that that would fly. I hope he didn't believe it seriously enough to give it a real trial."

"You don't think it would work, then?" asked Philip.

The young man laughed. "Dear me, no," he said. "It couldn't work."

"At any rate," said Philip, "it's an amusing curiosity."

"Oh, yes; indeed, yes," the young man assented cordially. "I wish it were mine. Only I wouldn't try to fly with it."

His duties called him away then, rather suddenly, and Philip was left to furl his wings alone. From the process he looked up into Jeanne's face.

"Why, Jeanne!" Her eyes were bright, bright with unshed tears, and there was a little flush of bright color in her cheeks.

"Oh, I know," she said, with an unsteady laugh, "it's absurd to be indignant, but I wished—oh, how I wished, when he was so patronizing and so sure, that you might have slipped your arms into their places and gone curving, circling up, all gold and gleaming, into the air. I knew you wouldn't, but I hoped you would."

"Jeanne, dear," he said, "you'll remember that always—my flight, I mean. But, sometimes you'll get to wondering if it isn't the memory

HENRY KITCHELL WEBSTER

of a dream. And then you'll go and find these old wings in an attic, somewhere, and stroke them with your hands, the way you did that night when I furled them first upon the ice-floe beside you."

She looked at him quickly, wide-eyed.

"What do you mean, Philip? Not that—not that I'm never to see you fly again?"

He nodded.

"Somehow, up there with all the world below me, it never seemed real. Even you never seemed real, who were the only real thing in all the world. The earth was only a spinning ball, and there were no such things as men. I wasn't a man myself, up there, not even—even after you had brought me back to life and given me a soul again. Somehow, to be a man one has to wear the shackles of mankind. I can't explain it better than that, but I know it's true."

For a long time she searched his face in silence.

"You used to seem a spirit rather than a man, to me," she said, "when I would lie watching you soaring there above me. And now—now it's I who brought you down."

"Do you remember how I told you once that a man like your father was worth a whole Paradise of angels? Well, I want to be a man, Jeanne, as near as possible such a man as he was. And I want to walk beside you, always."

A shift of wind from astern overtook them and the great ensign flapped forward, screening them for a moment where they stood, from the view of the rest of the deck. With a sudden passion of understanding she clasped him close and kissed him.

THE END

A Note About the Author

Henry Kitchell Webster (1875–1932) was an American novelist and short story writer. Born in Evanston, Illinois, Webster graduated from Hamilton College in 1897 before taking a job as a teacher at Union College in Schenectady, New York. Alongside coauthor Samuel Merwin, Webster found early success with such novels as *The Short Line War* (1899) and *Calumet "K"* (1901), the latter a favorite of Ayn Rand's. Webster's stories, often set in Chicago, were frequently released as serials before appearing as bestselling novels, a formula perfected by the author throughout his hugely successful career. By the end of his life, Webster was known across the United States as a leading writer of mystery, science fiction, and realist novels and stories.

A Note from the Publisher

Spanning many genres, from non-fiction essays to literature classics to children's books and lyric poetry, Mint Edition books showcase the master works of our time in a modern new package. The text is freshly typeset, is clean and easy to read, and features a new note about the author in each volume. Many books also include exclusive new introductory material. Every book boasts a striking new cover, which makes it as appropriate for collecting as it is for gift giving. Mint Edition books are only printed when a reader orders them, so natural resources are not wasted. We're proud that our books are never manufactured in excess and exist only in the exact quantity they need to be read and enjoyed.

Discover more of your favorite classics with Bookfinity™.

- Track your reading with custom book lists.
- Get great book recommendations for your personalized Reader Type.
- Add reviews for your favorite books.
- AND MUCH MORE!

Visit **bookfinity.com** and take the fun Reader Type quiz to get started.

Enjoy our classic and modern companion pairings!

Printed in the USA
CPSIA information can be obtained
at www.ICGtesting.com
JSHW022333140824
68134JS00019B/1452

9 781513 283531